# LETHAL
# PEOPLE

John Locke is a *New York Times* bestselling author, and was the first self-published author in history to hit the number 1 spot on Kindle. He is the author of the Donovan Creed and Emmett Love series. He lives in Kentucky.

JOHN LOCKE

***** Smart and ex[...]
Donovan Creed is or[...]
you'd love to hate bu[...]
exciting, humorous ar[...]
killer combination. I am looking for[...]
to reading the rest of the series.

***** I love this book. By Madeleine
Labitan This novel is chock-full of surprising plot twists and turns from beginning to
end. It grips you from page one. I read it
in an evening.

***** Bingo! Cool. Read this book and
you're hooked on Locke. By Karin
Locke keeps the story moving and in such
an effortless way. I'm passing it on to my
husband. It's been awhile since I've read
something sexy: this fits the bill.

***** So Entertaining I just went
and downloaded another one.
By Patti Roberts
I read this book over a period of 2 days
on my kindle and loved it! So I have
just downloaded another one. I hereby
declare that I am a John Locke fan. Do
yourself a favor....

***** Outstanding. By Coolfire
An outstanding read. A roller coaster of
action and stunning surprises.

***** 10 stars. By Ally
A wonderful mystery thriller. I love all of
them but I think this is just my favorite.

## THE DONOVAN CREED SERIES

# LETHAL
# PEOPLE
## JOHN LOCKE

HEAD
of
ZEUS

First published in the UK in 2012 by Head of Zeus, Ltd
9 7 5 3 1 2 4 6 8

A CIP catalogue record for this book is available from
the British Library.

ISBN (Paperback): 9781781852309
ISBN (eBook): 9781781852316

Printed and bound by CPI Group (UK) Ltd,
Croydon, CR0 4YY

Head of Zeus, Ltd
Clerkenwell House
45-47 Clerkenwell Green
London EC1R 0HT

www.headofzeus.com

# PROLOGUE

THE FIRE STARTED in Greg and Melanie's basement just after midnight and crept upward through the stairwell silently, like a predator tracking food.

Greg had never read the stats or he'd have known that home fires can turn deadly in just two minutes and that his odds of waking up were three to one.

Against.

And yet both he and Melanie had managed it. Was it because she'd screamed? He wasn't sure. But she was screaming now. Groggy, disoriented, coughing, Greg stumbled to the door. Like millions of others, he'd seen the movie *Backdraft*, and although the proper term for the event depicted in the film was a "flashover" and not a "backdraft," he'd learned enough to touch the back of his hand to the top of the door, the doorknob, and the crack between the door and door frame before flinging it open.

As he did that, Melanie rolled to the edge of the bed and grabbed her cell phone from the charging cradle on the nightstand. She pressed 911 and cupped her hand around the speaker. Now that Greg was in motion, she felt better, like part of a team instead of an army of one. Only moments ago, Melanie had taken her panic out on Greg's comatose body by kicking, punching, and screaming him awake. When he finally began to stir, she'd slapped him hard across the face several times.

Now they were working together. They'd silently assessed the situation and assigned each other specific roles in an unspoken plan. He'd get the kids; she'd get the firemen.

Melanie couldn't hear anything coming from the phone and wondered if she'd misdialed. She terminated the call and started over. A sudden blast of heat told her Greg had gotten the door open. Melanie looked up at him, and their eyes met. She held his gaze a moment and time seemed to stop while something special passed between them. It was just a split second, but they managed to get eight years of marriage into it.

Greg set his jaw and gave her a nod of reassurance, as if to say he'd seen what lay beyond the door and that everything was going to be all right.

Melanie wasn't buying. She'd known this man since the first week of college, knew all his looks. What she'd seen in his eyes was helplessness. And fear.

Greg turned away from her, shielded his face, and hurled himself into the rising flames. She couldn't hear the 911 operator over the roaring noise, but she heard Greg barreling up the stairs yelling to the children.

She yelled, "I love you!" but her words were swallowed up in the blaze. The searing heat scorched her blistered throat. Melanie clamped her mouth shut and turned her attention back to the phone. Was someone on the other end? She dropped to her hands and knees, cupped her fingers around the mouthpiece, and shouted her message as clearly as possible to the dispatcher she hoped was listening.

That's when she heard the crash—the one that sounded like columns falling in the foyer. Melanie figured the staircase would be next.

The kids' room was right above her. Melanie instinctively looked up to launch a prayer and saw a thick, rolling layer of smoke hugging the ceiling. She let out a long, piercing wail. A terrible thought tried to enter her mind. She forced it away.

Melanie screamed again—screamed for her girls, screamed for Greg, screamed even as hot air filled her mouth and lungs and tried to finish her off.

But Melanie had no intention of dying. Not here in the bedroom. Not without her family. Coughing, choking, she crawled steadily toward the doorway.

The theory that the air was better near the floor apparently didn't apply to basement fires because thick, gray ropes of smoke were sifting upward through the floorboards. Melanie's lungs ached in protest as the heat and flames stepped up the demand on her oxygen. Her pulse throbbed heavy in her neck. The hallway, a mere twelve feet away, had been rendered nearly impenetrable in the moments since Greg had left her. During that tiny window of time, the flames had more than doubled in height and intensity, and their all-consuming heat sucked so much oxygen from the air, she could barely maintain consciousness.

As she neared the doorway, a bedroom window imploded with a loud crash. Hot, broken glass slammed into her upper torso like a shotgun blast, pelting her face, neck, and shoulders with crystals of molten shrapnel. The impact knocked Melanie to her side. She shrieked in pain and instinctively started curling her body into a protective ball. The skin that had once covered her delicate face was gone, and the meat that remained broiled in the heat.

That would have done it for Melanie had she been fighting solely for her own life, but she was fighting for Greg and the twins, and she refused to let them down. Melanie shrieked again, this time in anger. She got to her hands and knees, made her way through the doorway, crawled to the base of the stairs, and looked up.

The stairwell was an inferno, and the bottom half of the staircase was virtually gone. Melanie's heart sank. She screamed for her family, listened for a response. There was none.

Then, as if an angel had whispered it, Melanie had an idea. She got to her feet and made her way to the powder room. She turned on the faucets, soaked the guest towels. She staggered back to the area where the steps used to be. Tapping into her last ounce of strength, she screamed, "Greg!" and flung the towels as hard as she could, upward into the rising flames, in the direction of the kids' room.

Had he heard her? Had he answered? She couldn't tell.

Emergency personnel arrived just four minutes after the 911 call was logged. Neighbors, hearing sirens, gathered in the street and watched in horror.

Later, when reconstructing the events at the scene, firefighters determined Greg had made it to the children's room, opened the window, and hung a sheet from it to alert rescuers to the location. He'd had the presence of mind to gather both girls in his arms on the floor beneath him before dying.

Firefighters entering the bedroom through the window were impressed to find wet towels covering the girls' faces. This is what saved their lives that night, they decided, though one of the twins died later on, in the hospital.

"Son of a bitch," Augustus Quinn said. "You are one tough son of a bitch, I'll give you that!" Shakespeare it was not, but Creed should have been dead by now and wasn't. "Let's call it a night," Quinn said.

They were on opposite sides of prison cell bars, sixty feet below the earth's surface. It took a while, but Donovan Creed staggered to his feet, a vantage point from which he now grinned at the hideous giant manning the torture device. "What was that?" Creed said. "Eight seconds?"

The ugly giant nodded.

"Give me ten this time."

"You'll die," Quinn said. Though the two men had worked together for years, Quinn's words had been uttered simply and gave no evidence of warmth or concern.

Creed supposed that for Quinn it was all business. Creed had paid his friend to administer the torture, and Quinn was expressing his opinion about continuing. Did he even care if Creed died tonight? Creed thought about that for a minute.

The ADS weapon had been created as a counter measure to the terrorists' practice of using civilians as human shields during the Iraq War. Effective up to a quarter-mile, ADS fires an invisible beam that penetrates the skin and instantly boils all body fluids. The idea was simple: you point the weapon at a crowd, flip the switch, and everyone falls to the ground in excruciating pain. You flip the switch off, collect the weapons, and sort out the terrorists. Moments later, everyone is back to normal. Unfortunately, during the testing phase, word got out about soldiers suffering irreversible heart damage and ruptured spleens. When human rights organizations got involved, the public outcry was so severe the weapon had to be scrapped.

Donovan Creed had been among the first to test the original ADS weapon without receiving permanent organ or tissue damage. From the first exposure, he believed the weapon held enormous potential as a field torture device, provided it could be modified to a handheld size. To that effect, Creed had persuaded the military to allow one of the original prototypes to go missing long enough for his geek squad to turn it into a sort of ham radio project.

The weapon currently aimed at Creed through the prison bars was one of a set of three that had been produced to date. The other two were locked in a hidden closet twenty feet away. These three weapons were second generation, meaning they were much smaller than the original but not as small as they would ultimately need to be for his purposes. Still, each phase required human testing.

"You don't believe that about me dying," Creed said. "You're just hungry."

Quinn ignored the remark. "Two hundred soldiers tested against the machine," he recited. "Forty-six with battlefield experience …"

Creed waved the words away with his hand. "Old news," he said.

Quinn turned to face the video camera. "I want it on record I'm advising you to stop."

"Don't be ridiculous," Creed said. "If you leave, I'll just figure out a way to do it alone."

"My point," Quinn said. "I leave and you pass out, who's gonna shut off the beam?"

Creed studied the giant's dark, dead eyes, searching for the proverbial ounce of humanity. "What," he said, "you going soft on me?" Quinn didn't answer, and Creed realized if there was an answer to be had, it wouldn't come from Quinn's eyes. Quinn's eyes were not the gateway to his soul. They were the place mirth went to die.

Look," Quinn said, by way of clarification. "I keep pushing

the switch till you die, and every assassin, every kill squad, and half the country's armed forces will try to plant me in the ground."

"Aw hell, Augustus, these guys try to kill me every time they invent a new toy. Don't forget, they pay me well for this shit."

"In advance, I hope."

Speaking to the camera, Creed said, "If I die tonight, hunt this ugly bastard down and kill him like the dog he is." Creed winked at his monstrous friend and set his feet.

Quinn shrugged. "I can always edit that last part." He held Creed's gaze a second and then checked his stopwatch and threw the switch.

Ten seconds later, Donovan Creed was on his back, lifeless, though his screams continued to echo off the prison cell walls.

Augustus Quinn, a man entirely unburdened by sentimentality, left Creed where he dropped and removed the video card from the camera. Tomorrow he'll send copies to NSA, the CIA, and Department of Homeland Security.

Quinn pocketed the video card but stopped short after hearing a small sound. In the absence of certainty, he preferred not to squeeze his huge frame through the narrow cell door opening, but this was Donovan Creed after all, so Quinn entered reluctantly, knelt on the floor, and tried Creed's wrist for a pulse. Failing to find one, he cradled the dead man's head in his giant hand and placed his ear close to Creed's mouth.

A raspy whisper emerged: "That all you got?"

Startled, Quinn drew back. "Son of a bitch!" he said for the second time that night. Some day he'll be drinking in a biker bar or hanging on a meat hook somewhere, and some guy will ask him who the toughest man he ever met was.

Quinn will say Donovan Creed, and he'll give a dozen examples of Creed's toughness, ending with these most recent events. He'll tell it just the way it happened tonight, no need to embellish, and he'll end the story with a recitation of Creed's final words, "Is that all you've got?" The guy hearing the story will smile because, as final words go, Creed's were gold.

As it turns out, those were not Creed's last words.

"This time," he said, "give me twelve seconds."

Quinn sighed. "I should've brought a sandwich," he said.

Quinn fears no human or beast in the world, save for the man at his feet. Specifically, he fears that thing inside the man on the floor that drives Donovan Creed to sleep in a prison cell every night when he's here at his headquarters in Virginia— or in the attics and crawl spaces of homes owned by clueless strangers the rest of the time. Nor can Quinn fathom what fuels Creed's insane desire to build his resistance to torture by scheduling these horrific late night sessions in order to play human guinea pig to the latest military death weapon du jour.

Quinn makes his way back through the cell door opening and places the video card back in the camera. He peers into the aperture, presses the record button.

The lens displays a stark prison cell measuring six feet by nine. A narrow bed with a bare mattress hugs the left wall, separated from the toilet by a stainless steel sink. The reinforced cinderblock walls and concrete floor are painted institutional gray. Two-inch-thick iron bars span the front of the cell. A center section can be slid to one side to accommodate prisoner access. The ceiling is high and holds fluorescent lighting above a grid designed to discourage prisoners from hurling food or clothing upward in an attempt to obtain shards of glass from which to fashion a weapon.

The grid diffuses the light into a greenish glow that slightly distorts the image of the man on the floor in the center of the prison cell ... as he struggles, once again, to his feet.

# 1.

I AWOKE IN mid-scream, jerked upright, and jumped off my cot like I'd been set on fire. My brain cells sputtered, overloaded by panic and crippling pain. I staggered three steps and crashed into the bars of my cell. I grabbed them and held on for dear life. It took a minute, but I finally remembered how I'd spent the previous night cozying up to the death ray.

My cell phone rang. I ignored it, made my way to the toilet, and puked up everything inside me, including, possibly, my spleen. The ringing stopped long before I felt like checking the caller ID. Nine people in the world had my number, and this wasn't one of them. Whoever it was, whatever they wanted, could wait.

From my prison cell in Bedford, Virginia, getting to work was as easy as stepping into the elevator and pressing a button. I did so, and moments later, the row of nozzles in my office steam shower were blasting me full force. After several minutes of that, I knew my body wasn't going to rejuvenate on its own, so I stepped out and shook a dozen Advil into my hand.

I looked in the mirror. Usually when I felt this bad I required stitches, and lots of them. I leaned my elbows on the sink counter and lowered my head to my forearms.

The ADS weapon was all I'd hoped for and more. I knew in the weeks to come I'd master the damn thing, but for the time being, it was kicking the crap out of me. I wondered if the suits at Homeland would be happy or miserable to learn I had survived the first session.

When the room finally stopped spinning, I swallowed the Advil. Then I shaved, put some clothes on, and buzzed Lou Kelly.

"You got anything on Ken Chapman yet?" I asked.

There was a short pause. Then Lou said, "Got a whole lot of something. You want it now?"

I sighed. "Yeah, bring it," I said.

I propped my office door open so Lou could enter without having to be buzzed in. Then I dragged myself to the kitchen and tossed a few ice cubes and some water into a blender. I threw in a packet of protein powder and a handful of chocolate-covered almonds, turned the dial to the highest setting, and pressed the start button. By the time Lou arrived, I was pouring the viscous goop into a tall plastic cup.

Lou had a thick manila folder in his hand.

"Local weather for a hundred," he said. He placed the folder on the counter in front of me.

"What are my choices?"

"Thunderstorm, ice storm, cloudy, or sunny," Lou Kelly said.

My office apartment was above ground, but windows could get you killed, so I didn't have any. My office walls were two feet thick and completely soundproof, so I couldn't automatically rule out a thunderstorm. But it was early February, and I'd been outside yesterday. I drank some of my protein shake. Yesterday had been clear and sunny.

"I'll take cloudy," I said.

Lou frowned. "Why do I even bother?" He fished two fifties from his pocket and placed them beside the folder.

"Nothing worse than a degenerate gambler," I said.

Lou pointed at the folder. "You might want to reserve judgment on that," he said. He reached down and tapped the folder twice with his index finger for emphasis.

Lou Kelly was my lieutenant, my ultimate go-to guy. We'd been together fifteen years, including our stint in Europe with the CIA. I took another swallow of my protein shake and stared at the manila folder.

"Give me the gist," I said.

"Your daughter was right not to trust this guy," Lou said.

I nodded. I'd known the minute I answered the phone last week that something was wrong. Kimberly, generally a good judge of character, particularly when it came to her mother's boyfriends, had felt the need to tell me about a curious incident. Kimberly had said, "Tonight Ken broke a glass in his hand. One minute he's holding a drink, the next minute his hand's full of blood!" She went on to explain that her mom (my ex-wife, Janet) had made a snide remark that should have elicited a withering response from her new fiancé. Instead, Chapman put his hands behind his back, stared off into space, and said nothing. When Janet whirled out of the room in anger, Chapman squeezed the glass so hard that it shattered in his hands. Kimberly had been in the loft watching the scene unfold. "There's something wrong with this guy, Dad. He's too ..." she searched for a word. "I don't know. Passive-aggressive? Bipolar? Something's not right."

I agreed and told her I'd look into it.

"Don't tell Mom I said anything, okay?" Kimberly had said.

In front of me, Lou Kelly cleared his throat. "You okay?"

I clapped my hands together. "Wonderful!" I said. "Let's hear what you've got."

Lou studied me a moment. Then he said, "Ken and Kathleen Chapman have been divorced for two years. Ken is forty-two, lives in Charleston, West Virginia. Kathleen is thirty-six, lives in North Bergen, works in Manhattan."

I waved my hand in the general direction of his chatter. "The gist," I reminded him.

Lou Kelly frowned. "The gist is our boy Chapman has serious anger issues."

"How serious?"

"He was an accomplished wife-beater."

"Was?" I said.

"There is evidence to suggest he's reformed."

"What type of evidence?" I asked. "Empirical or pharmacological?"

Lou looked at me for what seemed a very long time. "How long you been holding those words in your head, hoping to use them?"

I grinned and said, "A generous vocabulary is a sure sign of intellectual superiority."

"Must be a lot of room in your head now that you've let them out," he deadpanned.

"Let's continue," I said. "I've got a headache."

"And why wouldn't you?" he said. Then he added, "According to the letter his shrink presented to the court, Chapman appears to have overcome his aggression."

"A chemical imbalance," I suggested.

"Words to that effect," Lou said.

I gave Lou his money back and spent a couple minutes flipping through the police photos and domestic violence reports. The pictures of Kathleen Chapman would be considered obscenely brutal by any standard, but violence was my constant companion and I'd seen much worse. Still, I was surprised to find myself growing strangely sympathetic to her injuries. I kept going back to two of the photos. I seemed to be developing a connection to the poor creature who years ago had found the courage to stare blankly into a police camera lens.

"What do you say to a woman with two black eyes?" I said.

Lou shrugged. "I don't know. What *do* you say to a woman with two black eyes?"

"Nothing," I said. "You already told her twice."

Lou nodded. He and I often used dark humor to detach ourselves from the brutality of our profession. "Looks like he told her a hundred," he said.

I removed the two photos from the folder and traced Kathleen's face with my index finger. And then it hit me. I handed the pictures to Lou. "Have our geeks remove the bruises on these and run an age progression to see what she looks like today."

He eyed me suspiciously but said nothing.

"Then compare her to this lady." I opened my cell phone and clicked through the photos until I found the one I wanted. I handed Lou my phone. "What do you think?" I said.

He held my cell phone in his right hand and the photos of the younger Kathleen in his left. His eyes went back and forth from the phone to the photos. Then he said, "They could be twins."

"I agree," I said. I took the phone back and started entering some commands on the keys.

"So who is she?" he asked. "The one in the picture you're e-mailing me."

I shrugged. "Just someone I know. A friend."

"The geeks might question this project," he said.

"Just tell them we're trying to fit a specific girl into a terror cell."

He studied the photos of Kathleen some more. "A body double?"

"Right," I said. "And, Lou?"

He looked up. "Yeah?"

"Tell the geeks I need it yesterday!"

He sighed. "What else is new?"

Lou turned to leave.

"Wait a minute," I said. "What if Kathleen was not Ken Chapman's first victim?"

"You think he slept around during his marriage?"

"Maybe. Or maybe he dated someone after his divorce, before he met Janet. Can you find out for me?"

"I'm on it," Lou said.

When he left, I turned my attention back to the files. As I read the details in the police reports, the same thought kept running through my head: *If I do nothing, a couple of years from now this could be Janet, or even Kimberly.*

I could not believe Janet was planning to marry this bozo.

I remembered something Kimberly said a month ago when she told me about her mom's engagement. She said she didn't believe her mom was in love with Chapman.

"Why would she marry a guy she doesn't love?" I'd asked.

"I think Mom would rather be unhappy than lonely."

# 2.

THE STATE CAPITOL building in Charleston, West Virginia, is composed of buff Indiana limestone. Its dome rises 293 feet high and is gilded in 23.5-karat gold leaf. I was standing directly below it, in the capitol rotunda, staring at the statue of Senator Robert C. Byrd when I heard her high heels clopping across the marble floor.

Alison David.

"Call me Ally," she said, extending her hand.

I shook her hand and introduced myself.

"So," she said, "what do you think of our capitol building?"

Ally David had on a navy jacket with three-quarter sleeves and a matching pencil skirt. Her satin tank top featured a scoop neckline that offered the promise of superb cleavage. It took some effort not to drool while admiring the way she put her clothes together.

"Impressive," I said. "But I'm confused about the statue."

"How so?"

"Well, I know you can't toss a cat in West Virginia without hitting a building that has his name on it," I said. "But I thought you had to be dead at least fifty years before you got a statue."

She smiled and gave me a wink. "We West Virginians have a pact with Senator Byrd. He sends us the pork, and we let him name the pigs."

Alison David was the type of career woman who, without saying or doing anything out of the ordinary, gave the impression she was a creature of heightened sexuality. I wondered if this was a natural phenomenon or something she had purposely cultivated.

"Is it just me," I said, "or does it appear your illustrious senator's hand is pointing directly at my pocket?"

She forced a half-smile, but I could tell I was losing her. Small talk isn't my strong suit. "So," I said, "where are you taking us for lunch?"

"Someplace close," she said.

I waited for her to elaborate, but she chose not to. Unable to think of anything witty to say, I settled for, "Sounds perfect," which caused her to arch an eyebrow and give me a strange look.

We walked a block together and entered Gyoza, a small Japanese restaurant that proved trendier than its anonymous exterior might suggest. Inside, tasteful Japanese prints hung on bright red walls. The lighting was muted but was bright enough to read the menus. In the center of the restaurant, a bronze-laminate sushi bar separated the sushi chefs from the diners, and glass-fronted coolers atop the bar displayed tidy arrangements of colorful seafood. There were a couple of empty two-top tables with white linen tablecloths. Ally picked one, and we sat down.

"Gyoza?" I said.

Ally lowered her eyes and smiled at me, and the way she did it made me wonder if gyoza meant something dirty.

"Gyoza," she said, "is a popular dumpling in Japanese cuisine. It's finger food, like pot stickers, but with different fillings. Most people order meat or seafood, but I like the vegetarian."

A waitress appeared, and Ally did in fact order the vegetarian gyoza. I asked if the spider roll was authentic.

Our waitress looked confused and said, "This one very hot. Very, very hot! Yes, is spider roll."

"Spider," I said.

"Yes, yes," she said. "Spider. Is very hot."

I feigned shock. "Do you mean to tell me there's an actual spider inside?"

Ally David's eyes skirted the room. She gave the waitress a tight smile, and the two of them exchanged a female look, as if my comment confirmed some sort of conclusion they'd already drawn about me. Ally said, "Perhaps I should translate."

"Please do," I said.

"The spider roll is composed of tempura soft-shell crab," she said.

"Composed," I said.

"That's right."

I may have detected a hint of annoyance in her voice.

Ally wasn't finished with me. "Spider is the name of the roll," she said, "and nothing more." Then, as if she couldn't stop herself, she added, "Why would you even think such a thing?"

I shrugged. "Eel is eel, right? And tuna is tuna, yes?"

Ally David looked at her watch. "I don't mean to be brusque, but I've got a one o'clock and it's already twelve fifteen. You wanted to talk to me about Ken Chapman?" she said.

"I did."

I was not insensitive to the fact that our waitress continued to wait patiently for my order. "I'll have ..." I briefly looked through the menu again.

"Anytime today would be nice," Ally said.

"I think I'll try ... the spider roll," I said.

"For the love of God," Ally said.

"Very, very hot," our waitress warned. "Not recommend," she said.

"But it's on the menu," I said. "So people must order it."

"Yes, yes," she said. She pointed to a large man sitting alone at the sushi bar. "He already order. I bring to him very soon."

I smiled. "Then I'm sure it will be fine," I said.

She nodded and sprinted away to place the order.

"Are you always this ..."Ally searched for a word, gave up, and tried again. "Could you possibly be this *obtuse?*"

I shrugged and looked at her but she lowered her eyes and pretended to be intrigued by the place setting. I spoke to fill the silence. "Did you and Chapman date before his divorce became final?"

She took a deep breath and let it out slowly. "No. Ken was legally separated when we met."

There were delicate white china cups in front of us, and black lacquer soup bowls. I picked up my cup and tilted it so I could see if it said "Made in China" on the bottom. It didn't.

"How long did you guys date?" I asked.

Ally looked up from the place setting to stare at me. "Can you tell me again what my dating Ken has to do with national security?"

"Like I said on the phone, we're just building a profile," I said. "Mr. Chapman is currently engaged to a woman whose former husband was a CIA operative."

Ally made her eyes big and lowered her voice to an exaggerated whisper. "Is that against the law?" she asked. She rolled her big eyes at me the way my daughter Kimberly does.

Only instead of being exasperated, Ally was mocking me.

"Against the law? Not in and of itself," I said, sounding pathetic even to me.

"And yet," she said, "simply by dating me and becoming engaged to another woman, Ken has managed to become a threat to national security! Perhaps I ought to call Senator Byrd's office to sound the alert."

This wasn't going the way I'd envisioned. She was trying for smug and achieving it. She was also smarter than me, and I hate when that happens. There was but one thing to do: seize the initiative. I played the trump card God provided: I stared directly into her cleavage.

"During the time you dated Ken Chapman," I said to her boobs, "did he ever beat you?"

"No."

"You're sure?"

"Of course I'm sure!"

"But you're aware of his history, yes?"

She sighed. "I'm up here, perv."

I reluctantly lifted my focus to her face, and Ally said, "Ken told me about Kathleen's claims of abuse shortly after we started dating."

"And?"

"And he explained what happened."

I waited.

"I suppose you want to hear his version," she said.

"It's why I traveled all the way to Charleston," I said.

"Not the spider roll?"

I smiled and shook my head.

"Not the capitol rotunda?"

"As hard as it must be to fathom, no."

Our waitress approached carrying a heavy tray, which she

perched on a portable stand. She poured scented green tea into our cups and steaming miso soup into our soup bowls. Ally picked up a white ceramic spoon and stirred her soup. I took a sip of my tea and was instantly overcome by the horrific taste. I looked around for something in which to spit the rancid liquid but finally gave up and swallowed it. I made a face to demonstrate how I felt about the tea. Ally rolled her eyes again, reaffirming something I already knew about my charm: though highly infectious to females, it sometimes requires an incubation period.

My cell phone rang. I glanced at the number and put it back in my pocket where it continued to ring.

"You're an annoying person," Ally said. "Anyone ever tell you that?"

I reminded her that she was supposed to be telling me her version of the Ken Chapman saga. She rolled her eyes. She sighed. She frowned. But she finally spoke.

"Ken had been married about a year," Ally said, "when he learned Kathleen was mentally unstable. They had an argument, a shouting match, and he spent the night in a hotel. The next day, when he came home to apologize, he found her bloody and bruised."

"He claimed not to remember beating her up?"

"She beat herself up."

"Excuse me?"

"It was her way of punishing herself for making him angry."

I took some photos out of my suit pocket and spread them on the table. "This look like something a woman might do to herself?" I asked.

Ally's eyes avoided the photos. "I'm not an expert," she admitted. "But it seems plausible, and it wasn't an isolated case. Time and again during the marriage, Ken came home from work to find his wife had beaten herself for various reasons. When he tried to force her into therapy, she went to the police and told them Ken had assaulted her. This became a pattern. By turning him in to the police, or threatening to, she was able to control and manipulate the relationship."

I sat there in disbelief. My jaw dropped, and I think my mouth may have been open during her entire response.

Ally pursed her lips and tasted her soup in the sexiest manner possible, as though she were French kissing it. It was amazing what she could do with her mouth while nibbling at the liquid on her spoon. You put two women side by side, let them both taste some soup. The other woman can be twice as hot as Ally. Out of a hundred guys, Ally wins ninety times. Guaranteed.

"Are you dating anyone now?" I asked.

"Are you asking on behalf of national security?"

"This is a personal query," I said, flashing my high-voltage smile for good measure.

"Well in that case, yes, I'm dating someone."

She was clearly insulting me or at least pretending to. Truth was, I didn't even *like* her and certainly didn't want to date her. I really just wanted to see if I *could*. What can I say, maybe it's a guy thing, but she gives great soup.

"Your dating situation," I persisted, "would you classify it as a serious relationship?"

"Yes, I would," she said. "But I wasn't certain about that until just now."

"Well congratulations," I said dryly.

"Well thank you," she said, matching my tone.

Suddenly, the heavy-set customer at the sushi bar yelled, "Fuck!" and jumped off his stool. He grabbed his throat and spun around in a circle as if his left foot had been nailed to the floor. "Holy Mother of God!" he screamed and spit a mouthful of something onto the floor—something I was pretty sure had to be the spider roll. He jumped up and down in a sort of death dance, coughing and shaking his hands profusely. He yelled, "I'll sue you bastards! I'll sue you for every cent you have!"

The waitress ran out from the kitchen, took one look at him, and said, "Is hot, yes?"

He gave her a withering look. "Yeah, is hot! Is plenty, plenty hot! And I know you not recommend. But here in America, we have laws against serving battery acid. By the time I'm finished with you, you're all going to wish you'd never left China!"

The waitress and sushi chef looked at each other. She said, "We Japanese. Not Chinese."

The enraged customer flung his head toward the ceiling and yelled, "*Fuck you!*" He slapped his face twice, made a barking sound, and stomped off in a huff. Most of the customers laughed. Ally didn't, so I stopped laughing and changed the subject.

"So the police took Kathleen's word over Ken's," I said. "About the beatings."

"Wouldn't you?"

"I would, in fact," I said.

I tried a half-spoonful of the soup and wondered if miso might be the Japanese word for week-old sweat socks.

"I know what you're thinking," she said. "But I had reasons for believing Ken's story."

"Such as?"

"He never laid a hand on me. He never abused me verbally."

"That's it?"

"I never saw him lose control throughout our relationship. And even though Kathleen continued to accuse him of abuse, Ken never left her."

I raised my eyebrows and watched to see if her cheeks would flush. They did, just slightly. She'd basically just admitted to dating Kathleen's husband while they were still married. We both realized it, but I was the only one smiling about it.

"Look, Mr. Creed," she said, "whether you want to believe it or not, Ken's a decent guy. He was always there for his wife. He did everything he could to get Kathleen to seek treatment."

I looked at the photos. "He seems to have been very persuasive in that regard," I said.

She started to say something, then stopped and had some more soup. She looked at me and shook her head. Ally seemed comfortable with the silence, but I was even more comfortable with it. When she finally spoke, her voice was steady. "You may think I'm stupid, Mr. Creed, or gullible. But it was Kathleen, not Ken. You'd know it if you spent any time with him."

What I now knew, thanks to Ally, is what Ken Chapman would say to Janet if I confronted her with the photos and police reports. I couldn't believe this scumbag had invented a back story that made him the victim! I mean, I could believe it, but I couldn't believe it worked. But he had, and that put me in a quandary. If I couldn't use the police reports, how could I prevent Janet from marrying this creep?

I could always kill him. But I couldn't kill him. I mean, I'd love to kill him, but Janet would know I did it, and she'd never forgive me. No, everything in my gut told me that Janet had to be the one to find out about Chapman. She'd have to learn about him in such a way that he wouldn't be able to con her like he conned Ally David.

The waitress brought our main courses. Ally gave a coy smile and purred, "Dig in, Spider-Man! Show 'em how tough you are!"

I looked at the concoction on my plate. Every part of it was colorful, but the colors seemed wrong for the dish in a way that reminded me of Tammy Faye Bakker's makeup. I pushed a few items around the plate with my chopsticks and may have seen little puffs of smoke. I decided to concentrate on the soup instead.

When we left the restaurant, Ally said not to bother walking her back to the rotunda. I sat on a nearby bench and watched her walk away. About twenty steps into her departure, she lifted her arm and waved without turning her head. I wondered what gave her the confidence to assume I'd been staring at her ass that whole time.

I sat awhile and thought about my ex-wife, Janet. It was clear I'd have to come up with something novel to help her understand the enormous mistake she was about to make in marrying Ken Chapman. I had an idea playing through my mind, but before I could put it on paper, I'd need to spend some time with Ken Chapman's ex, Kathleen Gray.

Kathleen was currently living in North Bergen, just outside New York City. Lou Kelly had run a credit check on her and learned she had recently applied for a home loan with her local bank. The loan was still pending, and Lou suggested I pose as a loan officer and use that pretense to set up a meeting with her. Of course, I could simply threaten her, Lou had said. I thanked Lou for the advice and explained that I wouldn't need to rely on threats or a cheesy cover story. Truth, honesty, and an abundance of natural charm were my allies.

I dialed her number.

"Hello," Kathleen Gray said.

"Kathleen, my name is Donovan Creed and I'm with Homeland Security in Bedford, Virginia. I'd like to talk to you about your ex-husband, Kenneth Chapman."

The connection went dead.

Not a problem. I could always fly into LaGuardia tomorrow and sweet talk my way into a dinner date with her. Since I had my phone out anyway, I decided to dial my mystery caller, the persistent person who shouldn't have had my number.

I punched up the number and watched it connect on the screen with no premonition of the effect this simple act was about to have on my life.

# 3.

"MISTER...CREED... THANK...you for...re...turning... my...call."

At first I thought it was a joke. The voice on the other end of the line was metallic, choppy, like a guy on a respirator or maybe a tracheotomy patient who had to force air through a speaking valve in his throat.

"How did you get my number?" I asked.

"Sal...va ... tore...Bon...a ...dello," he said.

"How much did he charge you for it?"

"Fif...ty...thou...sand...dollars."

"That's a lot of money for a phone number."

"Sal says...you're...the...best."

The tinny, metallic voice revealed no hint of emotion. Each word bite was cloyingly monotonous and annoyed the shit out of me. I found myself wanting to imitate it, but resisted the urge. "What do you want?" I said.

"I want...to em...ploy you...part...time...the way...Sal... does."

"How do I know I can trust you?" I said.

"You can...torture...me...first...if you...want."

He offered to write down a name and give it to me and I could torture him until I was satisfied he'd never reveal it. This was supposed to prove he wouldn't sell me out later if something went wrong in our business arrangement. The man

28

was obviously insane, which meant he was pretty much like everyone else with whom I associated.

"Before we go any further," I said, "what shall I call you?"

"Vic...tor."

"There's a flaw in your plan," I said. "Torture is only one way to make you talk. What if someone kidnaps your wife or kids or your girlfriend? What if they threaten to blow up the day care center where your sister works? Trust me, Victor. It's hard to let your loved ones die a horrific death when you could save them by simply revealing a name."

There was a long pause. Then he said, "I'm...wheelchair... bound. There...is no...one...in...my life. When...you... meet me... you will...under...stand."

I thought about that for a moment and decided I already understood. "I'd rather limit our relationship to the telephone for now," I said. "I actually do believe you wouldn't talk. Something tells me you'd welcome torture and maybe even death."

"You are...very...percep...tive...Mr...Creed. So...when ...can you...start?"

I wasn't worried about speaking freely on my cell phone. The few people in the world capable of breaching my cell security already knew what I did for a living. "I have three clients," I said. "If you want me, you'll be fourth in line. Each contract is fifty thousand dollars, plus expenses, wired in advance."

"Can...I...de...cide how...the hits... go... down?"

"Within reason," I said.

Victor gave me the details for the first target. Then he hit me with a stipulation I'd never encountered: he wanted to speak to the victim minutes before the execution. I told him that would require kidnapping, which would place a major burden on me. It meant a second person, more time, and more exposure. I refused all the way up to the point where Victor offered to double my fee.

Victor proceeded to tell me exactly what he wanted me to do, and why. And as he spoke in that creepy, metallic voice, I realized that even though I thought I'd stared in the face of the deepest, darkest evil the world could possibly produce, I had never encountered anyone as vile. I came away thinking I'd have to scrape the bowels of hell with a fine-tooth comb to uncover a plan as morbidly evil as his.

I told him I'd do it.

# 4.

"BEFORE YOU MEET them, you need to see them," Kathleen Gray said as she signed me in. "They do this for the children, so they won't see you cry or recoil in horror," she added.

The William and Randolph Hearst Burn Center at New York-Presbyterian/Weill Cornell is the largest and busiest burn center in the country, entrusted with treating more than a thousand children each year. I got that and a bunch of other information from a brochure in the lobby while waiting for Ken Chapman's ex to show up. I had called her at work and explained I needed to meet her in person before I could consider approving her house loan.

"Bullshit!" she had said. "You're the guy from Homeland Security who called me yesterday. Don't bother denying it; I recognize your voice."

Nevertheless, Kathleen agreed to meet me after work at the burn center, where she volunteered two hours of her time every Tuesday. She escorted me through the lobby door and down a long hallway.

"What made you decide to work with burn victims?" I said.

"After my divorce, all I wanted was to get out of Charleston and make new friends, so I moved here and got a job. But I didn't know anyone. Then one day my company offered tickets for a charity event, and I took one just to have someplace to go, thinking maybe I'd meet someone."

"And?"

"And here you are!" She burst out laughing. "Well, you're a liar, of course, but at least you're good-looking. And everything about you screams 'single guy!'"

We turned left and headed down another hallway. Several corridors ran off that one, and I tried to keep up with the route we'd taken in case I had to navigate back on my own. Doctors and nurses came and went, walking with purpose. A short, pudgy nurse in a light blue lab coat winked at Kathleen and made kissing sounds as she passed. We walked a few steps, and I cocked my head and said, "I bet there's a story there!"

"Oh, hush, you!" she said.

I raised my eyebrows, and she started giggling.

"Don't even," she said.

I didn't. "What makes you think I'm single?" I asked.

She laughed. "Oh, please!"

We passed a window. The sky was darkening outside, and the gusting wind made a light buzzing sound as it attacked the weaker portions of the window frame. Kathleen had entered the hospital wearing a heavy cloth overcoat that she now removed and hung on a wooden peg by the outer ward doors. She pushed a silver circle on the wall and the doors flew open.

"I didn't meet anyone special at the fundraiser," she said, "but I was touched by the video presentation. That night, I read the brochure from cover to cover and got hooked."

"So you just showed up and they put you to work?"

"Yeah, pretty much. Until that point, my life had been in a downward spiral. I'd felt sorry for myself, victimized, after the whole Ken thing. Then I met the burn kids and I was humbled by their optimism and their passion to survive."

"Sounds like you found a home."

She smiled. "Yes, that's it exactly. I made an instant decision that changed my life."

"And now you come here every Tuesday?"

"Yup. Every Tuesday after work for two hours."

Kathleen picked up a clipboard. While she studied it, I took the opportunity to study her face and figure. I had come here expecting to find a timid, broken woman, but Kathleen's divorce obviously agreed with her. She was attractive, with large eyes and honey colored hair that stopped an inch above her shoulders. I took her for a natural blonde because she wore her hair parted in the middle and I couldn't detect any dark roots. High on her forehead, just beneath her hairline, I could make out a light dusting of freckles. She had a few more freckles scattered across the bridge of her nose as well. Her body was gym tight, and she had a friendly, easygoing manner that revealed nothing of the difficult past I had witnessed in the police photos. Her voice was unique. You could get caught up in it, especially when she spoke about her volunteer work. We were about to enter the burn center treatment area, and despite my concerns about what might lie beyond the next set of doors, I found myself hanging on her every word.

"The pain these children live with daily is something you and I will never encounter or comprehend," she said. "And the toddlers, oh my God, you can't help but burst into tears the first time you see them. It's best to see them through a one-way mirror before you meet them because the worst thing you can do is let them see your pity. It erodes their self-confidence and reinforces the fear that they're monsters, unfit for society."

I admired her character, but the last thing I felt like doing was looking at severely burned children. Kathleen sensed it and said, "If you want to talk to me about Ken, you'll have to participate."

"Why is it so important to you that I do this?" I said.

"Because even though you look like a thug, who's to say you won't turn out to be the person who winds up making a difference?"

"Let's assume I'm not that person. Then what?"

"If you really are with Homeland Security, I'm guessing you spend most of your time distrusting people. I can think of worse things than exposing you to some wonderful children who deserve compassion, friendship, and encouragement."

"Friendship?" I said.

Kathleen smiled. "Could happen," she said. "And if it does, it will change two lives: theirs and yours."

"But ..."

"Just keep an open mind," she said.

Kathleen escorted me through the double doors and into a viewing room that put me in mind of the ones in police stations—only instead of overlooking an interrogation room, the burn center viewing room overlooked a play area. She asked if I was ready. I took a deep breath and nodded, and she pulled the curtain open.

There were a half-dozen kids in the play area. We watched them interact with toys and each other for several minutes, and at some point, I turned and caught her staring at me. I don't know what Kathleen Gray saw in my face that evening, but whatever it was, it seemed to delight her.

"Why, Donovan," she said. "You're a natural!"

I assumed she was referring to my casual reaction to the kids' severe disfigurement. Of course, Kathleen had no way of knowing that my profession had a lot to do with it, not to mention my close friendship with Augustus Quinn, a man whose face was singularly horrific and far more frightening than anything going on in the playroom.

Kathleen took me by the wrist and said, "All righty then. Let's meet them."

I have a soft spot for children and rarely find it necessary to kill them. That being said, in general I'm uncomfortable around kids and expect I come across rather stiff and imposing.

These kids were different. They were happy to see me. Or maybe they were just happy to see anyone new. They giggled more than I would have expected, and they seemed fascinated by my face, especially the angry scar that runs from the side of my cheek to the middle of my neck. All six of them traced it with their fingers. They were truly amazing, all of them.

But of course, there was one in particular.

Addie was six years old. She was covered in bandages and glossy material the color of lemon rind. She smelled not of Jolly Ranchers or bubblegum but soured hydrocolloid.

I knew what I was seeing.

According to something I'd read in the waiting room, fourth-degree burns affect the tissues beneath the deepest layers of skin, including muscles, tendons, and bones. This, then, was Addie.

Except for the eyes. Her eyes were unharmed, huge and expressive.

Though relatives were told that Addie and her twin sister Maddie would not survive the initial treatment, amazingly they did. They were ordinary kids who should have been running around in a yard somewhere, playing chase or tag, but sometimes life deals you a shit hand. Around noon the second day, while Addie stabilized, Maddie took a turn for the worse. She alternately faltered and rallied all afternoon as a team of heroes worked on her, refusing to let her die. Kathleen wasn't there but she heard about it, what a special, brave child

Maddie was.

In the end, her fragile body failed her. A nurse said it was the first time she'd seen a particular doctor cry, and when he began bawling, it caused the rest of the team to lose it. They were all touched and personally affected by the fight in these little twins, these tiny angels. They said they'd never seen anyone quite like them and didn't expect to ever again.

"Want to see the picture I drawed?" Addie asked.

I looked at Kathleen. She nodded.

"I'd like that," I said.

Before showing it to me, Addie wanted to say something. "All the camera pictures of me and Maddie got rooned in the fire, so I drawed a picture of Maddie so all my new friends could see what we looked like before we got burned up."

She handed me a crayon drawing of a girl's face.

"That's Maddie," she said. "Wasn't she beautiful?"

I couldn't trust myself to speak so I just nodded.

When we left the burn unit, Kathleen said, "I love them all, but Addie's the one who got me praying."

"What happened to her?" I asked.

Kathleen took a deep breath before speaking. "About two weeks ago, Addie's house caught on fire. Her parents, Greg and Melanie, died in the fire while trying to save the girls' lives."

"Addie was able to talk about it?"

Kathleen nodded. "There was also the 911 call Melanie made. Apparently she got trapped downstairs. Greg made it to the girls' room and put wet towels over their faces to keep them alive until the firefighters arrived."

"Smart guy to think about the towels," I said.

"Addie originally thought the wet towels flew into the room by themselves. When they explained her mom threw them, her face lit up. Until that moment, she thought her mom had run away."

We were both silent awhile.

"There was a lot of love in that marriage," I said.

Kathleen said, "I haven't experienced it personally, but I've always believed that during the course of a good marriage, especially when children are involved, husbands and wives often perform random acts of heroism that go largely unnoticed by the general public."

"And in a great marriage," I said, "when one spouse goes down, the other takes up the slack."

Kathleen gave me a look that might have been curiosity, might have been affection.

"You surprise me, Creed."

# 5.

"THESE LITTLE BOMBS weigh in at 490 calories," Kathleen Gray said.

I glanced at the paltry square.

"That number seems high," I said.

"Trust me," she said. "I used to work at the one in Charleston."

It was 7:45 pm and we were in Starbucks on Third and East Sixty-Sixth. Neither of us had much of an appetite, but Kathleen said she always treated herself to a raspberry scone after spending time at the burn center. She took a bite.

"Yum," she said. "Technically, it's a raspberry apricot thumbprint scone." She cocked her head and appraised me.

"You sure you don't want to try one?"

I didn't and told her so. "Plus there's the other thing," I said.

"What other thing?"

"The acronym for it is RATS," I said.

She studied me a moment, a faint smile playing about her lips. I saw them move ever-so-slightly as she performed the mental calculation.

"You're an odd duck," she said. "You know that, right?"

I sipped my coffee and made a note of the fact that I had now met three of Ken Chapman's women, and two of them had commented on my strangeness on successive days. The third of Chapman's women was my ex-wife, Janet, and her opinion of me was beyond repair.

Someone pushed open the front door, and a rush of wind blew some rain in, lowering the temperature by ten degrees. Or so it seemed. Something behind us caught Kathleen's eye and she giggled.

"The barista was talking to someone and pointing at you," she said. "I think it has something to do with the venti."

I frowned and shook my head in disgust. "Barista," I said.

Kathleen giggled harder. She scrunched her face into a pout.

"You're such a grump!" she said.

"Well, it's ridiculous," I said.

She broke into a bubbly laugh. I continued my rant.

"These trendy restaurants, they're all so pretentious! Just yesterday I saw a guy nearly die from eating some kind of exotic Japanese dish. And here," I gestured toward the coffee-making apparatus, "you have to learn a whole new friggin' language in order to justify spending four bucks for a cup of Joe."

She laughed harder. "Joe? Oh, my God, did you just say Joe? Tell me you just climbed out of a forties time machine."

I think she liked saying the word "Joe," because she said it two more times while laughing uncontrollably.

The other customers glanced at us, but I wasn't finished yet.

"Grande," I said. "Solo. Venti. Doppio. What the hell is doppio, anyway—one of the seven dwarfs?"

"No," she squealed. "But Grumpy is!" Kathleen's laughter had passed the point of no return. Her cheeks were puffy, and her eyes had become slits.

I frowned again and recited the conversation for her. "All I said was, 'I'll have a coffee.' 'What size?' she says. 'A regular,' I said. 'We have grande, venti, solo, doppio, short, and tall,' she says. 'Four hundred ninety calories,' you say. It's a flippin' two-inch square!"

Kathleen gripped the sides of the table. "Stop it!" she said. "You're going to make me pee!"

When her last bubble of laughter died down, she told me it felt good to laugh after two hours with the kids. I understood what she meant. Bad as her life had been with Ken, she still managed to feel guilty that she had it so good by comparison.

I said, "I hate to end the party, but I need to ask you a few questions about Ken Chapman."

She frowned. "Just when we were having such a good time."

"I know."

"I really hate to talk about it," she said.

"I know."

She looked at me and sighed. "Okay, Homeland. You put in your time. What would you like to know?"

For the better part of an hour, we talked about her marriage to Ken Chapman. It was hard on her, and by the time she dropped me off at my hotel, I could see she was emotionally drained. I didn't ask her to join me for a nightcap, and she didn't offer to, though she asked if I wanted to get together the next day.

"Tomorrow's Valentine's, you know," she said.

I told her I had to meet someone, which was true. In fact, I said, I had to pack my overnight bag and head back to the airport that very night—also true. She nodded in an absentminded way as though this were something she'd heard before, something she expected me to say.

What I didn't tell her: I had contracted to kill someone the

40

next morning. What I did tell her: "I'm flying back tomorrow after my meeting to take you someplace special for dinner." When I said that, her face lit up like a kid at Christmas and she gave me a big hug.

Then I said, "I'll call you at work tomorrow just before noon and we can work out the details."

An hour and change later, I was settling into my seat on the Citation. Ten minutes after that, I was sleeping soundly. But just before falling asleep, I thought Kathleen Gray had to be the nicest human being I'd ever met.

# 6.

MONICA CHILDERS DIDN'T want to die.

It was just past daybreak, Valentine's Day, and we were north of Jacksonville, Florida, at the Amelia Island Plantation resort. Callie had positioned herself near the ninth tee box, where the main road intersected the cart path.

Monica was no terrorist or threat to national security, but I had already agreed to kill her, so here we were. These freelance contracts meant money in my pocket. Although it's noble to pretend my fulltime job is killing suspected terrorists for the government, they pay me with resources, not cash. Of course, the resources are supposed to be used exclusively for monitoring or tracking terrorists. But Darwin, my government facilitator, knows full well how I earn my living. He rarely complains because killing civilians during the down times keeps me focused and sharp. At least that's what he believes.

Darwin provides me with unparalleled clout. A simple call from him and doors get opened, legal procedures become irrelevant, and no turns magically to yes. While I'm very good with my own crime scenes, there's always a random element to taking lives. On the rare occasions when something goes wrong, Darwin can be counted on to dispatch a crew to remove a body, clean a crime scene, or cover my tracks. He even controls a secret branch of the government that provides me and my crew with body doubles. Of course, the body doubles don't know they're working for us, but they remain safe until we need them. Darwin sees to that. He has a group of people who secretly protect them. I myself protected one of the body doubles the first year after leaving the CIA. I'll probably do it again if I get bored in my retirement years. Listen to me: retirement years, what a laugh!

About 70 percent of my income had been coming through Sal Bonadello, the crime boss. Most of the rest came from testing weapons for the army. But now Victor Wheelchair had entered my life with what he said would be a lifetime of contracts—contracts so simple to fulfill, a rookie could do them. My typical hit involved high-profile targets and often required days, sometimes weeks, of planning. By contrast, the types of hits Victor needed could be planned and executed in a matter of hours. I'd have to be careful not to over-think them.

Victor said Monica had done nothing wrong and wanted to know if that was a problem for me. I said, "She's obviously guilty of something or you wouldn't want her dead. That's good enough for me."

Something in my comment struck a chord that resonated with the metal-voiced weasel, and he asked me to "E ... la ... borate." I explained, "We who kill people for a living avoid making personal judgments about our targets. In Monica's case, I'm not her attorney. Not her judge. Not her jury. I'm not being paid to determine her innocence. I'm being paid to render justice. Whether it's you, Sal, Homeland, or Captain Kangaroo, all I need to know is that someone, somewhere, has found Monica Childers guilty of something and sentenced her to death. My job is to carry out the execution."

Victor told me where to find Monica and how he wanted her to die. He said she ran at daybreak every morning and would do so even while on vacation at Amelia Island Plantation. So Callie waited for Monica by the ninth tee box, decked out in the latest dri-fit Nike athletic apparel. To complete the ensemble, she wore custom running shoes and a high-tech runner's watch. When she heard Monica coming her way, she started running and timed her approach to hit the intersection a few seconds after Monica passed. The two ladies noticed each other and nodded. Callie rounded the corner, increased her speed, and fell into step with Monica.

"Mind if I run with you?" Callie asked.

Monica pressed her lips into a tight frown. "As you can see, I'm not very fast."

"Actually, you are!" Callie said. "I had to sprint like a boiled owl to catch you!"

Monica wrinkled her nose. "Boiled owl? I hope no actual event occurred to inspire such an expression!"

Callie giggled. "Oh my God, I hope so, too!"

Monica smiled in spite of herself.

"In any case," Callie said, "this is a good pace for me. Plus, I hate running alone, especially when I don't know the area."

That was all it took to form a runner's bond: two very pretty, fashionable ladies who shared a passion for running. I imagined them jogging fluidly over the plantation road, the cadence of their stride adding a human counterpoint to the morning sounds of the island's bird and insect population.

Monica cast an envious glance at her running mate. "You have perfect legs!" she said.

Callie, caught a bit off guard, responded, "What a nice thing to say!"

Monica flashed a friendly smile and said, "You're a model, right? I could grow to hate you!" After laughing, she added, "Are you staying at the plantation?"

Callie said, "We—my husband and I—checked in late last night."

"You always run this early?"

"Not really. But my in-laws are arriving soon and I want to get in a few miles before they do." The way she drew out the word "in-laws" made Monica smile.

"Oh God," Monica said. "The in-laws."

"Exactly!" Callie said. "By the way, I'm Callie Carpenter."

"Hi, Callie. I'm Monica Childers."

They exited the resort and turned left onto A1A. Looking down the highway a bit, Monica said, "Let's avoid the van. It shouldn't be there."

Callie agreed.

They were about to head the opposite way when Callie said, "Oh my God! That's my in-laws!" She sighed. "Oh well, so much for my run!"

Monica slowed. "Let's try again tomorrow."

"Come with me!" Callie suddenly blurted out, her eyes twinkling. "I want to introduce you. It'll just take a sec, and you'll be speeding down the road again in no time!"

As we planned, Callie ran ahead without giving Monica time to reply. Monica barely knew this girl and certainly wouldn't want to stop her run to meet the in-laws. But she also wouldn't want to appear rude, so we counted on her to follow Callie to the van.

And she did.

As the girls approached, I slid the side door of the van open and stepped out, smiling broadly. I'd dressed in what I considered to be coastal casual, a white, spread-collar dress shirt and tan linen slacks with matching Italian loafers. When I picked Callie up that morning, she had pointed at me and laughed a full minute. Even now, I saw her smirking at my choice of attire.

While waiting to be introduced, Monica ran her fingers through her fashionably short black hair. Though I knew her to be forty-one, she looked years younger. She was in excellent shape, with deep, expressive eyes and a willowy frame that boasted a set of Park Avenue's finest implants. I wouldn't classify her as stunning, but she was certainly pretty, possibly even striking for her age. She would probably hate to hear a man add the words "for her age" when describing her looks, but things were what they were.

Callie made the introductions, saying, "Donovan's handsome, isn't he! Check out that engaging smile and those penetrating, jade green eyes."

"Oh please," I said, rolling my penetrating, jade green eyes.

Monica smiled politely. As far as I was concerned, Callie could step back and let me take it from there, but she was on a roll. "And that outfit," Callie said, winking at me, "very stylish." Then she said, "Monica, what would you call that look?"

Monica smiled. "Umm… continental?"

"Coastal casual," I said.

Monica was itching to get back to her run, but she returned my smile. "Hello, Donovan," she said, extending her hand.

I took her hand in mine and made a slow, exaggerated bow as if intending to kiss it. Callie started to giggle, and Monica glanced at her and blushed. Monica seemed to want to say something, but I increased the pressure on her hand and suddenly everything in her world turned crazy. Monica gasped and tried to pull away, but I shifted my weight and clamped my other hand on her upper arm. Before her mind could process what was happening, I hurled her into the van with such force her body crashed into the far wall and rebounded to the floor.

Wide-eyed, terror-struck, Monica scrambled for the door. But I was already in the van, blocking her escape. Stunned mute by the sudden explosion of violence, Monica tried to scream. My hand was already at her throat, and the pressure was so intense she couldn't achieve more than a squeak.

Monica's eyes frantically searched for Callie. What was going on here, she must have wondered. Why wasn't Callie helping her?

I pushed Monica's head against the exposed metal floorboard with my left hand and slid the van door shut with my right. She tried to wriggle out of my grasp, so I applied more pressure to hold her in place. I heard something crunch and guessed it was the cartilage in her ear. Cartilage or not, it seemed to take the fight out of her. Monica's chest heaved, and her breath came in quick bursts, like a child gasping after a hard cry. She let out a low moan like a terrified animal caught in a trap: too frightened to scream, too disoriented to react.

She must have heard the engine turn over, must have felt the van jerk into gear. Somewhere in the part of her brain that was still functioning, a puzzle piece fell into place. I know because I saw it register on Monica's face: Callie was driving the van, and there would be no escape.

Something worked its way up her throat and triggered her gag reflex. A mixture of drool, nose fluid, and blood collected at her chin and hung like a thick strand of rope. Victor would be proud to see how far Monica had fallen in such a short period of time. As if on cue, her tears began flowing freely. She whimpered in a little girl's voice, "Please, please stop! You're hurting me! You're hurting me! Please! Let me go!"

Callie scanned the highway and checked the rearview

mirror before slowing the van. She made a sharp left onto the meager trail we'd cased earlier. As she worked the van into the thicket, scrubby pine boughs and overgrown bushes and vines parted before us and instantly closed behind us, effectively swallowing us up. Callie pushed us in about a hundred yards, then, with great effort, turned the van around, pointed it back toward the highway, and put it in park.

"We're good," Callie said. She kept the engine running so the heater could work. Then she turned halfway around in the seat to watch.

"Monica," I said, "I'm going to let you sit up now if you promise not to scream."

She nodded as best she could, and I helped her get to a sitting position. She glared at Callie. Callie shrugged and mouthed, "Sorry," then handed me some tissue to pass to her former friend. We watched Monica dab at her face until she'd got it as presentable as it was going to get under the circumstances. She tentatively touched some tissue to her ear. She winced and lowered her hand to inspect the blood. There wasn't much on the tissue, but it was enough to cause some more tears to well up in her eyes. When she blinked, most of them got caught up in her eyelashes and only a few wound up tracing down her cheek. I'd been watching her all this time, waiting for her to catch her breath, maybe relax a bit. It seemed to be working. I think she was finding some hope to cling to. After all, why would we bother with tissue if we intended to kill her, right?

I called Victor. "She's ready to talk," I said. I handed the phone to Monica, and Callie and I climbed out of the van and closed the doors behind us.

"Did you see the look on her face when you handed her the phone?" Callie said.

I nodded. It was a look I couldn't easily describe: a mixture of shock, confusion, hope, fear. This whole experience had been a first for me.

"You think she'll try to lock us out?" Callie said.

"I doubt it. She knows she can't get to the front seat faster than we can open the door."

Callie nodded. We watched the poor soul holding the phone to her good ear, straining to understand the clipped, metallic voice at the other end of the line. I knew the feeling.

"How are you coming with the body double?"

"The one for you?" I asked. "I'm still working on it."

Callie laughed. "I'll bet you are."

"Not easy finding a nice, sweet librarian looks like you."

"Librarian, huh?"

"Sure, why not?"

"Your last 'librarian' was Fifi the French whore. Had a tattoo on her pussy that said, 'Read My Lips!'"

I smiled at the thought. "Fifi's right, but I don't remember her calling herself 'the French whore.'"

Callie frowned. "It's a librarian expression. But she wasn't the first hooker librarian with a crotch tat. Do you even remember the name of that other one?"

I did. Constance would have been a perfect body double for Callie … except for the crotch tat that said, "Is it hot in here or is it just me?"

"I think I deserve more credit," I said. "It's not easy finding a body double for you. Not to mention the detailed inspections I have to make, you being so fussy about tattoos and such."

"Yeah, well I agree that when it comes to hookers, you put everything you have into your work."

Inside the van, tucked against the far corner, Monica had pulled her knees up to her chest. Tears streaked her cheeks, and her mouth formed words I couldn't hear. She seemed to listen for a while and then she started crying softly.

"What do you think he's saying to her?" Callie said.

I had no idea and hated myself for caring.

"This next body double," Callie said. "Does she have a tattoo?"

"Jenine? I don't know yet."

"But you're itching to find out."

"My devotion to detail is legendary," I said. "Timeless."

"So is the clap," Callie said.

Monica looked up at me through the window and nodded, and I opened the door. I heard her thank Victor and wondered what that meant. She handed the phone back to me. I put it to my ear.

"Creed," I said.

"You know…what…to do," Victor said.

# 7.

I DID KNOW what to do, but I was curious about a couple of things. I asked Monica if she knew Victor.

"I know of him," she said.

"How's that?"

"Through my husband."

I nodded. So Victor was killing her to punish the husband. At least that made some sense. I didn't want to ask too many questions, though. Questions lead to answers, and answers lead to doubt, and doubt will ruin a good contract killer. I looked at Callie. She was about to explode, she wanted to know so badly.

"Tell me about Victor," I said.

"I can't. If I tell you, you'll kill me."

Callie and I exchanged a look. Callie couldn't hold it back any longer; she had to speak. "This Victor guy, you're saying he told you we'd let you go if you kept quiet about your conversation with him?"

Monica looked confused. "Is this a trick question?"

Callie looked at me in disbelief. "What a twisted fuck."

"Hey, watch it," I said. "You're talking about our employer."

We all sat there looking at each other for a minute. I could have forced it out of her, but I didn't want to torture her. I could have threatened her into telling me, but that would require giving her false hope, and that didn't feel right to me somehow. I decided to let the motive slide.

"Okay, Monica," I said. "You didn't tell us anything about your conversation with Victor or about your connection to him, so you did well. I won't ask you again. But tell me this: why is his voice so weird?"

"He's a quadriplegic."

I nodded. "Still," I said, "it's eerier than that. There's more to it."

Monica was loosening up now, convinced she was about to be released. She had stopped crying, and her voice was steadier. She seemed encouraged. "It's probably because he's so young," she said, "and a midget."

Callie and I looked at each other. I said, "Midget?"

Monica gasped. "Little person," she said. "I'm sorry. I didn't mean to say that."

Callie asked, "Young? How young?"

Monica looked at me before speaking. "I don't know," she said. "Early twenties?"

"Your husband must have done something terrible to make Victor this angry," I said.

She nodded. "He saved Victor's life," she said.

# 8.

I GENTLY LOWERED Monica's head back to the floor and held it there. I stroked her hair a couple of times to help calm her. And she was calm … until she caught sight of the syringe in my free hand. At that point, her eyes grew wide with terror. She started thrashing around in the van. Then she lost control of her bladder. Too frightened to care, she peed explosively. I heard it strain against her clothing, burbling hot against her crotch, down her thigh. Because of our close proximity, she managed to drench my pants leg in the process. I looked over at Callie, exasperated.

"Believe me, Donovan," she said, "that can only improve your 'coastal casual' look."

I frowned and loosened my grip ever so slightly—but just enough—and this time Monica's scream was loud and piercing. Of course, it had no effect out there in the middle of nowhere. I got her back under control, parted her hair, and pricked the side of her scalp with the tip of the syringe. A few minutes later, I slid open the side door and pushed Monica out. Her body tumbled into a thicket and skidded to a stop. She staggered to her feet and managed to walk a few shaky steps before falling down to stay.

Callie put the van in gear and steered it carefully through the underbrush and back onto the highway. She kept to the speed limit, drove south, and put the crime scene behind us.

"A real fighter, that one," I said, making my way to the front passenger seat. "She impressed me just now, the way she got to her feet."

Callie nodded.

The van's tires thrummed rhythmically over the patchy road tar. We passed a golf course on the right and an ambitious condo development on the left, which appeared to be unfinished and abandoned. The few residential community entrances we passed were camouflaged by foliage so dense and overgrown, even in February, I had to wonder what sort of people would pay these astronomical prices to live a half-mile from the beach, among the spiders and mosquitoes, without benefit of an ocean view.

"She had gorgeous hair," I said.

"Very stylish," Callie agreed. "And classy." She paused a minute before asking, "How long you think before someone finds her?"

"This close to the plantation? Probably two days."

"You think they'll notice the needle mark on the scalp?"

"What are we, CSI? I doubt the ME will notice it."

"Because?"

"I put it in one of her head wounds."

Callie thought about that and said, "She must have hit the wall head first when you threw her in the van."

"That'd be my guess," I said.

We rode in silence awhile, content to watch the scenery unfold. We were on A1A, south of Amelia Island, where the two-lane road cuts a straight swath through the undeveloped scrub and marsh for fifteen miles. There was a primal element to this stretch of land that seemed to discourage the rampant commercialization running almost nonstop from Jacksonville to South Beach. A couple miles in, we passed three crosses and a crude, homemade sign that proclaimed "Jesus Died For Your Sins!"

"Monica seemed nice," Callie said. "A little snooty, but that could be the money. Or the age difference. Still, I liked her. She had great manners."

I laughed. "Manners?"

"She had a premonition about the van," Callie said. "But she didn't want to offend me, so she came anyway."

I tried the sound of it in my mouth. "She was killed because of her good manners."

"I liked her," Callie repeated.

"I liked her, too," I said, "until she peed on me!"

I placed two bundles of cash in Callie's lap. She picked one up, felt the weight in her hand.

"I like this even better," she said.

We dropped the van off behind an abandoned barn a couple miles beyond the ferry boat landing. We removed the explosives from the wheel well in Callie's rental car and positioned them throughout the van.

"How much you have to pay for this thing?" Callie asked.

"Four grand," I said. "Not me, though. Victor." Right on cue, my phone rang.

"Is it...fin...ished?" Victor asked.

"Just a sec," I said. I climbed in the passenger seat, and Callie drove us a quarter-mile before putting the rental car in park.

"Are we far enough away?" I asked.

"If we go too far," she said, "we'll miss the fun part."

She got out of the car and dialed a number on her phone and the van exploded in the distance. Callie remained out of the car until she felt the wind from the explosion wash lightly over her face.

"You're insane," I said to Callie.

"It's done," I said to Victor.

Victor said, "Good. I...have...two more...jobs ... for you."

"Already?" I retrieved a small notebook and pen from my duffel and wrote down the information. The names, ages, occupations, and addresses were so different, it seemed as though they'd been plucked out of thin air. I asked Victor, "Do you even *know* these people?"

"All...part...of a...master...plan," he said. I covered the mouthpiece and said to Callie, "I take back what I said before, about you being insane." Then I said to Victor, "Are there many more?"

"Many," Victor said in his weird, metallic voice. "Real...ly ...Mr...Creed...evil  is...every...where...and...must...be pun...ished."

# 9.

"I *MUST* SEE the Picasso," Kathleen said.

"Then you shall," I said.

"And the maître d'," she said. "They have one, right?"

"They do indeed."

"Is he stuffy? I hope he's insufferably stuffy!"

"He will be if I don't tip him," I said. We were in the Seagram Building on East Fifty-Second, in the lobby of the Four Seasons restaurant.

She touched my arm. "Donovan, this is really sweet of you, but we don't have to eat here. I don't want you to spend this much on me. Let's just have a drink, see the painting and maybe the marble pool. We can share a pizza at Angelo's afterward."

"Relax," I said. "I'm rich."

"Really?"

"Really."

The Four Seasons is famous, timeless, and the only restaurant in New York designated as a landmark.

"Do you mean really, you're rich," she said, "or that you're really rich?"

"I'm rich enough to buy you whatever you'd like to have tonight."

She laughed. "In that case, I'll have the Picasso!"

Did I mention I liked this lady?

I gave my name to the maître d' and led Kathleen to the corridor where the Picasso tapestry had hung since the restaurant opened back in 1959. The twenty-two-foot-high Picasso was in fact the center square of a stage curtain that had been designed for the 1920 Paris production of *The Three Cornered Hat*. When the theater owner ran out of money, he cut the Picasso portion from the curtain and sold it. Now, with the economy in distress, Kathleen had heard the tapestry was about to be auctioned for an estimated eight million dollars. This might be her only chance to see it.

"Oh my God!" she said, her voice suddenly turning husky. "I love it!"

"Compared to his other work, the colors are muted," I said. "But yeah, it's pretty magnificent."

"Tell me about it," she said. "Impress me."

"It's a distemper on linen," I said.

"Distemper? Like the disease a dog gets?"

"Exactly like that."

She gave me a look. "Bullshit!"

"Well, it's spelled the same way. Actually, it refers to using gum or glue as a binding element."

She made a snoring sound. "Boring," she said.

"Okay," I said, "forget that part. Here's what you want to know: Picasso laid the canvas on the floor and painted it with a brush attached to a broom handle. He used a toothbrush for the detailed work."

Kathleen clapped her hands together. "More!" she said.

"It took three weeks to paint."

She looked at me expectantly.

"He wore carpet slippers so he wouldn't smudge the paint."

I struggled to remember what else I'd read about the thing. I shrugged. "That's all I've got," I said.

Kathleen smiled and nudged up against me. "You did well," she said.

We had a drink at the bar. Among the small crowd waiting for tables, Kathleen spotted Woody Allen, Barbara Streisand, and Billy Joel. I said, "See those two guys by the palm frond? That's Millard Fillmore and Jackie Gleason!"

She sniffed. "At least the famous New Yorkers I'm lying about are still alive."

A number of seasonal trees surrounded the white marble pool in the main dining room, and the head waiter sat us beneath one of them. Spun-metal curtains hung in rows against the walls, undulating softly as the air flow from the vents teased them.

"This is fantastic," she said, looking around the room. "Everything is so elegant, especially the breathing curtains!"

"Especially those," I said.

I tossed back a shot of bourbon and watched Kathleen sip her pomegranate martini. The waiter had brought us drinks and given us time to study the menus. Now he returned, ready to take our order.

"Of course I've never been here before," Kathleen said, "so you'll have to order for me."

I nodded. "We'll start with the crispy shrimp," I said.

"Oops. No shellfish," Kathleen said.

"Sorry," I said. "How about the foie gras?"

"Goose liver pâté?" she said. "Ugh!"

"Peppered quail?"

"Sorry," she said. "Meat product."

"Perhaps you should just pick something," I said. She may have detected some annoyance in my voice.

Kathleen burst into a hearty laugh. "I'm just messing with you, Donny. I'd love some crispy shrimp."

The waiter and I exchanged a glance.

"She might very possibly be insane," I said, and Kathleen laughed some more.

Then she told the waiter, "Watch out for this one. He's very grumpy in restaurants."

The waiter left to place our order.

"Donny?" I said. I huffed a bit, and she placed her hand on mine.

"Okay, I won't call you Donny," she said. "But if we're going to start seeing each other, I'm going to want a pet name for you."

We looked at each other, and I rotated my palm so I could hold her hand. She cocked her head slightly and raised an eyebrow.

I said, "I have to admit there's something special about you … Pablo!"

"Oh, God," she said and laughed some more. "Okay then, no nicknames!"

I tried to remember the last time Janet and I shared a laugh.

"Something about me," Kathleen repeated. Her eyes hinted amusement. She winked at me and sipped her cocktail. "Mmm," she said. She touched the napkin to her mouth. You could add up all her looks and mannerisms and never total gorgeous, but you'd get to adorable pretty quick, and that was enough for me. Hell, I couldn't take my eyes off her.

"Go ahead," I said. "Ask me."

"Ask you what?"

"Something's bothering you. I can see it in your eyes."

She twitched her mouth to one side and held it there, a sort of half-frown. "I don't want to ruin the moment," she said.

"The moment will survive."

"Okay then, brace yourself."

I took my hand away from hers and grabbed both sides of the table and pretended to hold on tight. "Let 'er rip!" I said.

She took a deep breath. "Last night at Starbucks, you told me about Janet and Ken dating. You were worried about his temper, what he might do to her if they decide to get married."

I kept quiet.

"Do you still love her?" she asked.

"No. But I don't want my daughter's mother to marry a wife-beater." She made a face, and I said, "I'm sorry. I can't imagine what it's been like for you."

Kathleen was wearing the same cloth coat she'd worn the night before. She'd been cold and hadn't wanted to surrender it to the coat check girl downstairs. But now she stood and removed it and folded it over the back of her chair, revealing a white blouse, a tan faux suede skirt, and a wide brown belt with two gold buckles. She wore very little makeup, or maybe it hadn't been freshened up in a while, since she'd come straight from work. It didn't seem to make her uncomfortable the way most women would be. She sat back down and surprised me by taking my hand in hers and kissing it.

"I don't wish him dead or anything," she said. "But Ken is …" She sighed. "Ken is not a part of my life anymore. I mean, there's not a day goes by I don't think about him or the terrible things he did to me. But." She paused and showed a bittersweet smile as the memories danced across her face. "There were some good times, too. In the beginning."

I nodded.

Then she said, "I've heard he's gotten treatment, and I'm glad. I hope he's okay. I hope he finds peace."

I nodded again.

I had already finalized a plan for handling the Ken and Janet situation, and now I realized I'd been right all along not to involve her in it.

We had a wonderful dinner, and afterward, my driver took us to her place and she invited me in. Home for Kathleen was a modest duplex cottage with faded green siding. Her side of the duplex had three rooms: a kitchen, living room, bedroom—and a bath. A small stack of books sat on one end of a threadbare couch in the living room. She picked up the books and stacked them on the coffee table so we'd have room to sit.

"I'm sorry it's not nicer," she said.

"Don't be silly."

"It's just, everything is so expensive here."

"It's wonderful," I said.

And to me it was. When I'm in Virginia, I sleep in a prison cell. When I'm anywhere else for more than a day or two, I generally break into the homes of strangers and sleep in their attics. Sometimes I'll live in an attic for weeks at a time. By comparison, Kathleen's duplex was a palace.

"I can offer you a gin and tonic, bottled water, a hot chocolate with skim milk," she said, "or a diet Coke."

I asked, "Do you have an attic?"

"What a strange question," she said.

"No, I just meant, there's not a lot of room for storage."

"I have half an attic and half a basement," she said. "Does that win me some kind of prize?"

I placed my hand to her cheek, and we looked at each other. "Don't ask me to show them to you," she said. "The attic is totally junked up, and the basement has rats, I think."

I asked if I could kiss her. She said, "Okay, but just once. And not a movie kiss," she added.

# 10.

"I'M NOT SURE I appreciate your tone, Mr. Creed."

"Why should you be the exception?" I said.

It was morning, a few minutes past eight. I was in the hospital coffee shop chatting with Addie's Aunt Hazel.

"And just how is it you're connected to Addie?"

"She's my friend."

After learning how special Addie was to Kathleen, I'd come to the hospital to check on her. During a discussion with one of the nurses, I learned that Addie's father, Greg, had won ten million dollars in the New York State Lottery six months ago. I also learned that Hazel and Robert Hughes had originally planned to adopt their niece after her release from the hospital but had changed their minds after learning the money was gone. So when Aunt Hazel showed up, I ambushed her in the coffee shop.

"We're not wealthy people, Mr. Creed," Hazel had said. "Addie will require specialized care for the rest of her life, and yes, we were counting on the inheritance to provide it."

"Perhaps your interest in Addie's welfare extended only as far as the inheritance," I'd said, and that's when Aunt Hazel told me she didn't appreciate my tone.

"What happened to the lottery money?" I asked.

"Greg used part of it to pay off the house, the cars, and credit cards. The balance, more than nine million, was placed in an annuity."

I had a sudden revelation and immediately began experiencing a sick feeling in my stomach.

Hazel said, "The annuity was supposed to provide a huge monthly check for the rest of Greg and Melanie's lives. But the way it was structured, the payments ended with their deaths."

"Can you recall some of the specific provisions?" I asked.

"No," she said. "But the whole business sounds crooked to me."

"Who can tell me?" I asked.

She eyed me suspiciously. "I suppose Greg's attorney can give you details."

She rummaged through her handbag and gave me the business card of one Garrett Unger, attorney at law. I put some money on the table to cover our coffees.

"I'll have a talk with Unger and let you know if anything develops."

"We can't afford to pay you," she said.

"Consider it a random act of kindness," I said. "By the way, can you give me the address of the house? I may want to poke around a bit."

"Now who are you, exactly?" she asked.

"Someone not to be trifled with," I said.

Hazel gave me a look of concern, and I smiled. "That's a line from a movie," I said.

"Uh huh."

"*The Princess Bride*," I added.

"Well it doesn't sound like a wedding movie to me," she said. I pulled out my CIA creds and waited for her to *ooh* and *ah*. Instead, she frowned and said, "This looks like something you'd find in a five and dime."

"What's a five and dime?"

"Like a Woolworths."

I shook my head. "Doesn't matter. As I said, I'm a friend of Addie's. I met her through Kathleen, one of the volunteers here. I want to help."

"What's in it for you?"

I sighed. "Fine, don't tell me." I took out my cell phone, called Lou. When he answered, I said, "There was a fire two weeks ago at the home of Greg and Melanie Dawes." I spelled the last name for him. "Both adults died in the fire. Their twin girls were taken to the burn center at New York-Presbyterian. I need the address of the house that burned down. No, I'm not sure of the state. Try New York, first." I got our waitress's attention and asked her to bring me a pencil and paper. By the time she fetched them, I had the address. I hung up and smiled at Aunt Hazel.

"Who was that?" she asked.

"Inigo Montoya."

# 11.

VALLEY ROAD IN Montclair, New Jersey, runs south from Garrett Mountain Reservation to Bloomfield Ave. Along the way, it borders the eastern boundary of Montclair State University's sprawling campus. Coming west from NYC, you're not supposed to see any of this on your way to the fire station, but if you make the wrong turn off the freeway like I did, you get to see the sights. While I was doing so, my cell phone rang. Salvatore Bonadello, the crime boss, was on the line.

"You still alive?" Sal said.

"You call this living," I said. It was still morning, not quite ten. I'd left the coffee shop, and Aunt Hazel, less than two hours earlier.

"I been hearing some things," he said. "You stepped on someone's toes big time." He waited for me to respond, playing out the moment.

"Joe DeMeo?" I said.

Sal paused, probably disappointed he hadn't been the one to break the news. "You didn't hear it from me," he said.

"Don't tell me you're afraid of DeMeo," I said. "Big, tough, hairy guy like you?" I turned left on Bloomfield, heading south east.

"I don't gotta fear the man to respect the power. And I got—whatcha call—compelling evidence to respect it.

66

Whaddya mean, hairy?"

"Figure of speech," I said.

I hadn't been certain that arson was involved in the Dawes' house fire but figured if it was, DeMeo was responsible. The fact DeMeo knew I was looking into the fire confirmed my suspicions. Still, I was shocked at how quickly he'd gotten the word. "How long you think I have before the hairy knuckle guys show up?"

"You in someone's attic or what?"

"Rental car."

"Okay. You prob'ly got a couple hours. But I was you, I'd start checking the rearview anyway."

"Thanks for the heads-up."

"Just protectin' my—whatcha call—asset."

"DeMeo called you personally? He doesn't know we're doing business?"

Sal paused, weighing his words. "He knows."

I was stuck in a line of cars at the intersection of Bloomfield and Pine, waiting for the light to change. I had nothing else to think about beyond Sal's comment or I might have missed the clue. I kicked it around in my head a few seconds before it hit me. "DeMeo offered you a contract on me."

"Let's just say your next two jobs are—whatcha call— *gratis*."

Two jobs? That meant ... "You turned down a hundred grand?"

Sal laughed. "It ain't love, so don't get all wet about it. I just don't have anyone—whatcha call—resourceful enough to take you outta the picture. Plus, where am I gonna get a contract killer good as you? Unless maybe that blonde fox you use. You tell her about me yet?"

The light turned green, and I eased along with the traffic

until I got to the curb cut. "I've got to go," I said.

Sal said, "Wait! We got a deal on the contracts?"

"I'll give you one free contract," I said. "You already made fifty Gs giving my name to that homicidal midget."

"Which one?"

"You know more than one homicidal midget? Vic ... tor," I said, imitating my newest client.

Sal laughed. "I met the little fuck. He's got dreadlocks."

"You're shitting me."

"Long, nasty dreads, swear to Christ!"

We hung up, and I parked my Avis rental in one of the visitor's parking slots and asked the guys out front where I could find Chief Blaunert. They directed me to the kitchen area of the station house. I walked in and asked the one guy sitting there if he happened to be the fire chief.

"Until October," he said. "Then I'll just be Bob, living on a houseboat in Seattle. You're the insurance guy, right?"

I nodded. "Donovan Creed, State Farm."

"Seattle's cold this time of year," he said, "but no worse than here. The wife has a brother, owns a marina up in Portage Bay near the university."

From under the table, he positioned his foot against the seat of the chair across from him. His brown leather shoes were well-worn, but the soles were new. By way of invitation, he gestured toward the chair and used his foot to push it far enough away from the table for me to sit down. "Ever been there?" he asked. "Portage Bay?"

"Haven't had the honor," I said. I grabbed a Styrofoam cup from the stack near the sink and helped myself to some coffee from the machine.

"Well, some don't like the rain, I guess. But to us, it's as close to paradise as we're likely to get." The old Formica table in front of him had probably started out a bright shade of yellow before decades of food and coffee stains took their toll. I sat in the chair he'd slid out for me and tasted my coffee. It was bitter and burnt, which seemed fitting for fire house coffee.

"How's the java?" he asked.

"Wouldn't be polite to complain," I said. "Of course, in seven months, you'll have great coffee every day."

He winked and gave me a thumbs-up. "You know it," he said. "Seattle's got a lot of nicknames, but Coffee Town's the one I use." He savored the thought a moment. "Course they've got Starbucks and Seattle's Best. You probably don't know Tully's, but that's a great coffee."

We were both quiet a minute, two guys sipping bad coffee.

"You have much fire experience, Mr. Creed? Reason I ask, we weren't expecting an insurance investigator."

I raised my eyebrows. "Not ever?"

For the slightest moment, he seemed uneasy, but he adjusted quickly. "Not this soon, I meant."

Chief Blaunert didn't look much like a fire marshal. He looked more like the love child of Sherlock Holmes and Santa Claus. He had white hair, a full white beard, and thick glasses with large, round frames. He also had an engaging smile and wore a wrinkled brown tweed suit over a white shirt and knit tie. All that was missing was a pipe and the comment, "Elementary, my dear Creed."

Lou Kelly had set up the impromptu meeting while I picked up the rental car in West Manhattan. Lou had given Chief Blaunert my State Farm cover story, and Blaunert put Lou on hold a long time before agreeing to meet me. He said he was doing a field inspection at the Pine Road Station, but if I hurried, I could speak to him before the meeting. Finding him wearing a suit instead of his uniform, I doubted he was conducting an inspection. At the moment, I noticed he was eyeing me carefully.

"I'm more of a grunt than an arson investigator," I said. "I interview the firemen, the neighbors, check the site. In the end, I tell the company if I think a fire's accidental. Of course, even if I think it is, they'll still want to send a forensic accountant to check the insured's books, see if there's any financial motive."

Chief Blaunert nodded. "I wish I could save you the trouble," he said, "but I know your company's going to want a full report. Still, you can take my word for it—this fire was definitely an accident."

"You checked it out yourself?"

"Had to, the media was all over it. Pitiful tragedy," he said. "The whole family dead, all but one child, and she was burned beyond recognition."

"No motive you're aware of?"

Chief Blaunert's face reddened. "Motive? You tell *me* the motive! What, they're trying to screw your company out of a few hundred grand? They won the whole damned New York Lottery a few months back, ten million dollars!" He seemed genuinely upset by my question. "You think they're going to torch their own home, kill their own kids?"

"No, sir, I don't," I said. "Truth be told, I'm just going through the motions. I'll need to see the first firefighters on the scene, ask them a couple questions. I assume they're here, this being the station that took the call."

He stared at me until his anger subsided. When he finally spoke, his voice was clear and steady. "Yellow flame, gray smoke," he said. "No suspicious people at the scene. No open windows. No sign of forced entry. No doors locked, no rooms

70

blocked. Single point of origin, basement. No accelerants."

"You definitely know the drill."

"Ought to; I been doing it my whole life. You want, I can give you a couple names. You can say you interviewed 'em, take a quick peek at the scene, snap a few shots, and be back in Bloomington by dinner time."

"Sounds like a plan," I said. "I'll have to interview one or two neighbors, though." He nodded, and I handed him the pen and spiral notebook I'd bought for the occasion. I'd also bought the camera sitting on the front seat of the rental car in case one of the firemen wanted to accompany me to the scene. Chief Blaunert wrote some names in the notebook.

"Three enough?"

"That should do it."

He tore out a clean sheet from the notebook and wrote down my name. "Got a cell number?"

I gave it to him and thought about Sal's warning. I could see where this was going.

"Need an escort over there?"

"Naw, it's only a few blocks," I said. "I'll get out of here and let you get on with your inspection." I stood up, reached over to shake his hand. He hesitated, deciding whether to say something else.

"As to the neighbors," he said, "my guys were on the scene in four minutes twenty after the call was logged. You can check it out: four twenty." He stared at me through serious eyes.

"That's really quick," I said, just to fill the silence.

"It was after midnight," he said, "darker than a closet in a coal mine. We set up a perimeter, pushed the neighbors back pretty far. They won't be able to tell you anything different that's reliable."

"Chief, no worries. We're going to pay this claim. That little girl's been through enough. Meanwhile, you've saved me some time and trouble, and I appreciate it." I smiled, and this time he shook my hand. "See you in Seattle, chief!"

"That's where I'll be," he said. "Up by Portage Bay."

"Drinking coffee with the wife," I said.

He smiled and gave me another thumbs-up. "You got it."

# 12.

GREG AND MELANIE'S burnt-out home was one neighborhood removed from the posh Upper Montclair Country Club. These were two-story, upper-middle-class homes with basements, brick exteriors, and asphalt shingle roofs. I'm no expert, but I'd price them around seven fifty, maybe eight hundred thousand.

I got out of the car and locked it with the remote. Before heading to the house and without staring at anything in particular, I scanned the area and didn't like what I saw out of the corner of my eye: a 2006 metallic blue Honda Civic Coupe parked where one hadn't been parked a few seconds earlier. I suddenly spun around, pretending to have forgotten something in the trunk. This didn't require an Oscar-winning performance on my part, since I had a small-frame Smith & Wesson 642 hidden in the wheel well.

As I opened the trunk and retrieved the handgun, I noticed the Honda moving toward me. Though the sun was reflecting off the windshield, I was able to see that the driver was a woman.

The Honda came to a stop about ten feet in front of mine, which meant it was positioned where I couldn't see anything without exposing at least part of my face from behind the raised hood of my trunk. I put the gun in my right hand and waited. Could DeMeo have sent a woman to do the job? I wracked my brain. Were there any women in the business brazen enough to drive right up to me in broad daylight and make an attempt on my life? Callie, maybe, but she was on my team. No one else came to mind.

Suddenly, I heard the car door open, and every synapse in my brain became locked and loaded for deadly confrontation. I waited for footsteps, thinking, yeah, DeMeo could have sent a woman. But while there were dozens of contract killers who might come straight at a guy, Joe DeMeo knows me, knows what I'm capable of. Would DeMeo send just one person to do the hit?

No way.

Which meant there was probably someone else working their way behind me, getting into position to make the kill shot.

Which meant I should turn my head and see what was happening behind me. Unfortunately, just as I was about to do that, I heard her step out of the car, heard her footsteps coming my way. I didn't dare look behind me and didn't dare not to. The way things were developing, I didn't like my chances.

She walked purposefully, coming straight at me, but so far no one had tried to shoot me from behind. A number of thoughts flooded my brain, forcing me to make split-second decisions. I was going to have to rely on skill sets and survival instincts honed over fifteen years of daily application.

She was in the vicinity of my right front bumper, which would normally cause me to move to my left. But no, that's what they'd expect me to do. It's what they'd be counting on.

But I'd already looked in that direction and hadn't seen anything to worry about. What was I missing? What was to the left of me that could possibly pose a threat?

The house.

Someone was probably inside the house, waiting to get a clear shot. She comes from the right, I move to my left, and bang.

White shirt time.

I waited another second until she was nearly on top of me, then ducked down and moved to my right and peered out from behind the rear bumper—then did a double-take.

It was Kathleen Gray.

"Donovan, what the hell are you up to?" she said, giving me just enough time to drop the gun into the trunk without her noticing. It would take a few seconds to gather myself and get my pulse back to normal. I took a deep breath and stood up.

"Of all the gin joints, in all the towns, in all the world, she had to walk into mine," I said.

She didn't fall for the misdirection. "Is that a gun in your trunk? Jesus, Donovan! Really, what are you up to?"

"What do you mean?"

"I got a call from my friend at the burn center. Addie's Aunt told her you were coming to look at the house. By the time I got Hazel on the phone, she was seconds away from calling the police! I told her she must have misunderstood your conversation, yet here you are."

"Relax. I'm just checking the scene."

"Excuse me? What are you, some kind of closet detective? What is it you're looking for?"

"Arson."

That threw her for a moment, made her pause. I said, "I spoke to Hazel because I wanted to see if anyone had set up a fund for Addie. I wanted to make a contribution."

"Imagine your surprise when you learned her family won the lottery."

"Yes, but then I found out the payments ended when her parents died, and now Hazel has changed her mind about adopting Addie."

"What does all this have to do with arson?"

I lowered my voice and looked around to make sure no one else was lurking about. "It's probably nothing," I said. "But I know a guy who buys structured settlements. Then he kills the annuitant and keeps the money."

She looked at me like I'd lost my mind. "That sounds like a bad movie script," she said.

"Uh huh."

She shook her head. "Look, I know you're some kind of muckymuck from the State Department or the CIA or Homeland Security or whatever. But this is Montclair, New Jersey, not Gotham City."

I said nothing.

"You said you know this is happening. How do you know it's true?"

"A couple of years ago, this same guy tried to hire me to do the killing."

She looked startled for a moment. Then she burst into laughter. "Fine, so don't tell me. Jesus, Donovan. You are so full of shit!"

She was wearing a burgundy patent tweed coat that showed her legs from the knees down. She had on textured panty hose that looked hotter than they sound, with burgundy ankle boots.

I said, "You heading back to work now?"

"What, and miss the big caper?"

I scanned the area around us again, knowing my time was running short. It wouldn't be long before Chief Blaunert called Joe DeMeo, who might very well dispatch some thugs to kill me. I had to get Kathleen out of there, and quickly.

"You got any idea what soot will do to those boots?" I said.

"God, Donovan, you must date the girliest girls! I'll just find a clean spot in there and watch you poke around, trying to impress me. Then you can take me to lunch."

"Look," I said, "I'll make you a deal. You pick out a busy restaurant and go there now. I'll get this done in twenty minutes and meet you there."

She looked at me for what seemed like a long time before glancing at the house.

"Look at all the flowers and stuffed animals by the porch," she said. "That's so sad." She paused a moment, thinking about it. "I know it's only been a few weeks, but she's so adorable. If anyone on earth deserves a mother's love, it's Addie."

I nodded. "Pick a booth if they have one, and make sure my seat has a view of the main road."

"Are you for real?"

"I am. And make sure I can see the restrooms and the kitchen from my side of the booth."

She hesitated. For a second, I was afraid I'd frightened her. Then she shrugged and said, "You're a lot of work, you know that?"

"I do."

"Promise you'll show?"

I did.

She named a restaurant and told me how to get there. She started to go, then spun back around, smiled a mischievous smile. "Kiss me," she said.

I felt myself smile. "Okay, but not a movie kiss," I said.

I watched her drive away and kept watching to make sure

no one followed her. Then I inspected the house. Most of the exterior walls were in place, but the interior had been decimated. I couldn't get down to the basement or up to the second floor, but sections of the second floor had fallen into the master bedroom. It took me less than ten minutes to figure out what had happened and how, but I interviewed one of the neighbors anyway.

# 13.

"OKAY, SO THE attic window was open," Kathleen said. "What does that prove?"

We were in Nellie's Diner. Nellie's was my kind of place, though worlds apart from the Four Seasons. The outside looked like the club car on a passenger train. Inside made you feel like you'd taken a step back into the fifties. I hadn't been alive in the fifties, but Nellie's was how I imagined the restaurants of the day: gleaming places filled with chrome. Vinyl booths, easy-to-clean laminate tables and countertops, and smiling, clean-cut waiters dressed in white shirts, black bow ties, and white paper hats. On the tables: plasticized menus propped against mini jukeboxes that showcased rock 'n' roll music. Menu fare included fried onion rings, baked beans, corn bread, patty melts, club sandwiches, pork chops, pot roast, chicken pot pie, spaghetti with meatballs, and fried chicken. Drinks included cherry and vanilla Cokes, root beer floats, and old-fashioned milk shakes. On the bar counter under glass covers were displayed chocolate fudge brownies, chocolate chip cookies, and cherry, lemon meringue, and coconut pies. Each of the pies had at least one slice missing so the customers could see what was inside. The waiter took our orders, and I told Kathleen, "Wait a sec," so I could hear him tell the cook. She rolled her eyes.

"One cowboy with spurs, no Tommy; a mayo club,

cremated, and hold the grass!" he said.

"What on earth?" Kathleen asked.

I beamed. "It's authentic diner talk. The 'cowboy with spurs' is my Western omelet with fries. 'No Tommy' means I don't want ketchup. 'Cremated' means toast the bread. And 'hold the grass' means no lettuce on your club sandwich."

"How do you *know* this stuff?" she asked. "And why would you *want* to?"

"Say it," I said.

"Say what?"

"I'm fun."

She looked at me until a smile played around the corners of her mouth.

"You *are* fun," she said. "Now tell me why the open attic window means something, and tell me what else you think you found."

"Okay. First of all, a fire requires three things to burn: oxygen, a fuel source, and heat. That's called the fire triangle. An arsonist has to tamper with one or more of those elements to fake an accidental fire. For example, this fire was set at the end of January and the attic window was open. Who leaves a window open in January?"

"Maybe the firemen opened it after the fact."

"No. The arsonist opened it to provide an oxygen source."

On the juke in the booth across from us, Rod Stewart was singing. Maggie May had stolen his soul and that's a pain he can do without.

"Tell me you've got more than the open window," she said.

"In the basement there were at least two points of origin. Also, in the floorboards in the master bedroom, under the bed, I saw some curved edges. I found some more in the hallway, and I'd bet the stairwell was full of them."

"So?"

"So I think someone used a circular drill bit to drill holes in all those floorboards. That's what created the air flow to feed the fire and make it spread much faster than it should."

"Well duh," she said. "If a guy was traipsing all over the house, opening windows and drilling holes, especially under the bed, don't you think Greg and Melanie would have heard him?"

"The prep work was done earlier, before they got home. They wouldn't have noticed the open attic window or the drill holes under the bed. The steps were carpeted, so those holes were hidden. The arsonist probably broke into the basement before they got home so he wouldn't have to chance waking them up later. I noticed the attic access doors were open, and that's something Greg and Melanie would have noticed when they tucked the kids in for the night. So the arsonist must have waited for the family to fall asleep. Then he sneaked up the stairs and opened the attic doors and doused the carpet in the kids' room with gasoline."

"What? Excuse me, Columbo, but how do you know he doused the carpet?"

"I pulled some of it up and guess what I saw?"

"A stain that looks like Jesus on a tricycle?"

"No, I found char patterns."

"Char patterns," she said.

"When you pour a liquid accelerant on carpet, it soaks into the fibers. When it burns, it makes concentrated char patterns on the sub-floor."

Kathleen frowned, still unconvinced. "What was all that with the neighbor guy and the color of the smoke?"

"The color of the smoke and flames tells you what's making it burn. Wood makes a yellow flame, or a red one, with gray or brown smoke."

"So what's the problem? The neighbor guy said he saw a yellow flame."

"Right, but he also said black smoke."

"So?"

"Black smoke means gasoline."

The waiter brought our orders and set them on the table. I tore into my omelet, but Kathleen just stared at me. Her face had turned serious.

"Donovan, all these details, this isn't your first rodeo," she said. "You obviously know a lot about arson. You said this guy tried to hire you a couple years ago."

"So?"

"To kill people."

I didn't know what to say, so I waited for her to speak. She gave me a look like she wanted to ask me something but wasn't sure she wanted to hear the answer.

When my daughter Kimberly was eight, she started to ask me about Santa Claus. Before she voiced her question, I looked her in the eye and said, "Don't ever ask me anything unless you're ready to hear the truth." Kimberly decided not to ask. Kathleen, on the other hand, had to know.

"Have you ever done this to someone?" she asked. "Set their house on fire?"

"You should eat," I said. "That sandwich looks terrific."

She didn't respond, so I looked up and saw her eyes burning a hole into my soul. "Have you?" she repeated.

I signaled the waiter and handed him a twenty. "Before you do anything else," I said to him, "I need a roll of duct tape or sealing tape." He nodded, took the bill, and moved double-time toward the kitchen. To Kathleen, I said, "I've done some terrible things. Things I hope I never have to tell you about,

82

and yes, I've been trained to set fires. But no, I've never done it."

"You swear?"

I swore. Happily, it was the truth. Still, I decided not to tell her how close I'd come a few times. And I was well aware that by swearing on the past I hadn't ruled out the future.

She stared at me awhile before nodding slowly. "I believe you," she said. "Look, I'm sure you're a world-class shit heel. It wouldn't even surprise me if you'd killed people for the CIA years ago, and God help me, I might even be able to live with that, depending on the circumstances. But since I started working with the kids at the burn center ... well, you know."

I did know.

Kathleen's club sandwich had been cut into four pieces. She picked up a wedge and studied it. "What about the fire chief?" she asked. "If you're right, that makes him wrong, and he's the expert."

I speared a couple of fries and popped them into my mouth. There's nothing like the taste of diner French fries. "They put hamburger grease in the oil," I said. "Makes the French fries burst with flavor. You want some?"

"No. What about the fire chief?"

The waiter returned with a thick roll of clear sealing tape and said he'd be right back to refresh our drinks. I nodded and began taping the fingers on my right hand.

"What are you doing?"

"Making sure I don't splay my metacarpals."

She showed me her bewildered look and watched me tape my wrist. After doing that, I removed a thin sheet of plastic from my wallet and began fitting it to the bottom part of my palm, from pinky to wrist. "Can you wrap this for me?" I asked.

"You're insane," she said, but she wrapped the tape around the palm of my hand, covering the plastic and holding it in place. I flexed my hand to test it and decided it would do. "What about the fire chief?" she repeated.

"He's in on it."

"What?"

"They paid him off after the fact. They didn't want to, but they had to."

"What are you talking about?"

"This arsonist was good. The only reason he appears sloppy is because the fire department got to the scene so quickly. Four minutes and twenty seconds, if you can just imagine. Another five minutes and the fire would have killed all the evidence. The chief knew it was arson, some of his men probably knew. So whoever ordered the torch—I'm guessing Joe DeMeo—had to get to the chief."

"You said the chief was talking about his retirement."

"It's all he talks about."

"So this Joe DeMeo character, he gave the chief enough money to look the other way?"

"I expect the money was a bonus, like a reward for doing the right thing. DeMeo probably got the chief's attention by threatening his wife, kids, and grandchildren."

The composite plastic affixed to the edge of my hand was invented by an engineering team at the University of Michigan in mid-2007. It's strong as steel and as thin and pliable as a small sheet of paper. Made from clay and nontoxic glue, it mimics the brick-and-mortar molecular structure found in seashells. The nanosheets of plastic are layered like bricks and held together with a gluelike polymer that creates cooperative hydrogen bonds between the layers. It takes several hours to build up the three hundred layers needed to make the thin sheet I kept in my wallet at all times.

Kathleen watched me studying my hand. She said, "If Chief Blaunert's involved in the cover up, why didn't he destroy the evidence? It's been two weeks."

"I'm guessing he hasn't had a chance, what with all the press coverage, candlelight vigils, and people coming day and night to place shrine items on the lawn."

"But he must have known the insurance company would send someone to investigate."

"That's the thing. He told me he wasn't expecting anyone this soon, which tells me no one has filed the claim yet. Or if it's been filed, someone at the insurance company has either submitted a phony report or they're delaying their investigation."

"Are you sure this DeMeo guy has that much clout?"

"That much and more."

Again she looked at the piece of sandwich in her hand but didn't taste it.

"There's something bothering you," I said. "What is it?"

"Are you in danger?" she asked.

"I could be. The chief probably called DeMeo this morning right after my guy set the appointment. DeMeo probably told him to meet me and find out what I was up to."

"Doesn't DeMeo know you're with the government? Doesn't he know you'll turn him in?"

I smiled. "These things aren't as black and white as you might think. Taking Joe DeMeo down won't be easy. He's killed enough people to fill a cemetery."

Kathleen's eyes began to cloud up. "Are you going to die on me?"

"Not on purpose," I said. "But nine million dollars is a lot of money, even to Joe DeMeo."

"What will he do?"

"Send some goons to try to kill me."

She put her uneaten sandwich wedge back on her plate. "Donovan, I'm scared. What if he really does send some men to kill you?"

"I'll kill them first."

"You can do that?"

I smiled. "I can."

"Are you sure?" she said. "You aren't even scared?"

"Not even," I said, trying to sound not even scared. Then I asked her to help me tape the fingers and wrist of my left hand.

"Why are we doing this?" she asked.

"Don't turn around," I said, "but DeMeo's goons are here."

A look of panic flashed across her face. "What? Where? How many are there?"

"Two in the parking lot, one in the kitchen."

"Jesus Christ, Donovan! What are we going to do?"

"The right thing."

"What, call the cops?"

"No. The right thing in this situation is kill the guy in the kitchen first."

"*Kill him*?" Her words came out louder than she'd intended. I noticed the couple across from us glancing in our direction. Katherine lowered her voice. "Why would your first thought be to kill him?"

"I don't want him sneaking up behind me while I'm attacking the others."

"You're planning to attack the others? Trained killers? No way," she said. "I'm calling the cops!"

I put my taped hand on her arm, shook my head. "Don't make such a fuss. This is what I do."

She looked … everything at once. Angry. Frightened. Exasperated. The businessman at the table across from us got to his feet. He put a little menace into his voice for my benefit while speaking to Kathleen. "Are you okay? Do you need any help?" She looked at him and back at me, and we locked eyes. She smiled at the man and shook her head no. Then she settled back in her seat, took in a deep breath, let it out slowly. When she spoke, her voice was small but steady. "Okay."

"Ma'am?" the businessman said.

"I'm fine. Really," Kathleen said, and the guy eased back into his seat, much to the relief of his wife. He did the right thing, too: stood up for a woman in distress, impressed his wife. If all went well, we'd probably both get laid tonight.

"You okay now?" I asked.

"I trust you."

I nodded and looked back at my plate. It was harder to finish my greasy fries with my hands taped up, but I managed it. Then I asked, "You going to eat that sandwich?"

# 14.

"CARE FOR ANY dessert today?" Our waiter looked nervous.

"What's your name, son?" I asked.

"Jared, sir."

I passed Jared a Franklin and asked if he'd seen the big guy in the kitchen, the one in the dark suit with the black shirt who kept peeking through the glass every thirty seconds. Jared's face clouded over. He tried to give me back the hundred. "I really don't want to get involved in this," he said.

"Don't look toward the kitchen," I said. "Just answer me. Where is he standing in relation to the door?"

"When you go through the door, he's on your right."

"The door pushes open to the right," I said. "So when I first walk through, he'll be hidden from view, yes?"

"Yes, sir. What are you going to do?"

"Has he caused any trouble yet?"

Jared lowered his voice to a whisper. "He's got everyone scared. He's got a gun."

"Anyone call the cops?"

"They don't dare. And I don't blame them."

"Good," I said. "Okay, here's what we're going to do."

"We, sir?"

"That's right, son. You're going to be a hero today."

I told Jared and Kathleen my plan. She asked, "What's a

Glasgow Kiss?"

"I'll tell you later."

"Assuming it works," she said.

"It'll work. These aren't DeMeo's best people."

"How do you know?"

"First, I know his best people, and they're in LA, guarding him. Second, there are three guys here."

"So?"

"If they were really good, he'd only need two. The one in the kitchen is the least experienced. He's related to one of the goons in the parking lot, probably his kid brother. I can tell by the resemblance. That bit of knowledge will work in our favor." I removed my belt and measured a space about twelve inches from the buckle. I pushed the tip of my knife there and worked it enough to create a small hole. Then I draped it loosely around my neck. To Jared I said, "Ready son?"

He looked at my hands. Swallowed. Looked at Kathleen. She shrugged. He looked back at me. I nodded. He said, "Yes, sir."

I waited until the goon checked the window again. When he ducked back behind the door, I jumped to my feet. Jared began walking straight to the kitchen door, deliberate pace, me right behind him. As he pushed the door open, I spun around and backed into it. Everything else happened in real time, in sequence, and though I didn't see it all happen, I heard or felt it playing out around me. Jared lowered his head and ran full speed through the kitchen, screaming at the top of his lungs. A waitress shrieked and fell to the floor in a dead faint. The cooks waved their hands and ran in all directions. I ducked under the roundhouse right my grandmother would have seen coming.

Jared's job was to run into the parking lot screaming, "Oh

my God, he's dead!" That would create a diversion and force the parking lot goons out of their plan. This was important because the fundamental lesson every successful street fighter learns is you do not want to fight your opponents the way they are trying to attack you.

I trusted Jared to do his part and began focusing on mine. While the kitchen goon was off-balance, trying to recover from the haymaker he'd launched in my direction, I straightened to my full height and slammed the top of my forehead down into the bridge of his nose full force, instantly shattering it.

The Glasgow Kiss.

I'd done this in the gym a thousand times, though maybe only twenty in real life. The Glasgow Kiss always works, even against experienced fighters, provided they're not expecting it. I would never attempt to lead with my head against a real pro, but this guy was easier to hit than the heavy bag in my gym.

The momentum I'd created carried my forehead downward into his cheekbones, which meant his nose fragments had to follow the same path. He crumpled to the floor. I noticed a gun bulge in the small of his back, under his suit jacket. I stuck his gun in my pocket and rolled him over with my foot, glanced at his face. I didn't recognize the guy, but even his wife or girlfriend would have a hard time recognizing him now. His nose and the blood from it had spread outward from the center of his face like pancake batter poured into a hot skillet.

Breaking the bridge of a man's nose in this manner creates a surprising amount of pain, dazes him, and blurs his eyes, which gives me time to explore other options. Like removing the belt from my shoulders, wrapping it around his neck, threading it through the belt buckle, and pulling it tight while pushing his head in the opposite direction with my foot. I forced his huge neck to fit into the tiny space created by the hole I'd cut into my belt moments earlier.

The goon was choking. His face sprayed blood like the blow hole of a whale, and I guessed he'd be dead in two minutes. I jerked him to his feet, but he was too heavy to hold with one hand, twitching and kicking as he was. I pulled the door open, got it between us, draped the belt over the top of it, and held him in place by pulling on the belt with my left hand. This way, the door was doing most of the work and the goon was hanging on the front of it, with me behind. I backed us up into the wall, which was a good place to be because the two parking lot goons had just burst through the back door of the kitchen with their guns drawn.

The first thing they saw was their partner hanging from a belt over the door, choking, spewing blood everywhere, grabbing at his neck, kicking and gasping for breath. The second thing they saw was part of my head poking out from behind the guy.

The one who looked like the dying goon's brother screamed, "Ray!" The other one called me a bad name and threatened to shoot me if I didn't let Ray go. Everyone else in the kitchen had long since hit the floor and found cover—everyone except the waitress who had fainted. She was starting to regain consciousness. The customers in the front part of the diner were just beginning to realize something very wrong was happening in the kitchen. I heard the sounds a group of strangers make when they're trying to decide what to do. If they were smart, they'd follow Kathleen's lead and jump under their tables.

"Here's how it's going to happen," I said to the gunmen. "You're going to drop your guns and kick them across the floor to me. Or else Ray chokes to death."

Ray's friend sneered. "I don't give up my gun to no one."

I squinted to get a better look. "That a Monster Magnum?" I asked. "Hell, I don't blame you. That's a damn fine gun."

The guy with the magnum ignored me, kept talking while he took a step away from Ray's brother, trying to create distance between them and work his way into my blind side. "Broken nose, belt around his neck—he's not gonna die. That's total bullshit."

Ray's brother wasn't so sure. "Joe, shut up. He's dying. Look at him! My brother's dying." To me, he said, "Let him go, Creed. Let him go and we'll walk away, I swear to God."

But Joe had other plans. He grabbed the fallen waitress and put his gun to her ear. "Let him go, Creed, or I'll kill her. Don't think I won't!"

She screamed. I laughed. "You think I care if you shoot her? Someone must have forgotten to tell you what I do for a living."

Ray, the goon on the door, was heavy, and my left arm was starting to gimp up from the strain of holding him there. I knew I wouldn't be able to keep him upright much longer. Ray had been packing a small-frame .38-caliber revolver, a good choice for a belt gun. I gripped it in my right hand.

Joe said, "Last chance, Creed. You know what this cannon will do to her head. It'll put you in mind of Gallagher smashing a watermelon." He pulled the hammer back and cocked it for dramatic effect.

It worked. It made the satisfying, precise clunk I'd come to love in that particular handgun. I'm sensitive to the unique sounds each gun makes, and my ears were able to isolate this one over the gasping death rattle in Ray's throat, above the sound of his legs kicking the bottom of the door from which he hung. I heard it above the commotion in the front of the restaurant as customers screamed and ran and knocked over chairs and trampled each other while trying to evacuate. I heard the sound of Joe's gun and loved it. Though the .500 was too big to use in everyday situations, I couldn't wait to add it to my collection.

Joe had made his threat and felt compelled to follow through on it. He instinctively leaned his head back, away from the waitress, which told me he was about to pull the trigger and didn't want some of her brains on his face. I felt the heft of Ray's gun in my hand. At twenty ounces and less than seven inches in length, its capacity was only five rounds, but I'd only need one to kill Joe. I didn't know what Ray was using for ammunition, but I put one of them in Joe's temple and his head jerked when it hit. He fell to the floor, and a thin wisp of smoke escaped from the hole in his head as dark blood started to puddle. I heard the nonstop shriek of the waitress and wondered how many years of therapy this experience might require.

But I didn't look at her. I was too busy looking at Ray's brother. He said, "Creed. Please. Let him go."

"You going to drop your gun?" I asked.

He shook his head no and I could see tears streaming down his cheeks. Ray's left leg had gone limp, and his right one was barely twitching. "I love you, Ray," he said.

I saw what was coming and released Ray just as his brother shot him. Then Ray's brother dove for the floor to my right, angling for position on me where I was most vulnerable. I couldn't let him get there, so I took a knee and squeezed a round into his left eye and another into the top of his head. I tried to push the door forward, but Ray's body kept it in place, so I eased my way out from behind it and checked myself to see if I'd been shot through Ray's body.

93

I hadn't.

I walked over Joe's body and spotted the magnum a few feet away. You don't just pick up the Monster Magnum; you have to lift it. I did so and took a few seconds to admire it. The .500-caliber Smith & Wesson Magnum was the biggest, heaviest, most powerful factory-production handgun in the world. It makes Dirty Harry's weapon of choice look like a BB gun. I hadn't been counting on a gun this size and wondered why Joe hadn't thought to shoot Ray. The 50-caliber bullet would have gone through him as well as the door, me, and the wall behind us.

I couldn't wait to tell Kathleen how lucky I'd been. I felt I finally had a woman I could talk to about these things besides Callie. Callie was great, but there was no warmth to her. She was part killer and part smartass. Callie wouldn't have considered me lucky; she'd have said Joe was stupid. And don't even get her started on Ray and his brother. She wouldn't have fallen for the Glasgow Kiss, she wouldn't have tried to cut a deal with a guy hanging her partner from a door, and she wouldn't have waited around in the parking lot in the first place. Callie would have marched right in the front door of the diner, put a slug between my eyes, and stolen Kathleen's sandwich for the ride home.

I told the people in the kitchen they could come out now, told them to take care of the waitress who was no longer hysterical but had turned catatonic with shock. I took my trophy gun, walked into the diner, and found Kathleen hiding under the table where I'd told her to wait for me. I got on one knee to get a better look at her. She was pale, shivering violently. I put the magnum on the floor and reached out to her. She screamed and slapped my hands away. I told her it was over. She was safe; everything was fine. I wanted to tell her what had happened, tell her how shocked I'd been when Ray's brother killed him to prevent his further suffering—I was even prepared to tell her more about how I earned my livelihood—but she kept screaming and told me she never wanted to see me again. I knew she'd probably be upset, but I'd failed to gauge the extent.

I removed the tape from my hands and wrists and put the plastic back in my wallet.

I left the diner, walked to my car, and began the relatively short drive back to Manhattan. When I hit the turnpike, I called Lou first, then Darwin, and caught them up to speed. I asked Darwin if he had the power to prevent police from stopping my car.

He said he'd try.

# 15.

IT WAS EARLY afternoon, and I was back in Manhattan, in my hotel room. I'd ordered a glass tumbler and a bottle of Maker's from room service, which for some reason took them over a half-hour to deliver. The tardy delivery guy tried to make conversation to increase the tip I noticed was already added to my order. While money is not an issue for me, the thought of paying one hundred and twenty dollars for a thirty-five-dollar bottle of whiskey is enough to discourage an extra tip. I dismissed him curtly, and we exchanged frowns. I went to the sink, turned on the hot water faucet, and waited for it to work.

It had been a hell of a day so far. I'd learned that Addie's entire family had been murdered in order to cheat them out of their lottery winnings. I'd been attacked by three goons who tried to kill me in a public diner. I'd lost Kathleen, the first woman in years who had offered a glimmer of hope for a possible relationship and normal future. I'd made an enemy of Aunt Hazel, which probably cost me visiting privileges with Addie.

The water from the faucet was steaming. I hoped that in a hotel like this, no one had peed in the glass tumbler, but I rinsed it thoroughly anyway. Then I poured a half-ounce of whiskey in it and swirled it around to flavor the glass and kill any stubborn germs that might be hoping to breach my bloodstream.

I sipped some whiskey.

There's something special about high-tone Kentucky bourbon. My favorite is the twenty-year-old Pappy Van Winkle, but Maker's Mark is easier to come by and is plenty sumptuous in its own right. Bourbon is not a pretentious drink, although there's a movement underfoot to make it so. Experts have started organizing tasting groups to explain the "softness" of the quality bourbons and the elegant flavors you're likely to encounter when tasting them, including such exotic notes as orange peel, licorice, almonds, and cinnamon.

In my opinion, listing all these flavor and aroma components leads to snobbery. As they might say in Kentucky, "Don't go around talking metric to decent folk." All a good Kentucky bourbon needs to show you is a smooth, mild burn on the tongue and the hint of a caramel taste. You drink bourbon straight, without mixers or ice, and if you've chosen a good one, it will taste like bourbon and not medicine or rubbing alcohol like most other spirits do.

I sipped some more.

I wanted to call Kathleen, wanted to work things out. I thought about calling her, wondered if humor might be the best approach. I thought about that awhile but decided she wasn't in the right mood to find any of this amusing. I could apologize, but what sense would that make?

First of all, I hadn't done anything wrong. I'd been investigating a crime someone else had committed, a crime that had permanently disfigured a darling little girl and caused the brutal murder of her entire family—a crime that caused the loss of her house and her inheritance, and would certainly have an impact on her future mental stability. And did I mention this was a little girl Kathleen was very fond of? And did I mention I had done all this while putting my own life in danger? And did I mention I had done all this for free?

Hell, she should be apologizing to me!

Second, because I had taken it upon myself to help Addie, three professional killers nearly destroyed a wonderful diner and traumatized an excellent cook and wait staff while attempting to whack me.

Third, Kathleen's life hadn't really been in that much danger in the first place. I thought about that and decided I might have to rethink being with a woman who could be so drastically affected by such a minor event. If someone attacked her on the street while we were out for a stroll, would I refuse to see her again?

Of course not.

Then again, if things worked out between us—even if I quit the business—there would always be the random murder attempt to deal with. After all, there were plenty of husbands, wives, parents, brothers, sisters, sons, daughters, business associates, and friends whose lives I had impacted by whacking someone close to them. Most of these people would pay to see me dead. Whether they come after me by themselves or in groups, or pay someone else to do it, I'd be a fool to assume they wouldn't even try.

Fourth, the violence at the diner could have been avoided altogether had Kathleen not driven out to the house, uninvited, to question my motives.

I was running out of whiskey in the glass so I added a couple inches and then dialed the number on the card Aunt Hazel had given me a few hours earlier. I sipped from the glass as Greg and Melanie's lawyer, Garrett Unger, told me he refused to discuss the details of Greg's estate with a non-relative.

"Even if you were a relative, I wouldn't discuss a sensitive topic like this over the phone," he said.

"I'm a relative by extension," I said. "I've been asked by Melanie's sister to look into the details regarding the structured settlement."

"Then you'll have to set up an appointment through the proper channels," Unger said, "and that will take some time. You'll have to file the proper documents as well."

"What documents would those be?" I asked.

"I'm sure you can appreciate it's not my job to explain the law to you. If you don't understand the procedures involved, I suggest you hire your own attorney."

"You don't appear to be very supportive of the family," I said.

"Terrible tragedy," Unger said, "but there's nothing anyone can do about the annuity. Believe me, I wish I could, but the language in the contract is quite precise and has stood the test of time."

"Aunt Hazel said Greg only received one payment before the accident."

"Not true," he said. "The family received three payments." Then he said, "Wait, you pulled that out of your ass just now, didn't you?"

I admitted it. Then I said, "Let me see if I can save us both the trouble of a visit. I have a theory."

"I'll entertain a hypothetical," Unger said, "provided it's a short one."

"Suppose I win ten million dollars in the state lottery."

"Go on."

"I get a lump sum payment of ten million and use one million of it to pay off my outstanding loans. I look for a way to invest the balance. My attorney tells me about an annuity he's found that's offered by a privately funded group of investors from California."

Unger had been saying, "Uh huh," to move me along, but when I said, "California," he suddenly became silent. I continued, "The lawyer says the return is astronomical, three times what I can get anywhere else. Not only that, but I'll get this huge monthly payment for the rest of my life! If I die before receiving the first month's payment, my wife gets the annuity payment for the rest of her life. But somewhere in the fine print, the contract says if my wife and I both die after receiving at least one payment, the entire principal is forfeited to the company. That sound about right?"

We were both silent awhile until I said, "How much did they pay you?"

"I beg your pardon?" Unger asked, working to put on a show of great indignation.

"Joe DeMeo," I said. "How much commission did he pay you to place the contract, to sell out your own client?"

"I don't have to listen to this!"

"You signed their death warrant," I said.

"I'm going to hang up now," Unger said.

"Before you do, I want you to give DeMeo a message for me."

"I don't know any DeMeo," Unger said.

"Of course you don't." I gave Unger my cell phone number and said, "If by some chance you happen to cross paths with DeMeo, have him call me before six tonight. If he fails to do so, I'm going to call the FBI and see what they think about my hypothetical theory."

# 16.

I HUNG UP and waited to hear from DeMeo.

Joseph DeMeo lived in LA, which got me to thinking about Jenine, the young model and potential body double from Santa Monica I'd told Callie about, the one I'd been sharing e-mails with for a couple of months. Listen to me: *model*. At best she was a model hopeful, and I was nearly twice her age. We both knew what this was. We'd shared a couple of photos and text messages, she'd invited me to visit her, and I'd said I'd try, next time I was in the area.

I took a catnap and woke up and waited for DeMeo's call. While waiting, I challenged myself to remember all the plates I was trying to keep spinning in the air. I was testing the ADS weapon for the army. Okay, that's one. Two, I was trying to keep Janet from marrying the shit bird from West Virginia. Three, I was trying to start a romance with the shit bird's ex. Okay, well that plate had already fallen and crashed, but I was going to have to deal with the effect it had on me, so maybe that's four. Maybe the model from LA could help me get over the feelings I had for Kathleen. I'd make that one plate number five.

I spied the empty tumbler by the phone. There was plenty left in the bottle. I poured another shot into the glass and worked it around my tongue, thinking, *Now let's see, where was I? Oh yeah, plates in the air.* Number six: I had started accepting murder contracts from an angry, quadriplegic midget with dreadlocks. Seven: I was still taking contracts for Sal Bonadello, the crime boss. Eight: I was trying to set up a face-to-face with Joe DeMeo, a meeting that would almost certainly result in my death. And of course, I still had my day job of killing terrorists for the government. So that made nine plates.

I was as out of control as the Looney Tunes conga line. It was time to wrap up some of these loose ends. I called Lou Kelly.

"You got my information yet?"

"If you're referring to the age progression on Kathleen, I e-mailed it to you an hour ago."

"What about the match profile on Lauren?" I asked.

"Well, I didn't know her name till just now, but you were right. If her picture is current, our guys can get her up to 91 percent."

"So that's a powerful resemblance," I said.

"It is."

"If I wanted to pass Lauren off as Kathleen, who could I fool?"

Lou thought about that a bit. "You wouldn't fool her spouse or a close friend or relative. Beyond that, you're probably okay."

"Good. That's what I was hoping to hear."

I asked Lou about getting me a jet. He put me on hold a few minutes while he made the arrangements. He got back on the line and said, "Got one. It'll be waiting for you at the FBO in White Plains, at the Westchester County Airport."

"How far is that from where I am?"

"Depends on where you are," Lou said.

I told him. He hit a few computer keys and said, "Fastest

way is to get you a chopper. The flight is only ten minutes, but it'll take me about forty to set up. If you're not in a hurry, you can use a driver, but I'd wait a couple hours before heading there, since it's rush hour now."

I looked at my watch. "If I leave the hotel around seven?"

"You're looking at an hour's drive to White Plains, maybe more."

I told him I could live with that. I hung up and started packing my gear. My cell rang.

Joe DeMeo.

"You've been busy," he said.

"Jesus, Joe, where'd you find those guys?"

"Ah, what can I tell you? Short notice and all. Look, sorry about today. Your whole thing caught me off guard, pissed me off. You shoulda called me first instead of poking around out there. I'd have cut you in. Now the whole thing's turning into a mess."

"You get my message about setting up a meeting?"

"Our phones are secure. We can work this thing out right now."

"I'd rather meet face-to-face."

"You got some balls, my friend. I always said so." He sighed. "Okay, Creed, we'll meet. You say when, I'll say where."

We worked it out for Saturday morning in LA, which gave me plenty of time to do some other things, including having another Maker's while waiting for my seven o'clock drive to White Plains.

And flying to Cincinnati to meet my good friend, Lauren.

And making plans to meet a certain young model wannabe at a beachside hotel in Santa Monica on Saturday afternoon— assuming I survived my Saturday morning meeting with Joe DeMeo.

## 17.

LAUREN JETER HAD been an escort since the early days of the Internet. Over time, she'd built a clientele that included a dozen of Cincinnati's most prominent public figures, most of whom managed to spend quality time with her several times a year. Add the income from these wealthy regulars to her hourly outcalls and Lauren was pulling down more than a hundred grand a year, all cash.

Not a bad business, but not without risk.

This particular morning, around ten o'clock, she knocked on the door of the upscale hotel room in downtown Cincinnati where I was staying. I handed her a quarter-inch stack of hundreds, and she smiled and said, "You've always been way too generous with me."

Lauren loved her Mimosas with fresh-squeezed orange juice, and she enjoyed several as we caught each other up on our families, our problems, our health, and the books we'd read in the months that had passed since my last visit.

At some point she smiled and asked, "So, you wanna …?"

Instead of answering directly, I told her I had a unique proposition for her: we could spend the next few hours in the traditional manner and afterward go our separate ways happy and richer for the experience, or I could pay her an obscene amount of money to let me beat the shit out of her.

For a split second, Lauren's smile remained frozen on her

face, caught in the moment like a deer in the headlights. Then she made a funny noise and bolted for the door. She fumbled a bit, trying to get it open. When she finally did, she flew out of the room and slammed the door behind her. I watched her do all that, and after a minute or so, I topped off my glass, sipped some more champagne, and moved closer to the phone. A few minutes passed before it rang.

"You didn't chase me," she said.

"Why would I do that?"

"I thought maybe you'd snapped or something. No offense."

"I'm sorry."

"No, it's just—I don't know, I guess I've always had the feeling you could turn violent on me, though you've always been a perfect gentleman in the past. Still, what you said a while ago, well, you sort of threw me for a minute there."

"And now?"

"Now I feel sort of bad that you paid for an overnight and I bailed."

"You were scared."

"I was *really* scared!" she said.

We were quiet awhile.

"You've got a good heart," I said.

"I'd like to be your friend, Donovan," she said, "but I might be just a little afraid of you right now."

"I can't fault you there."

"Should I be?"

"What's that?"

"Afraid of you?"

I paused a moment. "No."

"Well," she said, "you didn't grab me or hit me. You didn't force me to do anything. When I ran you didn't chase me. And you're very generous—the money, the champagne."

"Does all that add up to let's try again?"

"I don't know, Donovan. I'd like to save our relationship ..."

"But?"

"But I'd have to feel safe."

"Well," I said, "I didn't chase you."

She thought about that some more. Then she said, "I'm only about a block away, sitting in my car. If I agree to come back, will you promise I'll be safe? I mean, I'll treat you real good and all, but can you promise not to hit me?"

"Yes. If you want, you could bring someone with you."

"Another girl?"

I laughed. "No, I meant a guy. You can bring a guy with you, for protection."

She pondered that a minute. "Is there anyone I'm likely to bring who could protect me if you wanted to hurt me? Even if he had a gun?"

"No," I said, "but, Lauren, you have my word. This choice I mentioned, like anything else we've ever done or might do, is completely up to you."

"And you have my answer to your offer, right?"

I laughed. "You've made it abundantly clear. No hitting, no hurting."

Back in my room a few minutes later, she asked, "Do you get off on beating up women? Again, no offense meant," she added.

"None taken," I said, shaking my head. "No, I would never get any pleasure out of hitting a woman, and I don't understand those who would."

"Then why?"

I thought about telling her Kathleen Chapman's story, how

she had experienced years of physical abuse at the hands of her ex. I wondered if Lauren could possibly put herself in Kathleen's place, imagining the heartbreak, the pain and anguish, the humiliation Kathleen had suffered all those years.

My idea did have one major flaw: when you came right down to it, I'd be beating Lauren up now to protect Janet from getting beaten up someday. Of course, Lauren would have made the conscious decision to be beaten up. I wondered if that type of logic would provide sufficient justification for the way I'd feel later.

In the end, I just waved it off. "My mistake," I said. "Water under the bridge."

Lauren looked me over carefully. When she spoke, her voice was clear and steady. "You don't appear to be a freak," she said.

"Thank you."

"Of course," she said, "in my experience, most freaks don't appear to be freaks."

"I've found that to be true in my experience, as well," I said. She extended her hands in front of her, palms open, as if to say, *Help me out here, will ya*? Then she said, "But if someone were to ask me for an assessment at this stage of our relationship …" she paused a beat. "Can you understand why I might question your sanity?"

"You'd be crazy not to," I said.

She nodded slowly.

"Would you like me to take off my clothes now?" she said.

"I'd like that a lot. If it's your choice."

"It's what you've paid for," she said.

"Actually, I don't look at it that way."

She flashed me a skeptical look. "You don't, huh?" There was an edge of sarcasm in her voice.

I said, "Sex isn't the same as intimacy. Intimacy only works if it's a choice you've made about me."

She stiffened a bit. "A choice," she said.

"That's right."

"Like letting you beat me up?" I saw the anger flash through her eyes. Now that she trusted me not to hurt her, she was fired up.

"It's nothing personal," I said, hoping to diffuse the fireworks I could see coming.

"Really? Nothing personal, huh? So your offer had nothing to do with the fact that I'm just a low-life hooker? Tell me, Scarface, how many teachers, nurses, and housewives have you offered to beat up for money?"

I heard her. I don't mean I listened to her; I mean that what she said and the way she said it made me see it from her point of view. Now what could I say, except that she had a point.

"Lauren, you're right, of course. That was a big part of it, the fact you do things for money."

We sat there quietly and looked at each other, neither of us knowing quite what to say.

"There was something else," I said. "I didn't give you my reasons, but a big part of it had to do with an uncanny resemblance. But again, I'm sorry I brought it up. I feel terrible for scaring you. I really care about you and always have."

We were out of orange juice, but she reached for the champagne and poured some into a clean flute. She glanced at her champagne glass and a strange look crossed her face. She picked it up and held it to the light and stared at the amber liquid. *What now?* I wondered. Maybe there weren't as many bubbles floating to the surface as she thought there should be. Maybe …

"It's not drugged," I said.

"Then you drink it."

I sighed. "I've lost your trust, and for that I apologize." I took the champagne flute from her hand, put it to my lips, and drained it. Then I refilled the glass, handed it back to her. She nodded slowly and took a sip. Then, to her credit, she winked at me.

"Hookers have feelings, you know."

I smiled. "It's not because I think you're unworthy of being treated well. It was never that. If it makes you feel any better, you're the only person I've ever offered to pay to beat up."

Lauren had a light, airy laugh. Now, for the first time since she'd run out, she showed it. "Why the hell would that make me feel better?" she asked.

I laughed, too. "I'm sorry, Lauren. You're right. I prejudged you. Now I'm making it worse trying to talk about it. Big surprise: I'm not very smooth with women."

"Hey, ya think?" She smiled.

"Now you know why I have to pay for sex."

"Intimacy," she said.

"Yes."

"A choice," she said.

"It is," I said. "Or should be."

She nodded slightly, as if confirming some private thought. Then she took off her clothes and helped me with mine. Then she did the things Janet used to do to me all those years ago, things she was surely doing to Ken Chapman every night for free.

Lauren held me afterward and kissed my cheek.

"Just for the sake of argument," she said, "how much would you have paid?"

## 18

"I SEE YOU had better luck finding me this time," Joseph DeMeo said, flashing a grin I knew to be insincere. It was Saturday, and we were in the George Washington section of Hollywood Hills Cemetery near Griffith Park. DeMeo stood on the landing above the sidewalk next to the flagstone wall that shaded Buster Keaton's grave. He wore a black suit and a lavender silk shirt, buttoned all the way up, with no tie. DeMeo was flanked on either side by two dead-eyed thugs whose ill-fitting suits could barely contain their musculature.

"Your pets look uncomfortable," I said. "I hope they didn't squeeze into their prom suits just for me."

"No need to taunt," DeMeo said. "We're all friends here."

"That right?" I said to the goons. We all looked at each other a minute, trying to decide who could take whom, if it came down to it, and how best to do it. I didn't know these particular guys but I knew their type. Violence leaked out of them like stink on a wino.

Joseph DeMeo chuckled and walked down the steps toward me. "Walk with me," he said and passed me without shaking hands. I stood my ground. I wasn't comfortable walking with him if it meant turning my back on his goons. DeMeo chuckled again and said, "Don't worry about them. They'll follow at a respectful distance. Same as your giant," he added.

His comment rattled me. Quinn was my only backup, which meant he and I were as good as dead. Unless I could convince DeMeo I had another backup. In the meantime I had to display confidence.

"Big as he is," I said, "not many people can make Quinn. What'd he do, fall asleep?"

"I have the advantage that comes with setting the location," DeMeo said.

"Speaking of which," I said, "what's this fascination you have with cemeteries? Two years ago, it was Inglewood Park, James Jeffries' grave. This time it's Hollywood Hills, Buster Keaton."

"I meet people where it is fitting to do so. If you were an artist, I'd meet you at a gallery or art museum."

"Where do you meet Garrett Unger? Snake oil conventions?"

Forest Lawn Hollywood Hills is an oasis surrounded by bustling traffic. Though Disney, Universal, and Warner Brothers all have studios located just minutes away, the vast acreage has a self-contained quality that keeps it isolated and tranquil. Uncluttered by mausoleums, it features mountain views, gently rolling hills, fussy landscaping, and bright white statuary.

DeMeo suddenly stopped short and placed his hand on my arm, and I nearly came out of my skin. I spun out of his grasp and jumped into a fighting stance. I swept the area with my eyes to make sure the goons were where they should be. They were, but they had their guns drawn, waiting for any type of twitch or signal from DeMeo. I had no idea where Quinn was, but I believed he was wherever he needed to be to keep me safe. DeMeo seemed not to notice my jumpiness, focused as he was on something in front of us.

"Look at that," he whispered.

I tried to force myself to relax. I turned my head and followed his gaze and saw nothing, but his eyes were fixed on something. "What, the *bird*?" It was the only living creature I could detect in front of him.

"Not just any bird," he whispered. "A Western Tanager."

When I'm keyed up like that, I'm ready to kill or be killed. I *want* to kill or be killed. It was hard to focus on the bird. I looked behind us again. The goons' expressions had never changed, but at least their guns were holstered. For a moment, I almost felt sorry for them, having to guard their nutcase of a boss. I got my breathing under control and said, "Western Tanagers: are they rare or something?"

"Not rare," he said, "but very shy. You almost never see them in such an urban setting. See the bright red face and black wings? That's the male of the species."

I couldn't care less and hoped my expression showed it. DeMeo watched the bird fly off. Then he studied me a moment. "You've come a long way for this meeting," he said. "I should let you conclude your business so you can enjoy our warm climate and friendly atmosphere." He winked at me.

"Actually, I wanted to talk about *your* business," I said.

"To which business are you referring? I have lots of businesses."

I reminded him that a couple of years ago, he wanted to hire me to kill people who had signed contracts for structured settlements. I asked if he personally okayed each hit.

"This is a very disrespectful question," he said, "considering I haven't even patted you down."

I told him whoever he hired to kill the Dawes family in Montclair had been sloppy. I told him a little girl survived and I wanted him to personally underwrite her medical expenses for a complete facial reconstruction. Further, I wanted him to write a certified cashier's check to the estate of Greg and Melanie Dawes in the amount of nine million dollars so Addie could try to cope through life with the disability his actions had caused.

DeMeo laughed out loud. "You got some stones," he said. "I always said that about you."

"Me and my stones will give you five days to come up with the money."

DeMeo's eyes grew hard. "An ultimatum?"

I tried to think about it from his perspective. "Mr. DeMeo, I don't want to come across as disrespectful. Nine million plus the surgeries, that sounds like a lot of money. But let's be honest: it's no more than a bucket of sand off the beach to someone like you. I would consider it a personal favor if you do this thing for this one small girl. In return, I'll owe you a favor."

"I can make you stay out my business for all time with a simple hand gesture," he said.

"And you'll be dead before I hit the ground."

"Your giant? We've got three people on him."

"My girl."

"The blonde?"

I nodded.

DeMeo turned to me, made a show of opening his jacket. "I'm just reaching for my phone," he said. He pressed a key on the touch pad and said, "You have the girl?" Then he said, "Why not?" He turned his attention to me and said, "Nice bluff, but that's all it is. She's not here."

"You believe that, go ahead and give your signal."

He smiled that Cheshire cat smile again and said, "I don't think it would have worked out, you working for me."

Then we parted company.

I took a deep breath. I had faced down Joseph DeMeo and lived. Of course, it didn't mean much, since Joe had no intention of paying the money.

I made my way to the front of the cemetery and stood a block away from the black sedan and waited for Coop's signal. Cooper Stewart had been driving limos in the LA area for more than ten years. Before that, he'd been a capable light-heavyweight with a stiff jab. Coop was tall, maybe six five. His rugged face showed extensive scar tissue around the eyes, confirming his status as a journeyman, not a contender. Augustus Quinn knew Coop better than I did, but I'd ridden with him several times and trusted him. Coop gave the signal, and I walked over to the limo and climbed in.

"Your phone rang while you were out there," Coop said. "About twenty minutes ago."

I checked the display and found that Janet had called. A large shadow crossed the window, and I looked up and saw Quinn standing a few yards away. Coop flashed him a signal, and Quinn opened the side door and joined me.

"How'd it go?" he asked.

"Pretty much the way I thought it would. No sale."

"What's our next move?"

I motioned for Quinn to raise the privacy glass so we could talk. Though we trusted Coop, we were in DeMeo's town. No sense forcing him to choose between us.

"DeMeo made you out there," I said.

"Yeah, I know," Quinn said. "He had nine guys surrounding the place."

"Still," I said.

"According to Tony," Quinn said, "they been there since midnight."

Midnight! No wonder they saw him. "Who's Tony?"

"One of DeMeo's guys. At the end, we talked some. He recommended a restaurant, Miceli's."

"He'll probably be waiting there for you with an Uzi," I said.

Quinn shrugged. "So DeMeo won't pay. No surprise there. Got a backup plan?"

"We're going to rob him," I said.

"Joe DeMeo."

"Unless you're scared."

"How much you taking?"

"Twenty-five million," I said, "maybe more. Ten for Addie, two for each of us."

Quinn cocked his head. "That leaves more than ten million on the table."

"We'll need some help."

Quinn nodded. "I'm in."

We lowered the partition, and I told Coop where to take us. Quinn said, "Hey, Coop, you know a restaurant called Miceli's?"

"I do," Coop said. "Pizza's good; all the waiters sing to you. They got a pie they call the Meat House: pepperoni, sausage, meatballs, salami. If you decide to go there, get that one."

We turned the corner and passed a couple of protesters holding global warming signs. "Not much of a turnout," I said.

Coop chuckled. "There's usually a bunch of them. They got a chart from the fifties, tells them what the average weather used to be. Every day it's warmer than that, they gather at that corner to bitch about it. But when the weather's this nice, most of them sneak off to the beach."

I hit the voicemail button on my cell phone, and my ex-wife

Janet shrieked, "You bastard!" She went off on me with such gusto I had to hold the phone away from my ear. Quinn laughed, and Coop just shook his head. I grinned. I mean, I wasn't happy she was upset, even less happy she blamed me for it, but what was I going to do, right? She finished her screaming fit with a flourish, and Quinn said, "What the hell did you do to her, anyway?"

"She didn't go into detail," I said, "but the bottom line is she's not getting married."

Coop said, "So … is that bad news? Or good?"

"Bad for me, good for her," I said. In my mind, I allowed one of my spinning plates to crash.

# 19.

AFTER HER DIVORCE from Donovan Creed three years ago, Janet and Kimberly moved to the sleepy town of Darnell, West Virginia, where Janet's best friend, Amy, had made a comfortable, happy home after marrying one of Darnell's native sons.

Amy made it her mission in life to find Janet a husband. Janet gave it a shot, but after two years of dreadful set-ups, she was about to swear off men completely. Then, suddenly, Amy introduced her to a nice guy from Charleston.

Janet was caught completely off guard by the casually sophisticated Ken Chapman—so much so that a mere eight months of heavy dating led to a wedding announcement.

Kimberly thought her mom was rushing things, but she had to admit, Janet was happy for the first time in years. To her father, Kimberly played down the courtship, saying, "I think what's happening is Mom is talking herself into being in love, but it doesn't feel right."

One sunny morning while Janet was straightening up the living room, she opened the front door to find a thin, pretty girl in a sunhat wearing large, round sunglasses. The lady introduced herself as Kathleen Gray and said, "I don't want to cause you any problems; I just want to talk to you about Ken Chapman."

Janet stiffened. "Look Miss ... whatever your name is ..."

"Gray."

"Miss Gray. I don't know who you are or what you're talking about, but I'm rather busy right now, so if you don't mind ..."

"But I do mind. I need to ease my conscience. If you'll allow me the courtesy of three minutes, I promise to never bother you again."

Janet looked at the manila folder Kathleen was holding. "Whatever you've brought," she said, "I'm not interested."

Kathleen held out her hand. "Janet," she said, "Gray is my maiden name. My married name was Chapman. Mrs. Kenneth Chapman."

Janet's face flushed crimson. "Miss Gray, I have no interest in anything you have to say about my fiancé. I have an ex-husband of my own, but I don't go around saying disparaging things about him to everyone he dates."

Kathleen shook her head. "Really, Janet, you don't need to be upset. I'm not in Ken's life, and there are no children involved, so you and I don't have to be friends. I'm just trying to ease my mind, the same way you might do for the next one who comes along. My story's short and simple. May I come in?"

"Oh, do come in, by all means," said Janet, making no effort to hide her sarcasm.

Kathleen took a moment to study the photos of Ken and Janet on the fireplace mantle. Then she turned to face Janet Creed. "I hope it'll be different for you," she said. "I really do."

"Well I'm sure it will be. For one thing, I'm not a pushy person."

Kathleen smiled. "If you're ever in my situation someday, I hope you do a better job of it than me."

"I'm sure I will," said Janet. "Anything else?"

"Just this." Kathleen removed her hat and sunglasses. The sight of Kathleen's blood-red eyes surrounded by massive bruises stunned Janet into silence. There was an egg-sized lump on the side of Kathleen's head and strangulation marks on her neck. Kathleen unbuttoned her blouse and turned her back to Janet, revealing dozens of black and blue welts that covered her back and shoulders, each the approximate size of a man's fist.

Janet's pulse began to race. She felt her throat constricting. Her knees buckled, and she had to put her hand on the back of the sofa to steady herself. By the time Kathleen buttoned her blouse and put her hat back on, Janet regained some of her composure.

"I'm sorry for your condition, Miss Gray, but surely you don't expect me to believe Ken did this to you. I've known him, intimately, for eight months."

Kathleen's lip trembled slightly. She nodded.

"Have you been sleeping with him?" asked Janet. "Is that what this is about?"

"No. He did this to me yesterday, as a warning."

Janet's world started to whirl. "Warning about what?"

"He didn't want me to tell you he beat me throughout our marriage."

Janet felt a sudden rush of nausea. "I don't believe it," she said.

Kathleen sighed. "I'm not surprised. I wouldn't have believed it either. Look, I'm not trying to influence you or tell you how to live. I'm not saying Ken hasn't changed. I hope he'll be different with you."

While Janet found Kathleen's words impossible to believe, there was something in her voice that rang true. Janet said, "I don't understand. Did you threaten him somehow? Did you tell him you were planning to see me?"

"That's the crazy part. I had no intention of talking to you. When he told me he was getting married, I was so relieved! I figured he'd finally leave me alone and move on with his life. I would have been glad to keep my mouth shut. But he showed up on my doorstep yesterday, telling me about how your wedding announcement would be in the paper soon. He knew I'd see it and was afraid I'd make trouble. I told him to get the hell out of my life, but he told me he'd always be there, always around the corner or down the street. I laughed at him and turned away, but that's something you don't do to Ken Chapman. You don't laugh at him. He kicked the screen door open, grabbed me by the neck, and, well, this is the result. He said it was a hint of what would happen if I ever told you or anyone else about what happened in our marriage."

"And yet here you are."

"Yes."

Janet surveyed Ken's ex. "Miss Gray, I appreciate what you've said, but I sincerely doubt you're telling me the truth."

"I can live with that."

Janet shook her head. "Either way, I'm only getting one side of things."

Kathleen said, "Quite so." She extended her hand. "Janet, I've said what I came to say, and I appreciate your seeing me. My conscience is clear, and I wish you all happiness. I did want to leave these for you." She placed the manila folder on the table next to the front door. Then she carefully placed her sunglasses over her eyes and let herself out.

Janet didn't want to look at the folder, didn't want to touch it, didn't want to open it, didn't want it in her house. Even as she saw her hand reaching for it, she told herself not to do it, and that worked—she left it lying there a few extra minutes. Yet she knew she'd eventually reach out and take it and open it, and she knew that when she did, her life would change forever.

The folder contained numerous front and side views of Kathleen's battered face and torso, and several similar shots of her back and buttocks. Something cold and hard began forming in Janet's heart as she flipped through page after page of police photos chronicling years of brutal physical abuse. Medical records documented dozens of black eyes, split lips, knocked out teeth, a broken jaw, several broken noses, and numerous broken or cracked ribs. She reviewed the restraining orders, the violations of same, the police reports, and the arrest records.

In the end, Janet broke down and cried for two straight hours.

Then she made three phone calls.

Her first call was to her ex-husband, Donovan Creed. He didn't answer, so she left a message on his voice mail. She was short and to the point. "You bastard!" she said. "I know you told that woman to give me her files. Maybe I screwed up again, and maybe you saved me from a lot more hurt in the future, and maybe someday I'll even appreciate what you did. But right now my heart is broken and it's all your fault and I hate your guts! Don't call me, Donovan. Don't even think about it. I hate you! I *hate* you! So don't say a fucking word to me!"

Her second call was to her fiancé, the casually sophisticated Kenneth Chapman. "Ken," she said, "you know my ex-husband is Donovan Creed, and I've told you he is one of the top people with the National Security Agency. What you don't know is that he's a former assassin for the CIA. You can try checking it out if you don't believe me."

Ken paused before answering. "I believe you, honey, and that's pretty scary, but why are you telling me this now?"

"Because he's probably going to kill you."

"I beg your pardon?"

"It's possible that as a personal favor to me, he might agree not to kill you. But he's a nut job, and I can't guarantee your safety."

"Janet, what's going on? What are you talking about?"

"Donovan sent me a package today. A package filled with photographs and police documents describing in great detail all the violent things you did to your ex-wife, Kathleen."

"Look, Janet, that's bullshit. I can explain."

"Can you?" Janet said. "That's great, because I can't wait to hear your explanation. After all, I'm looking at more than thirty pages of documented police evidence. It's sitting in my lap right now, evidence spanning more than eight years of abuse."

The line was silent for awhile. Then, in a very small voice, Chapman said, "I'm not denying it. But that was a long time ago. You've got to understand, I was bipolar. I had a chemical imbalance. I had to take medicine for years, but I'm over that now. I swear to God. Look, you can call my ex-wife. She'll tell you."

Janet thought, *Can you believe this guy?*

"Yeah, Kenny, old pal, I'm sure Kathleen will say whatever you tell her to say. Listen, I've got to run. The wedding's off. I'll put the ring in the mail. Do not call me. Do not come near me, or Kimberly, ever again. If you try to contact me in any way, for any reason, I'll turn Donovan Creed loose on you. Believe me, you don't want that. Again, if you don't believe me, ask around."

The third call Janet made was to her best friend, Amy. She got into it quickly. "Did you know about Ken?"

"Know what, sweetie?"

"Did you know?"

"Uh, you're kind of weirding me out here, babe. Did I know what?"

"*Did ... you ... know?*"

Amy was silent a moment. "Oh, honey," she sighed, "that was such a long time ago. And anyway, there are always two sides, you know?"

"I have a *daughter*! How could you not tell me?"

"Janet, I'm begging you, think it over before you rush to judgment. Please. Don't screw this up."

"Too late."

"Let's get together and talk about it."

"Drop dead."

## 20.

IT HAD BEEN two days since Cincinnati, when I'd made the offer about beating her up and Lauren had asked, "Just for the sake of argument, how much would you have paid?" When I told her, she decided to at least hear me out. So I handed her Kathleen Chapman's police file and watched as she reviewed it. She took her time, studied all the photos carefully, read a portion of each page of the police reports. When at last she finished, she'd looked into my eyes and said, "If you know all this about her, and understand her pain, why would you want to physically assault me?"

I shrugged. "It's not about hurting you. It's about making my ex-wife happy. Happy in the long run, at least."

She gave me an encouraging smile and said, "Sugar, you really are pitiful when it comes to explaining yourself to women."

"That bad, huh?"

"World-class bad," she said.

She took both my hands in hers and looked into my eyes. She seemed to be searching for something better inside me than what I'd shown her so far.

"You'll have to explain how beating the shit out of me will make your ex-wife happy," she said. "It frightens me to think there's a woman out there who would appreciate that type of gesture, and it makes me wonder why you'd be attracted to her in the first place."

I nodded and told Lauren I cared a great deal about Janet and Kimberly and wanted only the best for them. I told her I wasn't interested in taking Ken's place; I just didn't want a man like him living in the same house with my family. I told her how horrified I'd been to learn that Janet was planning to marry a habitual wife-beater.

With that preamble out of the way, I explained my plan: Lauren would pretend to be Chapman's ex-wife, Kathleen, and pretend Chapman had beaten her as a warning to keep her mouth shut about the abuse. I assured Lauren that I was a professional, meaning I would assault her very carefully, going for the maximum effect with the minimum pain. I reiterated there'd be no enjoyment in it for me and that I didn't go around beating up women on a regular basis—but that I couldn't think of any other way to discourage Janet from marrying Ken Chapman.

Then I gave her a handful of pain pills and told her if she decided to go through with it, she should take two now and one every four hours for two days. I told her the pills would make her feel so good she'd probably call to thank me for the beating.

"Whoa, cowboy," Lauren said. "There you go again!"

I looked at her blankly. Then it registered. "Oh, right. Sorry." I shook my head. "That was a figure of speech about thanking me for the beating. I just meant that the pills are incredibly effective. I really am an idiot with women."

"I've had pain pills before," she said.

"Not like these," I said. "They're laced with something that gives you a feeling of euphoria."

Then I got out my duffel bag and handed her two bricks of money held together with rubber bands, each of which contained ten thousand dollars. She stared at the money. "It pains me to say this, but let's see if I can help you save a few bucks. Why not just call Janet and tell her about Chapman? Or better yet, send her this folder and tell her you did a background check on her fiancé and this is what turned up."

"She won't believe me," I said. "She knows my people can fabricate legal documents in a matter of hours. We can alter it, falsify it, destroy court records or create published testimony overnight. And don't forget, she loves the bastard, and he's persuasive. His last girlfriend still believes Kathleen beat herself up all those years to maintain control in the relationship."

Lauren was running out of ideas. I knew the feeling. "What if you sent the information anonymously?" she asked.

"Janet would know I did it," I said, "and she wouldn't believe it anyway. She really hates me."

"Honestly, sugar, if this is your best idea, I can see why she might feel that way." Lauren gestured toward the photos on the bed. "I admit there's a resemblance," she said, "but we're not even close to identical. Really, this whole thing is insane. Even if I agreed to do it, when Janet sees the real photographs, she'll know I'm not Kathleen."

"I'll take photos of you before and after the beating, and my people will alter the police photos to match your face and body. They'll even do an age regression on you to show the beatings over a period of years. Then they'll superimpose Kathleen's injuries on your photographs. The updated packet will be delivered to your home address by courier within eight hours."

"You can't possibly know where I live," she said.

To her horror, I recited her address from memory. "So the story and paperwork will be real," I continued. "Only the police photos will be doctored."

Lauren said, "How do you know that Janet never met Kathleen?"

"There's no way Ken would have let them meet. He wouldn't want Janet to learn about the beatings."

"Why can't I just pay her a visit, pretend to be Kathleen, and tell her the truth about Ken?"

"I thought about that, but we have to make Janet want to protect Kathleen."

"Why?"

"Because if Janet thinks Ken beat Kathleen half to death as a warning, she'd be putting Kathleen's life in danger by implicating her."

"You're talking about later on, when Janet breaks off the wedding," Lauren said.

"Exactly. If Kathleen just shows up on Janet's doorstep without any injuries, Janet will tell him, and he'd either say Kathleen was crazy or that it all happened years ago and he's cured. Remember, he can prove he's been to anger management courses."

"Required by the court."

"Right, and also counseling."

"Also a provision of his probation."

"You know the drill."

She nodded.

"He'll claim he was bipolar," I said, "and that he subsequently took drugs to alleviate his chemical imbalance."

"All of which might be true."

"It might be, but that's not the issue. I don't want this creep in my wife's life—or my daughter's."

"Your ex-wife, you mean."

"Right."

"So, if I pretend to be Kathleen, show up all battered and bruised, and tell Janet he did this to me as a warning, you think she'll buy it?"

"I know she will. He can't claim to be cured if he did this to you. But you've got to play it a certain way. We'll need to do a lot of rehearsing."

"I charge a two-hour minimum."

I smiled. "I thought the twenty grand might be enough."

She smiled back. "That'll help take away the sting," she said, "but you said the twenty was for the beating. Anything else, such as rehearsing, that's extra."

She saw me frown.

"Don't go cheap on me now, Donovan," she said. "I'm obviously the only game in town, the only escort that matches Kathleen enough for this crazy scheme to work."

"Fair enough," I said, noting she'd called herself a hooker earlier. "But if I'm paying for your time I want your full attention."

"Of course."

I nodded. "Good. And, Lauren, I'll make you a promise: if my ex breaks off the wedding, I'll owe you a favor."

"A favor," she said.

I nodded.

"You mean like some kind of Mafia thing?"

I didn't say anything.

"Like what, you mean you'd kill someone if I asked you to?"

I shrugged. "It's up to you how you use your favor."

"Mister, you are some kind of twisted freak, anyone ever tell you that?"

"I hear that a lot, actually."

She looked at me silently for a moment. "Well I intend to

128

hold you to it," she said, "'cause I've got a Ken Chapman in my life, too." Lauren tried to hand one of the envelopes back to me. She said, "Don't you want to just give me half now, half later?"

"I trust you," I said.

She nodded. "I guess if you're willing to beat me up and kill my ex, you're not the sort of person who gets double-crossed much, am I right?"

"You think you can pull this off convincingly?" I said.

"Are you kidding me?" She said her experience as a successful escort all these years made her a better actress than Meryl Streep.

The way she put it, "Every week, an eighty-year-old man thinks he gives me a screaming orgasm, okay? So this business with Janet's a piece of cake." Then she added, "Still, you need to prepare yourself for something."

"What's that?"

"She's never going back to you."

"I don't want her back."

"Then let me put it another way: she's never going to forgive you."

"You don't think she'll eventually thank me?"

"Not a chance."

I thought about that a bit. "Okay," I said. "It's still worth it."

In all, Lauren and I were together six hours. The first hour we rehearsed her lines, over and over. Then I ordered room service. We rehearsed another thirty minutes while waiting for the food. Lunch came and we ate it and chatted about life in general.

I couldn't get over how much she looked like Kathleen Gray. Lauren didn't have Kathleen's spark, of course, or her gift of gab, or her capacity to be adorable. Yet she had something special going for her in a Kathleen sort of way.

After lunch, since I was paying for her time anyway and since she looked so much like Kathleen Gray, we had a little casual sex.

Then I beat the shit out of her.

We rehearsed her lines again while I waited for her bruises to bloom. Then I took pictures and got the information about her ex and asked if she had a preference how she wanted the hit to go down. She said, "Two things. First, I want him to suffer."

"Of course you do."

"Wait," she said. "This is really going to happen, isn't it?"

I smiled. "What's the second thing?"

"I want to watch him die."

I smiled again. "Of course you do."

She asked, "Am I bad?"

I shrugged. "Hey, he's got to die sometime, right? Now don't over-think this. It'll be fun. You'll see."

# 21.

ONE QUICK GLANCE and I forgot all about Joe DeMeo.

It was Saturday, a couple hours after my meeting with DeMeo at the cemetery. I was staying in a luxury beach hotel in Santa Monica when she knocked on the door.

Jenine.

The first thing she noticed was the envelope fat with cash on the edge of the coffee table. She picked it up and her eyes widened as she riffled through the stack of hundreds. She glanced at me to see if I was serious.

I nodded.

She'd been advertising on Aspiring Actresses, the Internet escort site, and had purchased enough space to display three sultry photographs and a bio listing her vital statistics and limited acting experience.

In the e-mails we exchanged, she admitted being desperate for cash, and I had agreed to share some of mine in return for what might happen when we eventually met.

When she'd called from the lobby, I gave my room number and wondered—having been previously burned in similar encounters—if the girl who showed would bear any resemblance to the photos I'd seen.

I needn't have worried. If anything, she looked better than advertised—and that was saying a lot. Dressed casually in jeans and a halter top and sporting iridescent ear buds tethered to a surprisingly bulky MP3 player, she looked every bit the college student for whom a distinguished professor might willingly sacrifice his career.

Jenine removed the ear buds and placed the MP3 player on the coffee table before tucking the envelope securely into her handbag. She performed the obligatory small talk in a detached but efficient manner until I let her know it was time to move things along.

Standing before me in the parlor of one of Southern California's most exclusive boutique hotel rooms, biting her lower lip, she suddenly seemed quite small and vulnerable.

Before she arrived, I had propped open the French doors leading to the balcony. A slight breeze manipulated the sheer curtains into random patterns that caught her eye, causing her to look beyond the small wrought-iron seating area. From her vantage point, the Santa Monica Pier was visible, and she smiled wistfully at it or something else that attracted her attention.

On the beach below us, a guy played riffs on a saxophone.

Someone's stunning twenty-year-old daughter began lifting her halter top for my pleasure, and I thought about what I would do to a guy like me if this had been my daughter, Kimberly. After removing her top, she covered her breasts with her arms and paused.

I asked if there was a problem.

Just that she'd never done anything like this before, she said, and she was only doing it this once in order to make ends meet until her big break came along. I gave her the nod of understanding she expected, and she unbuttoned her jeans, slid them to the floor, and stepped out of them.

Promptly dismissing any misgivings I may have had regarding her age, I appraised her pert body and caught myself saying that what she was doing was no big deal; lots of famous actresses started out this way.

"It shows how committed you are to your craft," I said, shamelessly.

That wistful smile played about her lips again, and she wriggled out of her panties. "What do you like?" she asked, and something in the tone of her voice suggested she had in fact done this sort of thing many times before.

Demonstrating considerable expertise and a surprising degree of enthusiasm, Jenine did her best to earn the contents of the envelope, and afterward, I told her to lie on her stomach so I could get a better look at the small tattoo on her lower back.

When I aimed my camera phone, she said, "I don't do photos."

"Just the tattoo," I said.

She nodded but said she'd want to check the view screen to make sure I hadn't included any part of her ass in the shot. "I intend to be a famous actress some day," she said, "and I don't want any nude photos turning up."

I told her I didn't see any birthmarks on her body and asked if she had any I might have missed. She gave me a strange look and told me about the dime-sized rosy patch on the right side of her head, just above her ear, which would have been impossible to see without parting her hair at that precise spot.

After I snapped a close up of that area, she began collecting her clothes. I noticed her purse on the desk and brought it to her.

"Are we finished here?" she wanted to know.

"We are."

While she dressed, I moved to the balcony to signal the

saxophone player, the monstrous man with severely deformed facial features named Augustus Quinn. I watched my giant pack up his instrument and walk away, knowing he was making his way around the hotel to the waiting sedan. Quinn and Coop would follow Jenine for a couple of hours, find out where she lived, who her friends were. Then they'd come back and pick me up and we'd drive to the airfield for the return flight to Virginia. The only negative was the time difference. By the time we got back, I'd be too tired to test the ADS weapon.

Re-entering the parlor, I found Jenine standing in the center of the room, fully dressed, attempting to make eye contact. There's an art to saying goodbye in these situations, a sort of silent protocol. You don't kiss, but a hug is nice. There's the verbal dance you both do when neither of you want her to linger but neither wants to be rude, either.

You don't want to be too abrupt, so you tell her it was great and you'd love to see her the next time you're in town. She reiterates she doesn't really do this sort of thing, but for you she'll make an exception.

My cell phone performed a dance of its own, vibrating on the desktop. "I need to get that," I said.

She flashed a shy smile. "Okay … thanks?" It was almost a question. I gave her a slight frown to imply I wished she didn't have to go. She shrugged and offered a cute little pout to express the same sentiment. Then she blew me a kiss, let herself out, and closed the door behind her.

When she did that, something clicked inside my head. I thought about Kathleen Gray and felt a wave of sadness wash over me.

# 22.

THE CELL PHONE call that caused Jenine to leave had been prearranged. It was Quinn calling to let me know he was in position. I donned my jeans, pocketed the camera phone, poured myself a double whiskey from the wet bar. I sat on the edge of the bed with my drink and propped my free hand on the sheets we'd rumpled moments earlier.

The scent of Jenine's youth hung in the air, and I inhaled it fully, savoring her essence. Maybe Kathleen needed four hundred and ninety calories to de-stress, but not me.

I felt a vibration in my pocket, slid the phone open, put it to my ear.

"It's me," said Callie.

"You need to get a butterfly tattoo on your ass," I said.

She paused for a beat. "Donovan, if this is how you normally start conversations, I think I may have isolated your problem with women. No wonder you can't find a nice girl to marry."

If Callie Carpenter had been born three inches taller, she wouldn't have to kill people for a living. With her spectacular looks, she'd be a one-name supermodel by now. I drained my glass and placed it on the end table. I stood and walked back through the parlor to the balcony and chose the chair that angled toward the Santa Monica Pier.

"What's up?" I asked.

"Reach over the naked whore and flip on your TV."

I sighed. "How little you think of me. Truth is, I'm here all alone on a hotel balcony, enjoying the unseasonably warm February temperature. Which channel?"

"Take your pick."

I went back to the parlor, found the remote control, and pressed the power button. The words *Breaking News* flashed below the live feed of an interview in progress. The man being interviewed was telling reporters that the event that had just occurred was unprecedented. The electronic runner at the bottom of the screen flashed the words *Homeland Security confirms unauthorized spy satellite breach.*

The man identified himself as Edward Culbertson, head of Research Operations for Skywatch Industries. He said Skywatch had a government contract to provide artificial intelligence applications to enhance radar imaging. He said, "This is one of the five so-called Keyhole-class satellites that fly above us every day. The exact specifications are classified beyond top secret, but we know a few things about them."

"For example?" a reporter said.

"We know they travel one hundred miles above the Earth at a speed of Mach 25," Culbertson said. "We know they cover every inch of the Earth's surface twice a day, taking digital photos of specific locations that have been programmed into their tracking mechanism."

"Is that what happened in this case?" the reporter asked. "Did someone hack into the satellite computer and direct it to take the pictures we just showed on live television?"

"That's the current speculation."

Another reporter spoke: "Dr. Culbertson, there's a lot of argument regarding the accuracy of spy satellite imaging. What's the truth? For example, can they effectively display a car's license plate?"

"Under normal conditions, they have a resolution of five inches, meaning they can accurately distinguish a five-inch object on the ground."

On the phone, I said to Callie, "Did you know that?"

"No, but if I did, I wouldn't be telling the whole world about it."

A different reporter asked if the surveillance satellites could be tapped by authorities to help solve other crimes.

"No," he said. "The odds are probably impossible to one."

"Why's that, doctor?"

"Because," he said, "the crime scenes would have to be programmed into the satellite's computer at least an hour in advance of the crime."

"So what you're saying is, whoever's responsible for the kidnapping—they're the ones who breached the satellite's security?"

"That's what we believe, yes."

"To what end, sir?"

"My best guess? Someone wanted to watch the kidnapping from a remote location, someone who knew ultra-secret details about the satellite's orbit path in advance."

"Do you suspect terrorists?"

The expert suddenly looked uncomfortable and backed away as an FBI spokesperson took over the mic. "At this time, we are unable to confirm whether the satellite breach or the abduction were terrorist events. I'm afraid we don't have time for further questions, but we'll keep you informed as future details develop."

Now, back at the TV studio, the newswoman said, "For those of you who just tuned in, Homeland Security has confirmed an unauthorized breach of one of their so-called spy satellites. This particular satellite had been tracking over the southeastern seaboard this past Tuesday when the following images were viewed remotely by an unknown person or persons."

On the screen behind the newswoman, they showed about forty photos in rapid sequence. For me, the pictures would have been riveting even if the abduction hadn't involved Monica Childers, the woman Callie and I killed for Victor four days ago.

Callie said, "Do we get to keep the money for the hit?"

That was Callie, always good for a smile.

The news reporter said, "As most people in the Jacksonville area already know, Monica Childers has been the focus of one of North Florida's most extensive searches." Behind her, they displayed a picture of Monica's husband, Baxter. The newscaster identified him as one of the most prominent and widely respected surgeons in North America.

"Baxter's a big shot," I said to Callie.

"Baxter? What channel are you watching?"

"I don't know, one of the big three."

"Flip till you find CNN."

"Why?"

"They're talking about us."

# 23.

THE STATION I'D been watching had shown photos that chronicled the entire event, starting with the two women jogging out of the resort entrance and ending with pictures taken from the opposite angle, as the satellite moved out over the Atlantic. The final photo showed the van turning left onto a narrow overgrown path.

But CNN had dug up a computer imaging expert who was displaying close-ups of the three people standing by the van. Baxter Childers was on a split screen with CNN news anchor, Carol Teagess.

"Dr. Childers, good as these photos are," she said, "we still don't have quality resolution on the faces, though we're told Homeland Security is moments away from providing definitive photos. Are you prepared to tell us at this point whether one of these women is your wife, Monica?

"There's no doubt in my mind," he said. "Monica's the one standing between the other two. The jogging outfit she's wearing in the photographs is the same one she laid out on the chair the night before she disappeared."

"And you said she left the hotel room early Tuesday morning while you were sleeping."

"She always jogs around sunrise, so yes I'm usually sleeping when she gets up."

"Dr. Childers, if you're right, this is visual proof that

Monica was kidnapped by a man and woman driving a white van."

A third person appeared on the screen, and Carol said, "We are joined by Duval County Sheriff Allen English, the officer in charge of heading up the search team. Sheriff English, you've had fifteen hundred people combing the area for four days. These satellite photos clearly show the kidnappers took Monica Childers a mere six hundred yards from the hotel room the Childers occupied last Tuesday. How is it possible you missed the van or any evidence of Monica?"

The sheriff gave a withering look and said, "Because the van and Monica were gone by the time we learned she'd been missing."

"We now know the van turned left on a small path," Carol said. "Any chance your people missed that particular spot?"

"None whatsoever. Our search began from the beach and moved inland to A1A, so we hit that area a few hours into the search."

"I'm told that since these photos were released, you've had a forensic crew working at the site. Any new evidence yet?"

"Nothing I can report at this time," he said.

"But you're working on it?"

"We are," he said.

"Thank you, Sherriff," Carol said, and I muted the sound.

To Callie, I said, "I gave her a lethal injection. There's no way she could have survived."

"What did you use?"

"Botulinum toxin."

Callie laughed. "Maybe she's been pumped so full of Botox she's become immune!"

"Maybe Victor had someone pick her up after we drove off, someone who gave her a dose of Heptavalent."

"Is that some sort of anti-venom?"

"It's an antitoxin, but yeah, it works the same way. Botulinum paralyzes the respiratory muscles, but its effects can be reversed with Heptavalent. It's not a perfect science, and it takes weeks or even months."

"Thanks, *doctor*," Callie said sarcastically. Then she added, "You think Victor's behind this satellite thing?"

"Has to be."

"But why take that chance? You think he just wanted to watch the hit go down?"

"Maybe. He doesn't have much of a life, so maybe that's how he gets his kicks. It's also possible he tapped into the satellite so his people could find her."

"But he knew where she'd be. He even marked the path for us."

"Yeah, but this was our first job for him. Suppose he wanted her alive? He couldn't be certain we'd do it exactly the way he told us to. Also, what if someone had a flat on the side of the road near the trail? Or what if someone was camping out in the area and would have seen us make the turn? A dozen things could have gone wrong that would have caused us to kill her somewhere else. If he wanted her alive, he'd want to know exactly where she was."

"So you think he had Monica kidnapped."

"I do."

"Why didn't he just ask us to kidnap her?"

"Maybe he wanted her for himself and didn't want us to know."

"So the midget captures the trophy wife of the doctor who saved his life."

"It's just a theory."

"Why would he want to punish her?" Callie asked.

"There's probably a lot to the story about Victor and the doctor. A lot we don't know."

"Think we ought to have a chat with Victor?"

"Eventually, but I want to put Lou on it first."

"Research his connection to Baxter?"

"Right. Lou finds the connection, he'll have Victor's real name. Then we fast-forward his life, learn his abilities, figure out his motivations."

"And his friends," Callie said. "Any guy who can hijack a top-secret spy satellite…"

"Yeah," I said. "This is no circus midget."

Suddenly, the television had my full attention. I turned up the sound. "Are you watching this?"

She was.

CNN news anchor Carol Teagess was showing a close up of Monica Childers from one of the satellite photos. "This just in," she said. "FBI officials working in conjunction with Homeland Security have released the following image taken from one of the spy satellite digital photographs." The TV screen displayed the new close-up on the left, and a recent photograph of Monica on the right.

"It's official," she said. "The lady who was abducted at Amelia Island on Valentine's Day has been positively identified as Monica Childers, wife of the nationally prominent surgeon Dr. Baxter Childers."

Carol touched her earpiece and paused. "We take you now to the FBI field office in Jacksonville, Florida, where I'm told that FBI Spokesperson Courtney Armbrister is ready to begin her live press conference. Sources familiar with the story expect her to give further updates and reveal the kidnappers' identities."

On the phone, Callie said, "Darwin's gonna shit!"

"Ya think?"

The TV screen showed a bunch of people milling around a large room at the FBI's Jacksonville field office. It was clear the press conference would be delayed a few minutes, so Carol began a voice-over dialog to keep the viewers from switching channels to watch *Hee Haw* reruns.

Callie used the time to ask, "What were you saying earlier? About getting a tattoo on my ass?"

"I found an adorable one on the lower hip of your new body double."

"You found a hooker who looks like me?"

"I resent the implication," I said. "In any event, she's close enough facially, and our people can do the rest."

"A tattoo," she said.

"And you're also going to need a small red birthmark on your scalp."

"No pubic piercings?" she said with great annoyance.

"I wish," I said. I took a few seconds to conjure a mental image of Callie naked, but she was so far out of my league I couldn't even fantasize it. "I'll send you digitals when I get back to HQ," I said.

Body doubles are disposable people we use to cover our tracks, or, in extreme circumstances, to fake our deaths if our covers get blown. We put a lot of time and effort into these people, monitoring and protecting them, often for years at a time, until something happens that requires us to place them into service.

Of course, our body doubles are totally clueless about their participation in our reindeer games of national security. If they knew about it, most civilians would disapprove of the practice, just as most disapproved of the army's plan for wide-scale use of the ADS weapon. However, from my side of the fence, collateral damage is a fact of war, and civilian sacrifice a necessary evil. When managed judiciously, body doubles can buy us time to eliminate paper trails or change our appearance so we can get back to the business of killing terrorists.

Callie asked if Jenine was prettier than her—just the sort of crap you'd expect from a gorgeous woman. "Don't be ridiculous," I said. "Remember, she doesn't have to look *exactly* like you. She only needs to be the same age, shape, and height. The fact that she's beautiful, with high cheekbones, is a plus. The tattoo and birthmark are small and easy to replicate."

"What sort of butterfly is it?" she asked. "Is it stupid -looking? A tattoo is a permanent fixture, Donovan. It sounds creepy."

"Think of it as a shrine to Jenine's memory," I said. "And try to show some respect, will you? She's putting her life on the line for you."

"Not knowingly," Callie said. "Not willingly."

"A technicality," I said.

"If we ever terminate her," Callie said, "I'm going to be stuck with a tattoo and birthmark that my next body double won't have."

I let that comment hang in the air unanswered, and soon we were back to exchanging theories about the Monica hit. I wasn't ready to completely dismiss the terrorist angle, so Callie asked if it were possible Sal Bonadello was involved with terrorists. After all, he's the one who gave Victor my cell phone number. I told her Sal was many things, all unsavory, but a terrorist sympathizer, no. I told Callie to keep watching the news and let me know if anything interesting developed.

"This isn't interesting enough for you?" she asked.

# 24.

I WAS ABOUT to turn off the TV and take a shower when I got sidetracked by Courtney Armbrister's live update on CNN.

FBI Special Agent Courtney Armbrister was a media dream. Playing to full advantage her shoulder-length auburn hair, perpetually pouting lips, and killer body, she managed to appear beguiling despite the seriousness of the occasion. Courtney sported the obligatory dark suit favored by the bureau, though hers was obviously tailored. Her jacket framed a white blouse that appeared more silk than cotton. Her eyes glared fiercely into the camera, and when she spoke, it was with such conviction you knew she had to be telling the truth, the whole truth, and nothing but the truth.

Although in this case, she was lying like hell through those perfect, dazzling teeth.

I knew the cover-up was in full swing when S.A. Armbrister informed the CNN audience that FBI computers had identified the kidnappers as former Soviet agents with confirmed ties to terrorist leaders. On the screen behind her, the bureau displayed phony names and doctored images of Callie and me. In these photos, I was younger, smaller, and had no facial scar. Callie had been aged at least ten years, and they'd done something to her nose and eyes she wasn't going to like. They also displayed fake profiles obtained through "classified sources" to show they were on top of things. She said the bureau was sharing these photos and documents with the public so we could be part of the process. It was a total load of crap, but as far as the Joe and Mrs. Lunchbox crowd were concerned, any words coming from that face would seem credible.

"Until we have proof to the contrary," Courtney said, "we have every reason to believe Monica Childers is alive and being held captive. So we're asking for your help. We want you to be our eyes and ears on this one. If you see anything, if you hear anything, please, call our hotline. There is no clue too small when it comes to saving an innocent life."

Almost brought a tear to my eye, she did.

Then she talked about the white van and showed her national audience a picture of it. She said police around the country were working on that lead but they could use the public's help on this, also. Finally, on behalf of FBI agents and law enforcement officers everywhere, Courtney promised to hunt the kidnappers down and bring them to justice. She ended by issuing a special alert: "If anyone has any information regarding these two former Soviet agents, please call the FBI hotline at…"

The phone vibrated again, and I answered it.

"Creed, you son of a jailhouse bitch! What did you do with the body?" The man I knew only as Darwin had only just begun yelling at me. He told me how much trouble they had to go to in order to doctor the photographs and plant the phony Russian suspects. Darwin called me stupid, careless, and a bunch of other names that would have hurt my feelings had I not been keenly aware of his indelicate nature. So he unloaded, and I sipped my bourbon and took my lumps and waited for him to get on topic, which he eventually managed to do.

"I want to know who hired you, because whoever it was, he managed to throw a monkey wrench into our national defense system. And don't tell me Sal Bonadello, a guy who thinks software means sweaters."

Darwin fell silent, but only for a moment. Then he said, "I'm waiting."

"I can't give you a name," I said.

"Can't or won't?"

"Can't. But on the bright side, I know how to get it"

"Creed, listen to me. You've done a lot of stupid things over the years, things I've turned a blind eye to because up to now, you've been more valuable than the shit storms you've created. But this is too much. We can't let someone hack into our national defense systems, and we can't let the government find out that you and your people are running around taking contracts from criminals to kill people," he said. "They're funny about shit like that. How the fuck did you let this happen? No, don't bother telling me. Just tell me this: what are you going to do about it?"

"I'm going to talk to an angry midget," I said.

"What? Are you insane? You trying to tell me some midget hired you to kill the doctor's wife?"

"Little person," I said. "They prefer the term *little people*."

"I prefer Viagra and a nice set of tits, but right now you and Callie are the only boobs in my life."

"Yes," I said.

"Yes what?"

"Yes, I'm saying a midget hired me to kill Monica Childers, but I'm not sure she's dead."

"I know how to tell: did you kill her or not?"

"We killed her, but we left her body. Now it's gone."

"Wait," Darwin said. "Maybe I should get some Roman soldiers to move the stone away from the tomb."

"Look, I gave her a syringe full of BT. I think someone got to her in time to administer an antidote. I think that's why Victor monitored the satellite, so he could get a chase team to pick her up as soon as we left."

"Victor? Who's Victor? The midget?"

"Little person."

"Let me get this straight." Darwin paused on the other end of the line. "You took a contract from an angry midget to kill a prominent surgeon's wife, but she was rescued and then kidnapped by other people working for the very same midget. That what you're telling me?"

"It sounds stupid when you say it out loud like that."

Then, in a tight voice, he said, "Kill her again, Creed."

"Okay."

"Because otherwise she'll be able to identify you."

"Okay."

"And kill the midget, too."

"That I can't do."

"Why the hell not?"

"First, I don't know for certain he's the hacker. Second, if he isn't the hacker and I kill him, I'll never be able to find the real hacker. Third, I've entered into an agreement with him."

"You'll be entering a pine box if you don't put a stop to this hacking business."

"I will."

"And don't forget to kill Monica Childers."

"Assuming she's still alive."

"Don't assume anything. Just kill her."

"Will do."

"Keep me in the loop. I don't want to have to keep calling you after the fact."

"Got it."

"Oh, shut up." He hung up on me.

# 25.

I'M A TIME Saver.

Time Savers are people who commit special moments to memory. A skilled Time Saver can freeze all the components of an event—the date, mood, time, temperature, lighting, sights, sounds, scents, the breeze—everything. Then we park this information in a corner of our brains and relive it whenever we wish. It's like opening a time capsule years after an event and having all the wonderful memories spill out.

Some guys like baseball, some ballet. Maybe they're content to grow old with memories of sweeping the Yankees or reliving the *Dance of the Cygnets from Swan Lake*. But me, I'd rather Time Save the memory of trysts with beautiful young ladies like Jenine.

Fully dressed now, sitting on the balcony again, I closed my eyes and began experiencing all the facets of our encounter, committing them to a permanent file in my mind. Just as I'd indoctrinated my body to survive torture and function at a high level by testing weapons and sleeping in a prison cell, I'd structured my mind to compartmentalize the significant experiences of my life. These I can relive as if they're happening in the moment—a wonderful skill to be able to call upon the next time I'm stuck in a real prison for any length of time.

Some people plan for their retirement. I plan for my imprisonment, for I am certain to end up dead or in prison,

150

and if it's to be the latter, I want my body and mind to be prepared.

I began by concentrating on her voice. Then I relived the heightened awareness, the anticipation—the entire range of feelings and emotions that raced through my mental synapses and physical receptors just after she called from the lobby phone. I marked these things in my mind until I knew I could call upon them at will.

Then I re-experienced Jenine's arrival in the doorway, my first view of her, and the immediate impressions I formed, and how I felt the moment I encountered her beauty, newness, and youth. I smiled, thinking how none of this mattered in the least to Jenine and the other beauties I'd met in my life, although I'm sure they have fond memories of the money I spent.

I focused on the way she entered the room while listening to music, just as you'd expect a college kid to do, with the ear buds, the oversized MP3 player, and …

And suddenly I realized she didn't have the MP3 player with her when she left the room!

A cold chill rushed through me. Could Jenine have put the MP3 player in her purse while I was on the balcony, signaling Quinn? I didn't think so. If she ever kept it in her purse, she'd have done so before meeting me. I had to assume the worst. As a trained assassin for many years, I survived the deadliest ambushes, the most terrifying physical encounters imaginable, by always assuming the worst.

I jumped to my feet and dialed the operator. A young lady answered. "Front desk. This is Jodie; how may I help you?"

"Jodie," I said in my most commanding voice, "this is Donovan Creed in room 214. I'm a federal agent. I need you to listen very carefully."

"Is this a joke?" she asked. "If it is, it's not funny."

Maybe I should have told her that after spending twelve years as the CIA's top international assassin, I ought to know a bomb threat when I saw one. Then again, the word assassin conjures up such diverse feelings. I decided to stick with the federal agent story and gave her another go.

"Jodie, I repeat, I'm a federal agent and there's a bomb in my room. I want you to activate the fire alarm, contact hotel security, and immediately begin evacuating the building."

"Sir," she said, "bomb threats are taken very seriously. If I report you, it could mean prison time."

"Jodie," I said, "I wrote the manual on bomb threats, okay? Now sound the fire alarm and make an evacuation announcement before I come down there and rip your face off!"

I slammed the phone down and ran to the door, flipped the lock latch outward so the door would stay propped open, and tore down the hall, banging doors, yelling at the top of my lungs, "Emergency! Evacuate the building immediately! Leave your things behind! Get out of the building now!"

By the time I got to the fifth door, the fire alarm started blaring, so I raced back to my room and started a frantic search. The bathroom seemed the likeliest place, so I started there. I checked behind the shower curtain, lifted the toilet bowl tank cover, looked up to see if any ceiling tiles had been dislodged, and checked the floor for debris in case I'd missed something. Then I realized this wasn't going to work. I simply didn't have the time to conduct a proper search. Jenine, on the other hand, had the entire length of our visit to decide where to hide it.

If she hid it.

If it was a bomb.

I ran to the balcony, felt my legs climb over the railing, felt myself hurtling through the air. I realized I'd just jumped off the second floor balcony! My legs had made the calculation without me, had hurled me as far out as possible in an effort to clear the sidewalk below.

Now, in midair, with my mind back on the job, I tucked and rolled as I hit and tried to ignore the searing pain that suddenly knifed through my shoulder. I scrambled to my feet, sprinted twenty yards, and dove behind the thick base of a giant palm, scattering twelve-inch sand tsunamis in my wake. I tucked my chin, protected my vital organs as well as possible, and waited for the explosion.

# 26.

AND NOTHING HAPPENED.

A handful of hotel guests began filing out the side and back entrances. There weren't many, but I supposed that during a fire drill the vast majority would have gone out the front.

A minute passed, and the fire alarm droned on. The speakers must have pointed to the front and sides of the hotel because the alarm was fairly muted from my position.

Some more guests joined the first group. I considered running over to warn them, but no, a discussion was bound to follow, and we'd probably all get killed while they questioned my credentials and the conclusions I'd drawn.

In the end, it didn't matter, because someone in the group made the decision to walk toward the front of the hotel and the others followed.

More time passed, seconds I'm sure, but it always seems longer while waiting for a bomb to explode. The muffled drone of the alarm gave way to other sounds you'd expect to hear from behind a palm tree fifty yards from the Pacific Ocean: breaking surf behind me and, somewhere, hidden from view, the musical clang of steel drums rising above the traffic noise. A quarter-mile to my left, I could hear the distant rumble of the roller coaster on the Santa Monica Pier.

I didn't know how long I had before the bomb detonated, but if I had any time at all I figured I should use it to find better cover. I slowly uncoiled my body and chanced a high-speed dash to a small concrete wall fifteen yards to my right. I dove behind it face first, like Pete Rose sliding into third base, and waited. I looked up. Twenty yards to my right, on the concrete walkway behind the neighboring hotel, a young man in a bright orange windbreaker had stopped holding his girlfriend's hand long enough to point at me and laugh.

I looked at the young couple. At what point, I wondered, had I evolved into an object of ridicule? When had I become some sort of cartoon character, a delusional mental case deserving the scorn of teenagers? Was it possible I'd imagined the bomb threat? Was I witnessing a glimpse into my future, where every sudden sound or random thought might cause me to frighten people or threaten to send me jumping out of windows or ducking for cover?

From this angle, I could see a few hotel guests glancing toward the rooftop, probably searching for signs of smoke. I followed their gaze and came to the same conclusion: there was nothing to worry about.

I smiled at the young couple and shrugged, then stood and dusted myself off. The girl smiled back and held her position a moment, as if trying to decide if I'd be safe left to my own devices. Her boyfriend, showing far less concern, gently tugged at her wrist. With her free hand, she tucked a wayward strand of hair behind her ear. He tugged again, and she turned her eyes away—reluctantly, it seemed to me—and they resumed their leisurely stroll along the sidewalk.

Eventually, the alarm stopped. It was quiet now, and things were starting to resume their normal order. I guessed I'd have some explaining to do to hotel security and possibly the local police and bomb squad. Darwin would probably have to get involved again, which he'd hate.

The roller coaster on the Santa Monica Pier must have stopped to reload passengers because its rumble had been temporarily replaced by calliope music and the mechanical sounds of the other amusement rides. A couple of security guys came out the hotel's back entrance, followed by a bald guy in a gray suit with black lapels—probably the hotel manager. Behind me to my left, two coeds on roller blades glided along the beach walk in my direction. Their arms glistened with sweat, and their matching turquoise spandex leggings were stretched tight over well-defined legs. As they whooshed by, I gave them a nod of approval. One of them frowned. The other one flipped me the finger.

I moved closer and glanced up at the balcony from which I'd jumped. The MP3 player had been bulky. Could it have been a bomb?

Of course.

So why, I asked myself, was I standing out here in harm's way? The answer was simple: because it didn't add up. If the MP3 player housed a bomb, why wait so long? I mean, why didn't Jenine detonate it as soon as she'd gotten out of range? Or wire it with an internal timer and set it to go off five minutes after she left? I wondered if something had gone wrong. Maybe a wire got crossed or disconnected. Maybe the remote didn't get the proper signal due to interference from the hotel wiring system.

No. In my line of work, you have to assume that everything that can hurt you will always work perfectly. Yet this seemed the rare exception because I could think of no reason for her to wait this long to detonate it.

Unless …

Something nagged at my brain, just beyond my awareness. Something I couldn't quite put my finger on. Something about the timing of the detonation was itching at me, trying to make sense. If I had a few minutes to work it out …

But I didn't. I'd have to put that thought on hold and come back to it later. At the moment, I had to either wait for the bomb squad or try to disarm the bomb myself. I thought about it and decided it made sense for me to do it since the explosion was well overdue. I was sure the hotel clerk had called the bomb squad, but by the time the call got routed to the right people, by the time the right people got here, it could all be over.

I headed for the back entrance at a fast clip. As I pulled the door open, a childhood memory popped into my mind, a perfect example of how this Time Saver thing works.

I'd been twelve the summer my best friend Eddie tied a dozen cherry bombs together with a single fuse and lit it. We howled with excited laughter and dashed for cover. We waited forever but nothing happened. Eddie finally went back to investigate and when he did, the bombs exploded. Eddie lost several fingers, a section of ear, and most of the skin on the left side of his face.

I can't explain how, but standing in the hotel doorway just then I could *feel* the bomb trying to explode. In my mind I pictured an old-time detonator, the kind with the big handle you push down to make contact. In my mind that handle was already in motion. I screamed for the benefit of anyone within the sound of my voice. "There's a bomb in the hotel! Run for cover!"

I slammed the door shut, reversed my direction, and ran full speed back toward the concrete wall I'd spotted earlier, the one that bordered the courtyard. It was waist-high, and from this direction, I couldn't just slide behind it like before. I'd have to dive over it like the commando I used to be.

So I did. I managed the dive. Then, laying flat on my chest, I pressed the left side of my body and head against the wall.

At which point, much of the hotel—and the upper third of the wall protecting me—vaporized.

# 27.

THE EXPLOSION FROM the hotel left a residue of soot and dust hanging in the air like a mushroom cloud. I coughed what I could out of my lungs. My ears rang. All color had been blasted from my vision. I turned to check behind me and saw white sand and sky, black palm trees and water.

I shook my head a couple of times and blinked the color back into my eyes. I got to my feet, checked for injuries, but other than the nagging pain in my shoulder, I had nothing to complain about. I seemed to be moving in slow motion and wondered if I was in shock. I willed myself to snap out of it so I could focus on the devastation fifty feet before me.

The side walls of the hotel remained intact, but most of the back had been scooped out. The roof and outer walls of the penthouse floor were still there but were listing precariously. With the internal support structure weakened, it would only be a matter of time, probably minutes, before the overhang crashed into the rubble below. The balcony I'd jumped from, like the ones above and below it, as well as the adjacent ones, was history. The exterior of the hotel had been cleanly dissected in a half-circle running maybe sixty feet in diameter.

What remained looked like a scene from a war zone, with bodies and body parts everywhere. Leaping flames erupted sporadically, revealing ruptured gas lines. People screamed from within, but the massive wall of sweltering heat would surely hinder rescue efforts.

Locals, tourists, and even vagrants began rushing to the scene to rubberneck. I spotted a homeless guy heading my way wearing a decent pair of boots. I fished a fifty from my jeans and quickly traded for them. As I laced up the bum's boots, I studied the roof. How long could it possibly hang there, defying gravity?

This was no time for heroes, I thought, and had I not felt directly responsible for the widespread destruction and loss of life, I might have walked away. Instead, I took a deep breath and entered the smoldering ruins. As my eyes adjusted to the soot and heat, I scanned the carnage and decided the far right edge of the blast perimeter offered the highest probability for survivors.

Disregarding the teetering roof structure above me, I picked my way through the mess. Within seconds I spotted the torso of an elderly man covered in soot. I tried for a pulse, but he wasn't offering any. In these situations, you have to move quickly, put your effort where it can do the most good.

I had to focus on the living.

Working my way deeper into the ruins, I moved beyond the mangled bodies of the obvious dead. Since most surfaces were too hot or sharp to grab, I took a few seconds to search for something I could wrap around my hands. Strips of curtain remnants did the trick, and soon I was tossing broken furniture out of the way and pushing slabs of concrete aside in order to inspect the smoky air pockets below.

I found an unconscious boy with severe burns lying beneath the upturned bed that had saved his life. Next to him I found a girl, probably his older sister, who had not been so fortunate. I carried the boy out of the blast site to a clearing on the sand. Some people rushed to help. A lady said, "Bless you." I nodded

160

and went back to search for others.

Some who had gathered to view the scene became motivated to help. Better than nothing, I figured, but the devastation was formidable and the rescuers were unskilled and tentative. Some with rubber soles beat a hasty retreat when they felt their shoes melting.

I continued working and managed to uncover several bodies, but no survivors. Quinn appeared out of nowhere, carrying two children, one in each arm, both disfigured with horrific injuries but alive. Someone pointed and screamed when they saw Quinn's face, mistaking him for a burn victim. We assessed each other with a quick nod and continued our search.

Soon police and firefighters were on the scene, yelling at us to clear the area. Knowing these guys were better equipped to handle things, Quinn and I withdrew and began picking our way through the mass of people converging on the area where one of Southern California's premier boutique hotels had stood majestically a scant fifteen minutes earlier.

"The whore did this?" asked Quinn.

"She did," I said.

"On purpose?"

I'd been wondering the same thing while searching the blast site for survivors. She didn't strike me as the type who would blow up a building on purpose, but she was obviously the type who would hide a bomb in my room.

Quinn's cell phone rang with a text message. He read it silently, and his lips moved as he did so. "Coop followed her home," he said.

"Text him and have him send us the address," I said. "Tell him to stay put till we get there. Tell him to follow her if she moves but keep us informed."

Quinn gave me a look that offered more attitude than a ghetto crack whore. "You see these fingers?" he said. "You know how long it would take me to text all that?"

We walked. Quinn called Coop and gave him the message. He had Coop order us a sedan from a local limo service and told him where to pick us up. Since no cars were moving, we'd have to walk at least a mile to get beyond the traffic jam.

Around us, news crews were scrambling to set up live cams. Television reporters rehearsed eyewitnesses, prepping them for their big moment on live TV. Sirens blared from all directions. Above us, thwacking blades from a dozen helicopters sliced the sky.

"How'd she detonate it?" Quinn asked. "Cell phone?"

"That's my guess," I said. "Or maybe she just placed the bomb and someone else detonated it."

Hundreds of locals rushed past us, jockeying for the best views from which to observe the unfolding drama. Shell-shocked tourists aimed cameras and video recorders at the human carnage, and I cringed, thinking about how these grizzly images would be played and replayed and plastered all over the news. Talking heads would speculate and argue, and politicians from both parties would point fingers and assign blame to the opposition.

I asked, "Any idea why she waited so long to detonate the charge?"

He thought about it a few seconds before answering. "She might have made me from the balcony," he said.

I remembered how she made a funny smile when she arrived at the room, standing near the balcony. Could that have been what made her smile? Quinn? Would she have reason to know him? If so, the terrorists had infiltrated our organization much deeper than I'd thought. "She saw you behind the hotel and then made you in the car afterward?" I asked. "That doesn't seem likely."

"No. When she came out the front of the hotel, we got stuck in traffic. I told Coop to just follow the beeps while I jumped out of the car to follow her on foot. She probably saw me getting out of the car 'cause she took off like a poisoned pig!"

"And you couldn't catch her? Skinny little girl like that?"

"Runs like Callie," he said.

"No one runs like Callie," I said. "But I get the picture."

Quinn said, "Last time I saw her, she was passing a Krispy Kreme donut shop. Then I heard the blast and ran back."

"What was that, two blocks? You call that a run?"

"Hey, you're my size, two blocks is an Olympic event."

"So Coop followed the beeps, and we've got the address where she stopped," I said, patting myself on the back for placing the tracking device in her purse.

"Might take us a while to get there," Quinn said.

He was right. In fact, it took an hour to get the car and another twenty minutes to fight the traffic. Finally, after what seemed like forever, we spotted the minuscule split-level ranch with the peeling yellow paint on Vista Creek Drive to which Coop had tracked Jenine. Coop had parked his car a block away from the house, so we had our driver park a block beyond that. Then we signaled Coop and waited for him to return the signal. He didn't, which meant either he was sleeping or …

He was dead. We knew it the minute we saw the bullet hole in the driver's window. Coop had been shot from the blind side, just behind his left ear. His head hung down, his chin resting on his sternum. His blood was everywhere. Quinn opened the driver's side door and lifted Coop's head.

"What's that in the bullet hole?" he asked.

I hated putting my face that close to poor Coop's, but Quinn was right; there was something protruding from the bullet hole. It turned out to be the tracking device I had placed in Jenine's purse.

Quinn backed out of the car, stretched to his full height, and looked at the house. "Any guess what we'll find in there?"

"Jenine's body," I said.

Quinn gestured toward Coop and said, "Good thing our limo driver didn't see this. Might have spooked him."

"Ya think?" I said.

"I think you picked up that expression from the new girl, Kathleen."

"I think you're right."

# 28.

WE ENTERED THE house and quickly found two bodies wrapped in thick plastic. Both were attractive young women, one being Jenine. The other girl seemed vaguely familiar. She could have been anyone, but with two bedrooms in the house, my money was on her being Jenine's roommate.

What we couldn't find in the house was anything else.

No furniture, dishes, pots, pans, or silverware. No mops, brooms, cleaning supplies, paper cups, toilet paper. No computers, printers, phones, photographs, or paper of any kind. It was mindboggling. To rid an entire house of so much evidence in such a short period of time—even a small house like Jenine's—would require a large, experienced crew. These guys were consummate pros. One or more hit men had killed three people while a full crew of crime scene cleaners waited in the wings.

In the refrigerator, there were two unopened bottles of water.

"For us?" asked Quinn.

"Apparently," I said.

Quinn started to reach for one. "You think they're poisoned?"

"I do."

"What do we do now?" Quinn asked. "Talk to the neighbors?"

I didn't think so. Surely someone spotted the dead driver before we did. They'd have called the cops. Fortunately for us, most of the police were either at the hotel or heading there. Whoever they could spare to check on our dead driver was probably on their way but likely stuck in traffic. Still, I figured we didn't have much time.

"You got a laptop in your luggage?" I asked.

"I do."

"Let's get out of here and drive somewhere we can get wi-fi."

"What about the water?" Quinn asked. "Should we leave them for the cops?"

"There won't be any prints on them. On the other hand, some rookie's liable to get killed drinking one." We opened them and poured the water down the sink and took the bottles with us to the car.

When we got to Starbucks, Quinn remained with the driver and I took his cell phone and laptop inside. My first objective was to access the website where I'd discovered Jenine's ad. I remembered seeing lots of girls on the site, and hopefully some were local. If so, I intended to contact them and see if they knew Jenine. Best case scenario, someone might give me a lead to follow.

There were two locals on the site, Star and Paige. Star wouldn't be talking, since I recognized her as the other dead girl in Jenine's house.

I called Paige and got her answering service. I left a message to return my call as soon as possible. Then I left the coffee shop and climbed into the front seat and waited. I looked at Quinn and tried not to smile. Times like these—his huge form crammed into the back seat, knees bent, head bowed, shoulders hunched—made me realize the effort it took just to be him.

He was so large he could barely fit in the back seat of the town car.

"You did a good job at the hotel today," I said. "Probably saved a half-dozen people."

Quinn shrugged. "I was on the clock."

In time, we would learn that local hospital personnel labored for days to service the injured, and many of the bodies they received were charred beyond identification. The initial death toll was one hundred and eleven, but within a week the final count turned north of a buck fifty.

The phone rang, and I answered it.

"This is Paige," she said.

"You sound gorgeous," I said.

She laughed. "Maybe we should stick to the phone then, just in case."

"Not a chance. I've already seen your picture."

"Ah," she said. "So what did you have in mind?"

"I was hoping we could meet for a cup of coffee, maybe chat awhile, get to know each other. If we're compatible, we can take it from there."

"My standard donation is five hundred dollars an hour."

"I'll double that if you can get here within the hour."

"Don't be offended," she said, "but are you affiliated in any way with law enforcement?"

"I'm not. Are you?"

She laughed. "No, but I played a sexy meter maid in a high school play a few years back."

"That might be fun to re-enact some time," I said, trying to guess where she might be heading with the comment. I wondered if her other clients sounded this retarded.

"I still have the costume, so maybe we can talk about it when I get there," she purred. "You're fun; I can tell. Where would you like to meet, and how will I recognize you when I get there?"

I told her and hung up. Then I told Quinn that Paige thought I sounded fun. He rolled his eyes.

Paige was plenty cute, but she didn't look like an aspiring actress. She didn't look like a hooker, either. What she looked like was a soccer mom, which, as it turned out, she was. I slipped her the envelope, and she palmed it and placed it in her purse. She excused herself and went to the restroom. When she got back, she said, "That's way more than we agreed on. Did you want to book more time?"

"Not really," I said. "I just wanted you to know I'm sincere."

We talked about our kids and our divorces. She talked about how different grade school had become since she was a kid. "When I was in school, if I wanted to do something after school, I had to ride there on my bike," she said. "Or I didn't participate. My kids have it easy. They'd never believe it, but I actually used to be somebody. These days I'm a glorified taxi driver."

"Well, I've probably got ten years on you," I said. "But one thing that was different for me: my schools never had any moms like you!"

She winked. "Maybe they did and you didn't know."

I let that interesting thought float around in my head a minute, but the only mom I could remember clearly from grade school was Mrs. Carmodie, Eddie's mom—Eddie being the kid with the cherry bombs. What I remembered most about Mrs. Carmodie was she had a double-decker butt. While normal butts curve like the letter C, Mrs. Carmodie's butt got halfway through the C, then extended several inches in a straight line like some sort of shelf before finishing the curve. The shelf on her butt was wide enough to hold two cans of soda. Yet try as I might, I couldn't envision Eddie's mom turning tricks during the day while we were in school.

The half-hour flew by, and after we finished our coffees, I walked Paige to her car. Her silver Honda Accord had sixteen-inch Michelin tires with bolt-patterned alloy rims. She noticed the limo parked beside her.

"I wonder whose car that is," she said. "You think it's someone famous?"

"It's mine, actually."

"No way!"

"Want to peek inside?"

She did, and when she did, Quinn grabbed her by the shoulders and pulled her onto the seat. I followed her in and pulled the door shut behind me. Paige was breathing rapidly, and her heart was probably beating as fast as a frightened rabbit, but she knew better than to scream.

"Where's the driver?" I asked.

"When you went in, I told him to take a walk and come back in an hour."

That left us a half-hour to find out what Paige knew. Turns out, we only needed five minutes to learn something that hit me like a left hook to the liver.

# 29.

"ALL OF US had to share details about our customers with a man named Grasso," Paige said.

"By 'all of us' you mean?"

"The local girls, the ones they consider hot."

"Jenine would obviously qualify."

"Yes. She's one of the faves."

"What can you tell me about Grasso?"

"Not too much. He works for a major gangster. I don't want to say who."

I peeled off another grand and placed it in her hand. She looked into my eyes. "You didn't get this from me."

"Of course."

She whispered, "Joseph DeMeo." Then she said, "Please, mister, keep me out of this. I've got kids."

"I will," I said, "but you've got to find another line of work. You're not safe doing this. We won't repeat anything you told us, but DeMeo knows you're friends with Jenine and Star, and they're gone now. You've got to get your kids and get the hell out of town. DeMeo won't leave any loose ends. Do you understand?"

She nodded.

I kissed her cheek and let her go.

An hour later, we pulled up to the guard station at Edwards. I flashed my credentials, and one of the guards informed me that all flights had been grounded due to the terrorist attack. I got Darwin on the phone, and within minutes the guard received orders from the base commander to open the gate. Our limo driver took us across the tarmac and parked us next to the company's jet. Quinn reminded me to pop the trunk so he could retrieve his saxophone.

"That reminds me," I said, and sang, "You cain't always get h'what you wa-hant!"

Quinn's facial deformity prevented him from smiling, but you could sometimes find amusement there if you knew how to interpret it. I was one of the few who did.

"Always figured you for a Stones fan," he said.

The pilots, who had been glued to the TV in the auxiliary terminal, were now racing across the tarmac to open the cabin door for us.

"It'll take us fifteen minutes to get her ready for takeoff," one of them shouted.

Quinn and I climbed into the cabin. While he got situated, I poured us a drink. He said, "Is your cell phone broken? Reason I ask, you've checked it half a dozen times since the explosion."

"I sort of thought Janet might call," I said.

"Heard about the attack, wondered if you're okay?" he said.

"Stupid, right?"

Quinn shrugged and held up his glass. "To ex-wives," he said.

We clinked glasses. "I'm not sure that counts," I said. "You've never been married."

Quinn drank some of his bourbon. "Never been bitten by a yak, either."

I held a sip of the bourbon in my mouth a few seconds to

enhance the burn. "Yak?" I said.

He grinned.

I swallowed the bourbon and took another sip. "Me, either," I said. "That strike you as odd?"

Quinn's eyes started smiling again, or so it seemed to me. He said, "One time Coop told me he got bit by a yak. Said he was in India in a town whose name can't be pronounced by anyone who's not from Tibet. Said they made him drink tea made from yak butter."

"Yak butter," I said.

"Coop says the average man in Tibet drinks forty to fifty cups of tea every day of his life. The teapot always has a big lump of yak butter in it. You're supposed to blow the yak butter scum out of the way before you take a sip," Quinn said.

"That's disgusting."

"Same thing I told Coop!"

I nodded. "To Coop," I said, and we touched glasses again. From the cockpit, I heard the pilots working through their preflight checklist. Quinn silently swallowed the rest of his bourbon. I followed his lead. The co-pilot opened the door and gave us a thumbs-up, and we buckled our seat belts and settled in for the long flight to Virginia. I looked out the window and for the first time it struck me that today had been clear and beautiful, just like New York City on 9/11.

# 30.

THE JET MADE quick work of the runway. Once airborne, I told the pilot to veer toward the hotel so I could witness the scene from above. However, within seconds, an F/A-18 Hornet pulled alongside us and escorted us northeast, out of LA airspace.

The co-pilot opened the cabin door. "Sorry about that, Mr. Creed."

"You pussy," I said.

He frowned and went back to work, leaving me to contemplate the smoldering bodies I'd seen just hours ago. I pictured families and loved ones across the country desperately dialing cell phones that would never be answered. I wondered if, when the roof fell, how many rescue personnel had to be added to the death toll.

After we hit cruising altitude, I called Victor. When he answered, I said, "How'd you do it?"

"If...you're...talk...ing...about the...spy...satel...lite... you can...tell...your...people...I'm...sorry. I...won't...do it ...again."

"You're *sorry*?" I said. "You're kidding, right? 'Cause they have ways to *make* you sorry. By the way, where's Monica?"

I heard a shuffling sound, and a guy with a high-pitched but otherwise normal voice took over. "Mr. Creed," he said, "My name is Hugo."

"Hugo," I said.

"That is correct," he said.

"Your voice," I said. "I'm gonna go out on a limb here and guess you're a little person."

"Also correct," he said.

"Okay, so I'm supposed to believe your names are Victor and Hugo. Who do you guys hang out with, H.G. and Wells?"

"I do not know any H.G. and Wells," he said. "I am Victor's spiritual adviser."

"Spiritual adviser," I said.

"That is correct."

In the background, I heard Victor say, "Tell...him...the... rest." Hugo attempted to cover the mouthpiece with his hand but it was a small hand and I could still hear them talking, plain as day.

Hugo said, "He'll *laugh* at me."

Victor said, in a commanding voice, "*Tell...him*!"

Hugo removed his hand from the mouthpiece and told me he was something, but his voice was so small I had to ask him to repeat himself.

"You're the what?" I asked.

"Supreme commander of his army."

"I'm trying to think of something funny to say," I said, "but you've rendered me speechless."

Hugo said he and Victor had amassed an army of little people all over the country. "We have soldiers everywhere," Hugo said. "Hundreds. Some are captains of industry. Others have access to information surpassing all but the highest pay grades. We've even got a little person on the White House kitchen staff," he boasted.

"What is he," I asked, "a short order cook?"

He covered up the mouthpiece again and I heard him tell

Victor, "Say the word and I'll kill the bastard. Turn me loose on him, that's all I ask. I'll cut out his liver and dance on it." He was shouting now: "I want to dance on his liver!" Victor took charge of the phone.

"Mr...Creed...you...have up...set my...gen...eral."

"C'mon, Victor, cut the crap," I said. "I need to know if Monica's alive. If so, I need to kill her. Thanks to you, it's become a matter of national security."

"We...should...meet," he said. "There...is much...ground ...to...cover."

We agreed to meet Tuesday morning at Café Napoli in New York City. "You got an address for me?" I asked.

"Hes...ter and Mul...berry," he said. "In...Little...Italy."

"Little Italy," I said.

"You...see I'm...not...without...a sense...of hu...mor, Mr. Creed."

"You gonna have soldiers at the restaurant?"

"Eight o'...clock be...fore the...place...opens up," he said.

"I'll be there," I said.

## 31.

AFTER COMPLETING MY conversation with Victor and Hugo, I placed a call to headquarters and told Lou Kelly that the hotel bomb wasn't a terrorist strike. "It was a personal attack against me by Joe DeMeo," I said.

I gave him all the embarrassing details regarding my tryst with Jenine, told him about Coop the driver getting killed and about Jenine and Star and how their house had been sterilized.

"This Jenine, she the one you'd pegged for Callie's body double?"

"She was, and she'd have been perfect." I didn't tell him about the birthmark photos I'd taken. It seemed like an intrusion, somehow.

"What you're saying," Lou said, "Jenine and her friends, and most of the prostitutes in LA ..."

"The pretty ones," I said.

"All the pretty prostitutes in LA: working for Joe DeMeo?"

"Not working for him as in being pimped, but yeah, he finances their websites, has his people monitor the sites and the girls, and pays them for information."

"Information he can use to buy influence with politicians, maybe the Hollywood elite?"

"Otherwise, how would he know where and when I was planning to meet Jenine?"

"He'd set this up even before your meeting at the cemetery,"

Lou said.

"Otherwise his guys would have shot me there."

"Not the easiest thing to do with Quinn guarding you."

"Yeah, but DeMeo had nine guys there the night before. DeMeo told me they spotted Augustus. Still, Quinn would have killed a couple, and I might have done the same, but we were outmanned and on Joe's turf. He could have killed us both. And should have," I said.

"Why have a big shootout in the middle of the day? Better to use Jenine to bomb you," Lou said. "He already knew you planned to visit a hooker in Santa Monica."

"Make it look like a terrorist attack," I said. "Kill Jenine, let her take the fall. They've got her computer, which ties her to me, and they can make it look like she was working with terrorists."

"And Joe DeMeo gets away with pinning the hotel bombing on the terrorists."

"Joe's a slick one," I said.

We were silent a moment while Lou's mind worked it. "You tell Darwin about DeMeo yet?"

"I wanted to bounce it off you first."

"Uh huh. Well, we better let him be the one to tell the world," Lou said.

"Or not tell them."

"You think he'll try to cover it up?"

"I think he'll keep the blame focused on the terrorists. He left the possibility open with Monica, and this is a logical extension. It's easy to believe, and it's good politically; it justifies his job and budget and brings the country together."

"He'll have to tell the Feebs something," Lou said.

"Whatever he tells them, our focus is Monica. After we confirm her death, we'll give them the hotel bombing and let them take the credit for solving it."

"That's worst case scenario," Lou said. "We might get lucky, find and rescue Monica. Then we give the Feebs all the glory and get a ton of future favors in return."

I said nothing.

There was a short pause and then he said, "Oh, right. I got it. There will be no rescue."

I said, "Just so we're on the same page."

Lou sighed. "This business," he said.

"Don't get me started."

I told Lou to get some full-timers working on any connection they could find between Baxter Childers and Victor.

"Tell me about Victor," he said, and I told him what I knew, except for the part about the spy satellite.

Then I asked, "How long you think it'll take to find a connection?"

Lou laughed. "Five, maybe ten minutes."

"You're joking," I said.

"Donovan, you and I each have our specialties, and for both of us, some jobs are harder than others. When you tell me that on the one hand you've got a world-famous surgeon, on the other an angry quadriplegic midget with dreadlocks, and you know there's a connection and want me to find it— well that's like asking you how long it would take to kill a hamster with a shotgun."

"So that's a yes."

"It is."

I told Lou to also contact the LAPD and bomb squad techs and get back to me ASAP. The more we learned about the bomb, the more we'd know about Joe DeMeo and the extent of his power.

"No way the attack on you could have been an inside job?" Lou asked.

"I don't think so. If our guys, including you, wanted to kill me, it would be a lot easier to just poison me." I glanced at Quinn and noticed him watching me with amused indifference. "Of course, Quinn knew about both Jenine and the hotel," I said, "but it's hard to pin it on him."

Quinn pricked up his ears.

"Not because he's my friend," I said, aiming a smile in his direction, "but because he didn't know my plans for after the DeMeo meeting. I didn't tell him about the hotel or Jenine until a few minutes before we got there. And he didn't know her name or what she looked like until she arrived. None of that really matters, because Augustus could kill me anytime he wants when we're testing the ADS weapon."

Quinn nodded and closed his eyes, glad to know he wasn't a suspect. Now maybe I wouldn't try to murder him in his sleep.

"One more thing," Lou said. "They've got your cell phone number."

I hadn't thought about that, but sure, if Jenine had my number, DeMeo's team had it.

"If he's got whores and bombs, he's probably got connections to a radical fringe element as well," Lou said.

"So?"

"You might want to shut down your cell phone, just in case."

"In case what?"

"In case DeMeo's aiming a Stinger missile at your cell signal right now."

"Shit!" I said. I hung up and ripped the battery out of my cell phone. The jet had a secure phone, and Quinn had one,

179

too, so I didn't need mine anyway. I took a deep breath, thinking, *Jesus, there's so much to think about in this business*! I let the breath out slowly, kicked off my shoes, and turned my attention to Quinn, hoping for conversation. However, my deadly giant was snoring away. I had to admire anyone who could fall asleep so quickly, especially at a time like this.

I couldn't sleep; I felt trapped inside the jet's luxurious cabin. Felt impotent, too. Stuck in this metal cocoon, I couldn't do anything about Janet or Monica or Kathleen or the hotel bombing. I couldn't even read the book I'd started on the flight here—it had vaporized in the hotel along with the rest of my personal items. I tapped my fingers on the burl wood table and glanced around the cabin for a newspaper. Started flipping through a *People Magazine*, hoping Augustus wouldn't catch me doing so, but I couldn't get into it. When you've survived a bomb blast and more than a hundred people didn't, it's hard to focus on rumors of a possible hickey on Paris Hilton's neck.

I was going stir-crazy. I checked my watch for the third time since Lou's call and tried to fall asleep, but the monotonous thrum of the turbofans kept mocking me. I tapped my fingers some more and tried to think about what sort of relationship might exist between Joe DeMeo and Victor, if any. Then wondered how to go about stealing twenty-five mil from Joe DeMeo. Then I worked on the problem of how to find and kill Monica Childers, assuming she wasn't already dead.

I'd never had trouble concentrating on business before, but here, locked in this environment, nothing was working. Listen to me: environment! Hell, who was I kidding? It wasn't the environment. I knew exactly what it was: whether I was having sex with Lauren or saying goodbye to Jenine or sitting alone bored out of my gourd on a luxury jet, all my thoughts eventually turned to Kathleen. There was something about her infectious laugh and winning personality that touched my heart and made me itch to know what might have been. That was over now and probably couldn't be salvaged. In dumping me, she'd made the right decision, because in the final analysis, I was no better than Ken Chapman. We'd both managed to hurt her in our own way.

Still, I couldn't stop thinking about her.

# 32.

"DADDY, THANK GOD you're okay! I mean, I knew you would be, but whenever something like this happens, I can't help but worry."

We'd been in the air forty-five minutes, long enough to feel comfortable putting the battery back in my cell phone. I'd been thinking about the boy I saved earlier and the girl who might have been his sister, the one who didn't survive. It made me think about Kimberly, how precious she was to me.

"Daddy? Are you okay?"

And how lucky I was to have her in my life.

"Dad?"

Kimberly doesn't know the details of my job, but Janet had told her plenty over the years. She had some sketchy knowledge about the killing I'd done for the CIA, and she knew my current position had something to do with counter-terrorism. Still, I never realized until now what I'd been putting her through. I hadn't realized that every time a bomb detonated or a bridge collapsed, she automatically wondered if I might be injured or dead.

"I love you, Kimberly," I said. "I'm sorry you were worried."

"Well, at least you called this time."

I felt guilty. Up to now, I'd thought Janet would call and I'd reassure her first, then I'd talk to Kimberly. My daughter is so together; I always seem to think of her as the parent and Janet as the child.

"I'm good," I said. "How's your mom?"

"Daddy, I'm worried. That hotel bomb, was it a terrorist attack? Are there going to be more?"

I looked at the color monitor on the wall panel. It showed our air speed, altitude, and ETA. We were making good time. If the computer was accurate, Quinn and I should be in Virginia by midnight. "We don't know much about the hotel yet," I said, "but I'm sure Homeland Security is doing everything they can to stop any further violence."

Kimberly groaned. "Jesus, Daddy, you sound just like that FBI bimbo on TV. I'm your daughter, remember? I can't believe you don't trust me enough to tell me what's really happening with all this."

Kimberly was a sophomore in high school. No way could I give her the type of inside information she wanted. If she told a friend and word spread, the wrong people could trace the story back to her and that would put her and Janet's lives in danger. Since I couldn't allow that, I decided to change the subject.

"How come you're not in school?"

"I knew it!" she said. "You're on the West Coast! It's night-time here. Not that you'd know," she added, "but it's also winter break."

"Oh," I said. "I thought that was in December."

She sighed. "That's Christmas break."

I loved my daughter, but what Janet had accused me of was true. I wasn't an involved father. Maybe someday I'd have the time to become one—at least that's what I keep telling myself. I knew Kimberly was experiencing some abandonment issues that were pretty much all my fault, and I'd eventually get around to solving them. But that would mean committing significant blocks of time to her, time I didn't have at this point in my life. I wasn't completely absent; I saw her once or twice a year, but in point of fact, where Kimberly was concerned, I was pretty much one and done.

Now I was about to do it to her again, because I knew Janet was hurting and I had to ask about her. Specifically, I wondered if Janet had told Kimberly about the break-up with Chapman. I decided to jump right in. "How are the wedding plans coming?"

She paused a beat. "Okay, I guess."

"Have the announcements gone out yet?"

"No, they're not at that stage."

"Have you picked out a bridesmaid's dress?"

"That comes later."

"Are you uncomfortable talking to me about this?"

"What do you think?" she said. "I'd rather she didn't get married, okay? I'd rather you didn't ask me about it. I'd rather have you both in my life. If you want to know about her wedding so much, why don't you talk to her about it?"

I heard teenage voices in the background.

"Where are you?" I asked. "At the mall?"

My daughter made a sad sound, the kind a teenager should never have to make. It was a sound that told me that in her eyes I was not only clueless as a father, but hopeless as well.

"Just call Mom," she said. Just like that, she was gone.

Janet regarded me as poisonous. Her take on our marriage: the single biggest mistake of her life. Had she the opportunity to do it over again, she'd have lived in sin and walked out on me the day she gave birth.

I'd be the first to admit things weren't always perfect, but really, whose marriage is? I attribute the bad times to the crazy hours I kept, the high stress component of my job, my anger issues, the void in my chest where a heart would normally be located, the lack of sympathy and tact most people expect to find in a spouse, and the depression I suffered when the opportunity to kill people for the CIA ended so abruptly.

However, these last few years had made me a better person. I'd been far less moody lately and wanted a chance to prove to Janet how much I'd changed since the divorce. Not because (as Lauren had said) I wanted her back—I didn't—but because of Kimberly, who was hitting the age where having an involved father was more important than ever. I just wanted to get to a place where Janet might be able to find it within her power to have some decent things to say about me to our daughter.

I glanced at the sleeping Quinn and hoped he wouldn't wake up in the middle of an argument between Janet and me. Talking out loud to Lou about my date with Jenine had been embarrassing enough. I took a chance and dialed Janet's number.

"What do *you* want?" she snapped, as if she was hours into a bad mood and suddenly turned to see me standing beside her. I ignored her tone, knowing Janet had to rev herself up in order to deal with me. I didn't blame her for keeping her guard up. According to her shrink, she may have divorced me, but she had never been able to drain "the reservoir filled with unresolved pain from the relationship."

Janet's question had been a good one. What, in fact, *did* I want? Down deep, I guess I wondered if her break-up with Chapman could somehow provide the catalyst for friendship. Maybe she'd thought about it this afternoon and realized I wasn't the bad guy in all this, that by making her aware of Ken's shortcomings, I was the one who'd been looking out for her and Kimberly. If Quinn hadn't been sitting there, I might have casually mentioned some of the good things I'd done since the marriage, like the way I helped save some lives today. I wondered if she'd develop a greater appreciation of my character if I did so.

"Did you hear about the hotel bomb in LA?" I said.

"Was that *your* doing?"

Or not. "Jesus, Janet."

"So that's a yes?"

Janet wasn't the most classically beautiful woman I'd ever known, but she was certainly the prettiest who ever professed to love me. While some might not care for her thin, cruel lips or sharp facial features, everything about her appearance used to tantalize me.

"I've obviously caught you at a bad time," I said.

"Are you for real? Any time spent talking to you is a bad time, you son of a bitch!" She screamed, "I'd rather spend ten days strapped to a machine that sucks the life out of me than spend ten seconds talking to you!" Then she hung up on me.

I thought about what she said. The part about the life-sucking machine. I wondered if such a device could be built. If so, how would it work? How large would it be? What would it cost? Would it have much value as a torture device? I couldn't imagine anything better than the ADS weapon. It was relatively portable now, but the army was already working on a handheld version that could be functional in a matter of months. Also, with ADS, the pain is instant and so is the recovery. Now that I'd compared the two in my head, I'd have to put the ADS weapon way above Janet's life-sucking machine idea. Then again, Janet probably hadn't heard about the ADS weapon.

I was pretty sure she'd choose talking to me over being exposed to the ADS beam.

I thought some more about Janet and the good times we shared. Then I pressed another number on my speed dial to shake away the image of her tight body and firm, slender legs.

Sal Bonadello answered as he always did: "What."

It was more a statement than a question.

"Tell me about Victor," I said.

"Who?"

"It's me, goddamn it."

"The friggin' attic dweller?"

"The same."

"Where are you?" he asked. I imagined him looking at the ceiling over his head, wondering if I were up there right now. I heard he woke up from a bad dream a few months ago and pumped six rounds into the ceiling above his bedroom while screaming my name.

"Relax," I said. "I'm in the air, somewhere over Colorado." I noticed Quinn was beginning to stir. Maybe he'd been awake the whole time and was giving me privacy with Janet and Kimberly. You never knew for certain about Augustus Quinn or what he might be thinking at any given moment.

"I heard what happened in Jersey."

"You sound almost disappointed."

"Nah, not really. But hey, it's hard to find good shooters, you know?"

"Which is why you put up with all my shit," I said.

"Tell me about it."

"Listen up," I said to Sal. "You said you met Victor. Where?"

"You know I can't—whatcha call—divulge my sources."

"Cut the crap, will ya?"

"He needed some heavy shit. I gave him a name."

"What kind of heavy shit?"

"Guns, drugs, explosives—shit like that."

"And your contact required you to be there?"

"Right. Look, what about that blonde of yours, the one on TV driving the van—the real one, not the bullshit picture the FBI showed. You talk to her about me yet?"

"Don't even," I said.

"What, I can't dream? What, I'm not good enough for her? How about you put in a good word for me, ah? I'll consider it a favor."

"Do you guys go to school somewhere to learn how to talk like that?"

"Yeah, wise ass. It's called the friggin' school of bustin' heads, and I'm the—whatcha call—headmaster. So, you want my help or what?"

I sighed again and realized I'd been doing a lot of sighing lately. "I'll mention your interest to the little lady."

"All I'm askin'."

"Next chance I get."

"Ask her nicely."

"Fine."

"'Cause you never know."

"Right."

"Tell her I'm a man of mystery."

"For the love of God!" I shouted. A few feet away from me, in the cabin, Quinn did that thing where he sort of smiled. I decided to come at Sal from a different angle.

"Did you happen to catch the hotel bombing in LA?"

"What am I, blind? Everywhere I look that's all I see on the friggin' tube. Was that you?"

I sighed again. I should be blowing balloons for a living.

"Sal," I said, "the hotel bombing, it was DeMeo."

"What? Joe DeMeo? That's nuts!"

"I had a meeting with DeMeo this morning. Afterward, I met a hooker. That bomb you saw on TV? She planted it in my room. I found out later she was one of DeMeo's girls."

"You sayin' they blew up that whole goddamn hotel just to kill *you*? And *missed*? I'd a used a friggin' ice-pick."

"That's a happy thought," I said.

"Hey, nothin' personal."

"Right," I said. I got us back on track. "Do you think Victor and DeMeo are working together some way?"

"Why?"

"Victor gave me the hit on Monica Childers. Suddenly the pictures are all over the TV. Turns out Victor hijacked a spy satellite and downloaded the photos. Then Monica's body goes missing. The government pins it on Russians, supposedly working with terrorists. Next thing you know, DeMeo tries to kill me and makes it look like a terrorist attack on a hotel. That sound like a coincidence to you?"

"What do I look like, Perry Mason? Whaddya think, I got a friggin' crystal ball in my pocket? What, I'm gonna check the horoscope for—whatcha call—worlds colliding?"

I took that as a no. "Can you give me anything at all on Victor?"

"You tryin' to find Childers' wife? Make sure she's gonna stay dead this time?"

"That's the plan."

"Might cause a—whatcha call—rift between you and the midget."

"I'll try to solve the one without losing the other."

"Well, nuthin' from nuthin', but things go bad between you, I don't give refunds. Anyway I already donated my share to charity."

"Spare me."

"The Mothers of Sicily. You should look into it. They do great work here in the neighborhood."

I said nothing.

Sal's voice changed to something resembling sincerity. "Truth is, I got squat," he said. "But I'll shake the trees, see what falls out. I hate that friggin' DeMeo. He's bad for business."

"You want to help me take him down?"

He paused. "That's the sort of question gets people killed if someone's taping."

"I'm not taping anything. I want to rob him."

"You better be planning to kill him, then."

"I won't rule it out," I said. "You want half?"

"How much we talking about?"

"Twenty million."

He was quiet a moment. "Twenty for me, or all together?"

"All together. Let's get together soon, work it out."

"Yeah, sure," he said, then added, "but stay outta my house. I don't want to come home one night, find you in my friggin' living room in the dark."

"I'll come to your social club."

"Bring the blondee with you."

"Sal, about the blondee. She's dead inside."

"You ever do her?"

"She's like a spider. If she does you, she kills you."

He thought about that awhile. "Might be worth it," he said.

I thought about it, too. "Might be," I said.

We hung up. My shoulder throbbed from hitting the sidewalk a few hours earlier. The engines continued their monotonous whine. I reclined my seat and closed my eyes. I think I might have heard Quinn say, "How can you sleep at a time like this?"

190

# 33.

A SHRILL SOUND jolted me awake. It repeated, and I pulled the air phone from its cradle. I checked my watch. Two hours had passed.

"What have you got for me?" I asked.

"We're guessing Semtex," Lou said.

Semtex is the explosive of choice for international terrorist groups. It's cheap, odorless, readily available, has an indefinite shelf life, and slides through airport security scanners like a pair of silk panties.

Lou said, "You were right; the hotel blast originated in the area of your bedroom."

"How'd they verify that?"

"Lack of a crater. Ground floor detonation would have left one a meter deep. A charge placed above the second floor would have taken out the roof."

"What are the Feds working on?"

"Hotel cameras, cross-referencing faces with suspected terrorists and sympathizer lists, checking for connections by address, criminal records, religious and political affiliations. Darwin said to give them Jenine, so they're working up a profile on her as well."

I looked across the aisle at Quinn. He appeared to be asleep again, in the exact same position as before. From what I could see he hadn't moved a muscle since finishing his second drink. I envy any monster that can crash like that.

"I wish he hadn't given them Jenine," I said. "They're going to want to talk to me about it, and we're liable to cross wires in the field. Better to solve the case for them and let them take the credit afterward."

"The Feebs have you on the lobby camera checking in. They've got your name and credit card on the registration. They've got Jenine twice on the lobby cameras. They know about your clearance to fly out of Edwards. Darwin said if we didn't give them Jenine, the Feds would detain you and Quinn as material witnesses when you land."

That made sense. Still, I hated having everyone in law enforcement know about my dalliance with a twenty-year-old escort. Every Feeb I deal with from now on will find a way to work that into the conversation.

# 34.

BY SURVIVING JOE DeMeo's attack, I'd put my family in danger, so I asked Callie to keep an eye on Janet and Kimberly until further notice. I'd also tipped my hand by demanding money for Addie, so I put Quinn in the burn center to protect her.

"Victor's story is a sad one," Lou said.

It was Sunday afternoon. My shoulder was freshly bandaged, and I'd gotten caught up on my sleep. Lou had gathered a ton of information for me on Victor, but all I wanted to know was the source of his funds and his connection to Monica Childers.

"They're both related," Lou said.

"Enlighten me with the short version."

"Victor was born with serious respiratory problems. About twenty years ago, he was in the hospital for a minor surgery when a nurse gave him an accidental overdose that put him into cardiac arrest. Someone wheeled him into an elevator on the way to emergency surgery and somehow managed to leave him there. Up and down he went from floor to floor in the elevator for more than thirty minutes before someone realized what had happened. They rushed him to the OR, but the surgeon botched the procedure and Victor suffered a stroke. Subsequent attempts to save his life rendered him a quadriplegic.

"Then the hospital made a feeble attempt to cover up the incident. Victor's attorneys sued both the hospital and the drug company and managed to win the largest settlement ever paid to an individual in the state of Florida. After being released from the hospital, Victor's parents placed the proceeds from the lawsuit into Berkshire Hathaway stock. By the time he was of legal age, he was worth more than a hundred million dollars. By then, his parents were dead, and he surrounded himself with the best financial people money could buy. He became a venture capitalist, funded several Internet start-ups that hit the big time."

"How big?"

"We're talking close to a billion dollars at this point. Beyond his incredibly sophisticated computer system, state-of-the-art apartment, and cutting-edge electronics that have allowed him to function at the highest possible level, he had nothing else upon which to spend his wealth."

"The doctor that severed his spinal cord," I said.

"Baxter Childers," Lou said.

"Ladies and gentlemen, we have motive," I said.

## 35.

TOURISTS ARE OFTEN surprised to learn the true size of Little Italy. The entire area runs only three or four blocks along Mulberry Street, between Canal and Houston.

One of the cross streets is Hester, where Café Napoli has been in business more than thirty years. It's open eighteen hours a day, beginning at 9:00 am. Victor had called in a favor and got us a table an hour before the breakfast crowd.

"Thank...you for...com...ing," Victor said. He did have the dreadlocks Sal Bonadello told me about, and they grew long and filthy and hung down the sides and back of his body like thick ropes of dust. Were he able to stand erect, at least two of the strands would drag the floor. I wondered if they ever got caught in the spokes of his wheelchair.

Speaking of which, his wheelchair was incredibly high-tech. I had no idea what bells and whistles it contained, but it seemed to have enough electronics on board to launch the space shuttle. It looked like something you'd find in the distant future. The back was enclosed and swept in an arc over his head, where it attached to a sort of roll bar that was at least an inch thick.

Victor moved his index finger on a touch pad, and several small computer screens silently retracted from the roll bar and positioned themselves at various angles about a foot in front of his head. Though I couldn't view any of the screens from

195

my position, one of them must have displayed a digital clock, because Victor glanced up at it and said, "Time…is limi…ted so…we should…get…star…ted."

He wore a long-sleeved navy warm-up suit with three vertical white stripes on one side of the jacket. It was very expensive-looking, probably hand-tailored, which made me realize how hard it must be for little people of limited means to find clothing. It's one of those things you wouldn't think about until you find yourself in this type of situation.

We were in the main dining area, where the walls were brick and covered with pictures and other memorabilia from Italy. Our table was larger than the others, but they all had white, floor-length tablecloths and small vases with colorful fake flower arrangements.

Hugo had been standing when I arrived, and he continued to stand. I wondered about that until I realized he didn't have a choice. The table and chairs were too tall to properly accommodate him. So he stood and glared at me.

I nodded at him. "Hugo," I said.

I saw a flash of dark yellow and realized Hugo had bared his teeth at me. If intense staring could cause a person to explode, I was doomed.

A young man approached us and said, "The kitchen's not open yet, but I can bring you a pot of coffee and a bagel or pastry if you wish."

"No liver?" Hugo snarled, without taking his eyes off me. I suddenly realized what made his stare so intimidating: he never blinked. In fact, he hadn't blinked once since I'd arrived.

The server seemed confused. "I'm not a waiter. I'm just a busboy, so I don't know the menu very well. I can probably scrounge up some lox or cream cheese."

No one said anything, so I said, "I think we'll just talk, but thanks for the offer." Then I thought of something and added, "Could you remove the flowers?" I didn't think Victor would put a bug in the flower arrangement, but why take a chance?

The busboy left with the flowers, and I started things off. To Hugo, I said, "You know, for a spiritual adviser, you're pretty pugnacious."

"Fuck you!" he screamed.

I shrugged. I was beginning to get used to the unblinking stare. To Victor, I said, "Do you need to frisk me? Make sure I'm not wearing a wire or tape recorder?"

Victor said, "Not…neces…sary. I…scanned…you… already." He lifted his head slightly to indicate the screens.

I didn't believe for a minute that he had the ability to scan me or he would have mentioned the gun I'd taped to the small of my back.

Victor said, "Just…don't… reach for…the gun…behind … you." Then he said, "Hu…go will…do most…of the…talking …for ob…vious…reasons."

"That's fine," I said, wondering what else his wheelchair could do. "So tell me: how did you hijack the spy satellite?"

"That's proprietary," Hugo snapped. "Military experiment. Need-to-know basis only."

"Yeah, well I need to know," I said. "I've been ordered to find the people who breached the satellite's computer system, and kill them. I'm asking you nicely here, but this is non-negotiable."

Hugo sneered at me as if I were an insect. "Is that a threat?"

I sighed. "I came here hoping to strengthen our relationship, but if it's not to be, I can always just snap your necks."

Hugo still hadn't blinked, but he turned to face Victor. "May I approach?" he asked. Victor nodded. Hugo unzipped Victor's jacket. Victor's entire torso was covered with explosives.

I tried to act unaffected, as if this sort of thing happened all the time. But I don't think I fooled anyone. Still, I pressed on. "Where's the detonator?"

Hugo looked down at the table. At first I didn't understand. Then I said, "You're joking." I slid my chair back a couple of feet and slowly lifted the tablecloth. There were two midgets under the table. One had a .38 pointed directly into my crotch. The other had a detonator taped to his left hand. His right index finger hovered just above a large red button. I took a deep breath and nodded to the two midgets under the table. "Relax, okay?" I said. Then I put the tablecloth back the way I'd found it.

"Actually," I said, "I don't care how you hijacked the satellite. I just want to be able to tell my boss why it won't happen again."

"He already knows. They installed a patch to block us."

"Does it work?"

"It does," Hugo said. He smiled and added, "For now."

Victor said, "We…won't…breach it. I pro…mise."

I studied my vertically challenged employer a moment. He had a boyish face, made puffy from what I assumed to be years of drug use. I was about to say something when he suddenly flashed a smile. Not just any smile, or a creepy one, but a full, genuine, winning smile. Encountering it this way, in such an unexpected manner, startled me more than seeing the explosives on his body or the midgets under the table. Victor scrunched up his face in a way that reminded me of kids on a playground, him being the last kid hoping to be chosen for a team, the kid no one wants to pick. Then, in a small, vulnerable voice, he said, "Can we…just…be friends?"

It was an amazing moment to witness, an instant

transformation from deadly to helpless. At that moment, he seemed sweet, almost adorable. If Kathleen had been there, I'm sure she would have said, "Aw, how cute." But Kathleen wasn't there, and she didn't have a gun aimed at her crotch.

"Good enough," I said. "I'll try to keep my people off your backs. So what happened to Monica?"

Hugo said, "You know Fathi, the diplomat?"

"Father or son?"

"Both. But the father, the UAE diplomat, we sold Monica to him."

Victor and Hugo were full of surprises, so why should I have been shocked? But I was. In fact, I was so stunned, I couldn't think of a sensible question. So instead I said, "Was she alive at the time?"

Hugo laughed. "He wouldn't have much use for a dead sex slave."

I tried to wrap my brain around it. "Is she still in the country?"

"Her body is."

So she was dead after all. Darwin would be pleased. But something still didn't compute. "You hired me to kill Monica, and I did. Then you tracked me on spy satellite, grabbed her body, brought her back to life, and sold her as a sex slave. Now she's dead again, right? Well pardon the pun, but that seems like overkill. Why didn't you just hire me to kidnap her?"

Hugo said there were two reasons. First, it would have been a conflict of interest, since they planned to sell her to terrorists and I'm a counter-terrorist. Second, they wanted to see if they could bring her back to life after a trained assassin had done his best to kill her.

"So I was what, part of a medical experiment?"

"Yes."

Hugo reminded me that their army of little people included scientists, microbiologists, and specialists in almost every field of research. One of their people had developed a revolutionary antidote to botulinum toxin, and since they had targeted Monica anyway, she would be their first test. They figured I'd give her the most potent injection possible, which I did. If she survived, they'd sell Monica to Fathi. If not, they'd keep working on the antidote.

"And it worked," I said.

"That is correct. We intend to make one hundred million dollars selling the antidote to the military."

"Our military?"

"Ours, theirs, whoever."

"Back to the conflict of interest," I said. "I'm not comfortable working with you if you're also working with terrorists."

Hugo sneered. "That is absurd. Your government works with terrorists every day. They call it infiltration. We do the same. We infiltrate them for our own purposes, which shall not be revealed to you."

Though my head was swimming, I managed to ask him about the two other targets they wanted me to kill. Hugo said they were part of a social experiment.

"First a medical experiment, now a social experiment."

Hugo said, "That is correct."

"Can you give me the Cliff's Notes on that?" I asked. Hugo looked at Victor before answering. Victor nodded. Hugo turned back to me and said, "Victor wishes to understand the true nature of evil. Before you injected Monica, we gave her a chance to name two people who caused her pain in her life. You will kill those two people and get two names from each.

200

Victor believes we all have at least two people who have caused irreparable harm in our lives. You will exact vengeance for all the victims."

"He started with Monica because of her husband, the doctor."

"Yes. We could not have you kill the doctor. It would be too easy to link Victor to the crime. There is a saying: 'If you would hurt your enemy, punish the one he loves.' Since Monica was innocent, we gave her a choice: live in captivity or die in the van."

"And she chose life."

Victor and Hugo nodded together.

"But you knew the Fathis planned to kill her."

Hugo and Victor nodded together. Hugo clarified, "We knew they would not use proper restraint. We knew they would not give her time to recover."

"So why have you involved me in all of this?" I asked.

"We've got big plans for you, Mr. Creed."

"Such as?"

"You're going to help us take over the world."

"Well, why not," I said. Then, for whatever reason, I thought of Joe DeMeo. I said, "I'd love to help you take over the world and all, but I'm going to be busy robbing and killing a very powerful crime boss."

Victor said, "Maybe…we can…help."

I thought about that a minute and said, "You probably could. You hijacked a spy satellite. Do you have access to drones?"

"Killer drones?" Hugo asked. "Loaded? That is impossible."

I laughed. Maybe they weren't as crazy as I'd thought. "I was thinking maybe you could divert one of the weather drones off the coast of California or a surveillance one flying between Alaska and Russia."

"To where?"

"Hills of LA," I said. "Just for a few minutes."

Hugo walked to the other end of the room with his cell phone. He was gone a couple of minutes. When he came back, he looked at Victor and nodded. Victor nodded back. "Yeah," Hugo said, "we can do that."

"Really?" I asked.

Hugo nodded.

"What will it cost me?"

"What's...the...take?" Victor said.

"Tens of millions, I think. If we do it right."

Victor thought a moment before replying. "We...don't want...the...mon...ey," he said. "We'd...ra...ther bank...the fa...vor."

"Works for me," I said. Then I dialed Joe DeMeo's number.

"Well, you said you'd call," DeMeo said. "So it must be Tuesday."

"You killed a lot of people in that hotel trying to blow me up," I said.

"Creed, listen to me. If you're still worrying about that ten million for the burned kid, I got a better idea. I did some checking," he said. "Turns out she's got all kinds of life-threatening injuries, so I'm wondering maybe we should see if she survives before you and me ruin a good relationship."

"She's well protected, Joe."

"Yeah, I heard your giant was there. A face like that, he ought to fit in with the rest of the burn patients."

We were quiet awhile. Then he said, "Are we done here or is there something else you want to say?"

I said, "I'm coming to get you, Joe."

"Oh yeah?" he said. Then he laughed. "You and what

army?"

I looked at Victor and Hugo, thought about the guys holding the gun and detonator under the table, thought about the mini scientists who could hijack spy satellites and create an antidote for the deadliest poison known to man. I thought about the dwarf who worked on the White House kitchen staff.

I nodded at Victor. He winked at me and nodded back.

"I got a hell of an army," I told Joe DeMeo.

Hugo's posture went ramrod straight, and his chest swelled with pride. He saluted me.

I hung up the phone. Hugo said, "Well? What did he say? Did he laugh when you said that part about the army? I bet he laughed. Tell me he laughed. Just say it, just tell me he laughed and I'll kill the son of a bitch with my bare hands. I'll rip his ears off his head. I'll ..."

"He laughed," I said.

Hugo looked at Victor. "They always laugh," he said. He seemed to instantly deflate.

"Don't let it get you down," I said. "They don't know what they're up against."

"Ac...tually...they...don't," Victor said.

# 36.

THERE IS NO scent of freshly baked bread in Little Italy, no Italians singing love songs or speaking boisterously while flapping their arms in the air. Still, enough charm remains to inspire a walk, if you've got the time. I did, so I told my driver to wait while I headed down Mott, and Mulberry, and Elizabeth and Baxter.

The area is gradually being swallowed up by Chinatown, and most of the people who can speak Italian have long since moved to the Bronx. But the streets are still lively and colorful, and the fire hydrants are painted green, white, and red, the colors of the Italian flag.

I didn't find anything to buy, but I had a decent lunch and managed to clear my head after the meeting with Victor and Hugo. I didn't think for one minute Victor and Hugo's army of little people could take over the world, but I was gaining confidence that they could help me take down Joe DeMeo.

A couple hours after lunch, I found my driver and had him push his way through the traffic to the Upper East Side of Manhattan, where I got a room at the Hotel Plaza Athenee. By five, room service had delivered an incredible panini sandwich filled with fresh spinach, mozzarella, and roasted red peppers. They also brought me a bottle of Maker's and a heavy glass tumbler. I ate the sandwich and washed it down with three fingers of bourbon. By six, I'd had a hot shower and was freshly shaved and dressed. I watched the news on Fox for twenty minutes and still had more than enough time to walk the quarter-mile east, to Third and Sixty-Sixth.

It was Tuesday, after all.

"For me?" she asked.

There was an empty chair waiting for her at the tiny table I'd staked out at Starbucks, and Kathleen had instantly spied the raspberry scone on the small square of wax paper across from me. To my utter surprise, she rewarded me with a radiant smile, removed her coat, and joined me at the table.

"Who'd a thought it?" she said.

"What's that?"

"There's a romantic component at work here," she said, "one that might even rival your desire to separate me from my panties."

"The mystery never ends," I said.

"Do I want to know where you've been since Wednesday, what you've been up to?"

The angel on my shoulder urged me to tell Kathleen everything and let her run out of my life so she could find true happiness. Of course, the devil on my other shoulder said, "When in doubt, just smile and change the subject."

"Can I get you a coffee?" I asked.

Kathleen frowned and shook her head. "That bad, eh?"

"I've had worse," I said, and immediately realized I was telling the truth. I thought, *What a rotten thing to have to admit, even to myself*. I looked at Kathleen across the table. Her eyes were locked onto my mouth, as if she could read my thoughts by watching me speak the words. If that could possibly be true, I wanted to give her something better—a happier thought, one she might enjoy hearing. It would have to be something sincere.

Lucky for me, I had one. "I missed you," I said. I'd wanted to say more about it, wanted to say it better, but at least I'd said it.

Her eyes remained fixed on my mouth while she processed the validity of my comment. Then she slowly twisted her lips into a smile, and I felt that thing I always felt in her presence.

Hope.

Maybe I still had it in me to be a better person than I'd been. Maybe I hadn't yet descended so deeply into the pit that I couldn't experience a woman's love, capture her heart, have a decent life.

She took a bite of her scone and made a production of licking the sugar from her upper lip. She gave me a sly smile. "You really like me, don't you!" she said.

I laughed. "Don't get cocky."

"Oh, I can get cocky," she said. "Judging by the way your tongue is hanging out of your mouth, I can get cocky anytime I want!"

"That's pretty big talk," I said, letting my tongue hang out of my mouth.

"Pretty big what?" she said, laughing.

"Keep talking like that and you're never going to get me in bed."

"Oh, yes, I will!" she said.

# 37.

*THE ARABELLE* IS the Plaza Athenee's signature restaurant. It was also far too ostentatious, Kathleen felt, for the way she was dressed. "However," she said, cocking an eyebrow at me, "the Bar Seine was voted 'Best Spot for Romance' by the *New York Post.*"

"Then we're in the right place," I said. We strolled across the lobby and entered the Bar Seine. I pointed across the leather floor to an empty couch that was covered with an animal print fabric.

"Wanna cuddle over there in the private alcove?" I said.

"Slow down, Romeo, and get me a sandwich first."

"You can think of food at a time like this?" I said.

She winked. "I need to build some strength for later, you lucky dog."

We sat beside each other in overstuffed chairs with ridiculously high armrests. There was a small octagonal coffee table in front of us. "Maybe I'll order a bottle of courage," I said.

"They don't serve bottles here silly," she said. "This is a high-class joint."

I looked around. "They've got a signature hotel, a signature bar, probably got a signature drink," I said.

"Here we go again," she giggled. "Actually, they *do* have a signature drink!"

"As long as it doesn't contain the words *venti* or *doppo*," I said.

"If I tell you the name, promise you'll order it?"

"Is it *really* pretentious?" I asked.

Her laughter started bubbling up, spilling out into the room.

"More puffed up than the coffees at Starbucks?" I said.

She feigned a snooty look. "Those are bush league by comparison," she huffed. "Mere pretenders."

I smiled. "Okay," I said, "hit me with it."

Our waitress came, and we ordered a watercress sandwich for Kathleen. "And to drink?" she asked.

"I'll have a pomegranate martini," Kathleen said.

The waitress smiled and looked at me. "And for you, sir?"

I looked at Kathleen.

"Say it," she giggled.

I sighed. "I'll have a crystal cosmopolitan," I said, and she howled with laughter.

The drinks came, and I didn't want to ruin the moment, but I had to know what happened to make her change her mind about seeing me.

"Augustus," she said.

"Augustus?"

"You sent him to guard Addie."

"I did."

"Even though you and I were through at the time."

"So?"

"So you really cared about Addie and wanted to keep her safe. That warmed my heart, Donovan. It says everything about your character."

I remembered how I'd ruined the moment with Lauren the week before and was determined not to react or say anything that could turn the tables on what promised to be an epic evening. I thought I'd stick to a safe topic.

"You had a chance to spend some time with Quinn?" I asked.

"I did," she said. "Augustus is wonderful with the children—so loving and gentle."

I couldn't recall ever hearing the words *Augustus* and *loving* and *gentle* in the same sentence before.

"Did you talk to him about me?" I asked.

"Of course!" she said, her eyes sparkling.

"And?"

"And I told him I thought you were seriously flawed."

I nodded. "And what did he say?"

Kathleen grew serious for a minute and paused to give weight to her words. "He said you were chivalrous. That you're always on a quest."

"Anything else?"

"Yes. That you're a good friend to have."

"Did he mention I liked puppies and butterflies, too?"

"No … thank God!"

An hour later, we entered my suite, and she mugged me with kisses before I got the door shut. Our hands were all over each other, racing to see who could touch the most skin in the shortest period of time. I pinned her against the wall in a full body embrace, and our mouths worked hard to keep pace with our passion.

Then Kathleen broke away and dragged me to the bedroom. She spun me around and pushed me onto the bed. I sat up and reached for her, but she slapped my hands away.

I said, "Damn, those pomegranates are amazing!"

"You mean these?" she said. She ripped off her bra, and my brain circuits spun like tumblers in a slot machine.

"Now, Donovan!" she said.

"Now?"

She stepped out of her clothes. Licked her lips.

"At your cervix," I said.

We made love like teenagers, wrecking the sheets, rolling all over the place. At one point, she started moaning like a porn star, and I said, "Hey, calm down. We both know I'm not that good!"

## 38.

THE WIND IN Cincinnati whipped and swirled under a gunmetal sky. Bits of paper came to life on currents of air. A bus stopped at the corner of Fifth and Vine, and a young lady stepped off, wearing a short gray sweater dress with pleats. The sudden gusts played havoc with her dress, causing it to flutter and dance about her legs in a way that revealed more than she'd intended. A cellophane wrapper rose from the gutter and became part of a tiny swirling cyclone that covered some twenty yards along Vine Street before coming to rest on the sidewalk in front of the Beck Building.

The Beck was an austere building located a stone's throw from the Cincinnatian Hotel, where I'd spent the previous night. It was also the building that housed the law firm of Hastings, Unger, and Lovell.

According to the concierge, my corner suite on the second floor of the legendary hotel was tastefully flamboyant. Still, the kitchen and parlor offered a great view of downtown Cincinnati, as well as the Beck Building's front entrance, so I did my best to ignore the décor while waiting for Augustus Quinn to call me.

Quinn had arrived in town an hour earlier, carrying only a duffel bag. Now he and the duffel were locked in the trunk of Sal Bonadello's black sedan.

I could only hope he was still alive.

Actually, I was almost certain he was alive, because that was part of the plan.

Every city has a rhythm, and I absorbed what I could of the sights and sounds of downtown Cincinnati from my window, trying to get a feel for it. Half a block away, a homeless person sat on a frozen park bench in what passed for Cincinnati's town square: a block-sized patch of green with a gazebo and enough open space to accommodate a small gathering for outdoor events. It was practically freezing outside, but he had a couple of pigeons hanging about, hoping for a bread toss. I wondered if he'd had a better life at some point, and hoped so.

I didn't expect Quinn's call for at least ten or fifteen minutes and didn't plan to worry unless a half-hour had passed without hearing from him. As I stood at the window, I was thinking that I had no reason to believe Sal would double-cross me, and yet I had just bet Quinn's life on that assumption.

I was also thinking what a fine target I'd make standing in front of the floor-to-ceiling windows.

I shut the blinds, moved to the interior of the room, and— to take my mind off the wallpaper pattern—went through my mental checklist one more time.

We were in battle mode, and I had things wrapped pretty tight. Callie was still in West Virginia keeping an eye on Janet and Kimberly. Quinn had spent the night at the burn center and had been relieved early this morning by two of our guys from Bedford. Kathleen was at her office, and Lou Kelly had put a guy on her just in case. Victor and Hugo were assembling the assault team and working out the final details for hijacking a government surveillance drone.

Sal Bonadello was on the seventh floor of the Beck Building with his bodyguard and two attorneys, hatching a plot to kill me. The attorneys were Chris Unger, whose private suite was located there, and Chris's younger brother, Garrett, who had formerly represented Addie's parents, Greg and Melanie Dawes.

Normally attorneys wouldn't be involved in discussing—much less planning—a criminal activity. But because I am known by the underworld as a counter-terrorist, Joe DeMeo wanted to be extra careful with the hit, wanted everyone to be on the same page. The attorneys were deep into organized crime but they couldn't afford to be seen meeting with Sal Bonadello and his bodyguard Big Bad—as in Big Bad Wolf—that is why I thought we had a good chance of pulling off the plan I had hatched the night before.

Sal had gotten the call from Joe DeMeo to oversee the hit on me, but Sal claimed my status with the government required a sit-down. DeMeo refused, wanting to lay low until he knew I was dead, but he sent his emissary from New York City, Garrett Unger. Since Sal lived in Cincinnati, and Garret's older brother, Chris, had his own law practice here, they decided to meet in Chris's private suite on the seventh floor.

The Beck Building tenants and customers were well aware of the four parking levels attached to the building, but they'd have been shocked to learn that the double-wide garage door labeled "Emergency Exit" actually led to a private parking area for the law partners and their underworld guests. The partners changed the access code before and after every meeting with their criminal clients.

Sal Bonadello was the key to my plan working. He and Big Bad had been met by Chris Unger's bodyguard and escorted to the private suites moments earlier.

The suites were soundproofed, surrounded by empty offices. No one who worked at the law offices knew of the existence of the private suites, nor could they access them from the occupied offices. The walls of the suites were heavily concreted to provide a high level of safety and privacy.

When a driver dropped off a mob client, the protocol was to stay put, in his car, until the meeting was over. The only other person in the suites during this or any other meeting was Chris's secretary, whose job was to keep an eye on the private parking area from a monitor at her desk.

The way I'd planned it, Sal would create a diversion and signal his driver, who would pop the trunk. Quinn would get out and call me with the access code. Then I would join him and put the plan into action.

My cell phone rang. I answered it, and the lady on the other end said she'd thought about me all night and wanted to know if I'd been studying how to be a better lover. Then she laughed.

"I confess, I haven't had time to *bone up* on the subject yet."

Kathleen laughed again, and I pictured her eyes crinkling at the edges. "That's perfect," she said, "because I can't wait to teach you!"

"I'm still trying to recover from the exam you gave me last night."

"Well, be forewarned," she said.

"Why's that?"

"The next test is oral!"

"Wow! You promise?" I said.

"Mmmm," she said.

I could have gone on talking like this a bit longer, but not without putting on a dress.

I flipped on the TV, found the headline news channel. They were hitting the hotel bombing four times an hour, so I

214

couldn't help but see it again. For the millionth time, they dragged out the footage showing rows of body bags lined up on the sand, waiting to be loaded into ambulances that were in no hurry to leave. There were mangled men and women, family members sobbing for loved ones, expressionless children with bloody faces—all the typical crap you'd expect from the nightly news crews that made shock and horror a dinnertime staple.

When they'd sucked every ounce of pathos from that story, they turned to Monica's husband, Dr. Baxter Childers, surrounded by shouting reporters as he made his way to a car.

Until recently, Baxter had gotten a free pass from the press, but I knew that wouldn't last long. Murder-for-hire speculation gives fresh legs to stories that have run their course. For this reason, some talk show hosts had begun digging into possible connections between Baxter and the kidnappers. One moron was even trying to make a connection between the names Monica and Santa Monica. Maybe the next victim would be Monica Seles, he speculated. Yeah, I thought, or maybe Santa Claus.

Even more delicious to newsrooms across the nation, rumors were circulating about a possible love triangle involving Monica Childers and a yoga instructor.

I already knew what was coming for Dr. Childers, it had all been prearranged. Abdullah Fathi and his son had gotten their money's worth from Monica until there was nothing left to enjoy. Then either she died or they killed her, and now Victor's people would plant enough phony evidence to get Baxter convicted. In the end, Baxter would get a life sentence and Victor would have his revenge.

News crews were standing by in Washington, waiting for Special Agent Courtney Armbrister's press conference, during which she planned to name persons of interest to both investigations. I suspected Courtney was delaying her press conference in order to build interest for a future career in broadcast journalism.

Mercifully, Quinn sent me the access code, which meant he was in position. I took the stairs to the lobby and crossed the street to the Beck Building's parking entrance. I walked to the end of the ground-floor parking lot, looked around to make sure I hadn't been observed, and entered the code. The big garage door opened slowly. Quinn was inside, waiting for me by one of the elevators. I joined him, and up we rode.

# 39.

THE ELEVATOR DOORS had barely opened before Chris Unger's secretary let out a blood-curdling scream and jumped below her desk.

"Poor dear," said Quinn. "I should comfort her."

"That work for you in the past?" I asked.

The muscle head who was obviously Chris Unger's bodyguard suddenly appeared. He looked at Quinn, did a double take, and said, "*Jesus H. Christ*!" There was something about the guy I couldn't place. Up close, he looked familiar. Perhaps he came to earth with powers far beyond those of mortal men, at least that's how he comported himself. In any event, he was a big, heavily muscled guy, built thick like a fireplug. His head was shaved completely smooth and on his forehead, above the bridge of his nose, someone had carved XX.

Quinn sat his duffel on the floor.

"What's in your purse?" asked muscle-head. "A tampon?" He pursed his lips and smacked a kiss in Quinn's direction.

Augustus noticed my left leg had buckled. He shot me a look.

"I'm okay," I said.

He nodded. Nobody moved. The muscle-head kept his voice calm. He said, "Miss, come on out and get behind me."

She scrambled out from the desk well and shielded her eyes

217

as she ran behind Mr. Muscles. From what I could tell, she had a nice enough figure, but I wasn't a fan of the tight, angry bun she wore in her hair. She was hyperventilating, and her voice made a funny huffing sound as she struggled to get herself under control.

"Your severe reaction toward my associate suggests poor training," I said, trying to be helpful.

To Augustus, she shrieked, "You keep away from me!"

The muscle-head whispered something, and she backed up a few steps and slowly circled around us and disappeared through the elevator doors. I could have stopped her, but I knew Sal's driver would handle it.

Now that he was alone in the room with us, the body builder let us hear his street voice.

"Who the fuck're you turds and what do you want?"

"We'd like to see Garrett Unger and his brother Chris," I said, trying to be polite about it.

"I work for Chris Unger," he said, "and you don't talk to Chris Unger without my okay. You got something to say to Chris Unger, you say it to me."

"Very well," I said. "Tell Mr. Unger his bodyguard is a pussy."

The muscle-head kept a watchful eye on my giant and the space between them. Then he said, "Okay, so you know who I am, right?"

I looked at Quinn. He shrugged.

"We don't know," I said, "but you look familiar to us."

"You always speak for the dummy?" he asked.

I noticed that he noticed my limp as I took a step toward him.

"I'm Double X," he said, as if that explained everything.

Quinn and I exchanged looks again.

"You carve that in your head when you turned twenty?" asked Quinn.

Double X frowned. "It's my nickname. On the circuit."

"The circuit," I said.

Double X sighed. "Hello-o, the UFW circuit? Ultimate Fighting Warriors?"

"Oh, that circuit," I said.

I took another gimpy step toward him. He shifted his weight into a fighting stance and said, "I'm the former heavyweight world champion." He said that part with a healthy measure of pride.

"How nice for you," I said. "Maybe we can talk about it after I see Mr. Unger. Would you be a good little warrior and take us to him?" Double X sneered.

I've had tough guys sneer at me lots of times, but I was pretty sure not many had sneered at Quinn. I glanced at my monster. He didn't appear to be offended.

Addressing me, but pointing at Augustus, Double X said, "I don't know your boyfriend, Mr. Ass Face, but I know who you are. You're the guy who kidnapped Monica Childers."

Quinn said, "Ass Face?"

To me, Double X said, "You're pretty tough when it comes to assaulting skinny, middle-aged women, but in me you'll find an unbeatable foe."

I said, "They teach you to talk like that in the UHF?"

"That's UFW, asshole." He appraised me as if he were sniffing an onion. "You got some size on you, and you may have kicked some untrained butt in your day, but you can't fathom the stuff I've seen. You wouldn't last thirty seconds in the quad."

"Quad?"

"That's right. They stick you in a cage with a world

219

contender and you don't walk out until one of you is basically dead."

He let that comment sit in the air a minute, and then added, "You guys are going to stay right here till I say you can move."

"I don't think so," I said.

"Mr. Unger's secretary is at this very moment talking to a member of organized crime about you. You guys are already dead; you just don't know it yet."

A good martial artist will always attack your weakness, and Double X didn't disappoint, rushing me the way I knew he would, leading with his right leg to sweep my gimpy leg out from under me.

Unfortunately for Double X, I didn't have a gimpy leg, and I easily moved inside his kick before it could do any damage. Double X suddenly found himself in a strange position, slightly off-balance, vulnerable, his leg still rising toward a target that wasn't there.

Before he had a chance to regroup, I punched the former quad cage heavyweight champion of the world in the neck, with full leverage behind the blow. I followed it up with a left hook to the other side of his neck, and his eyes went white. He tried to fall, but I caught his Adam's apple between my thumb and index knuckle and crushed it until his mouth formed a perfect O shape. When I released my grip, Double X fell in a heap and grabbed his throat. He made an attempt to speak, but the effort proved too great. He rolled onto his side, and his legs began twitching involuntarily, like a sleeping dog dreaming about chasing a rabbit.

I looked at Quinn. "Just before I crushed his larynx, he patted my shoulder several times. Why do you suppose he did that?"

"I think he was tapping out. It's what they do in the quad

cage when they've had enough."

"Oh. He should have said."

I stepped over him and went through the door from which Double X had appeared a moment earlier.

Quinn found Double X's gun and put it in his duffel. Then he grabbed Double X by the collar and dragged him and his twitchy legs through the door and down the hall until he saw me enter Chris Unger's suite.

First thing I noticed going in, Chris Unger was at his desk, his back to the windows. Three client chairs faced him. The first was occupied by Chris's brother, Garrett. The second chair was empty. Sitting in the third chair was my favorite crime boss, Sal Bonadello.

Sal nodded in my direction and said, "Hey, this is—whatcha call—serendipity. We was just talking about you!"

I recognized Sal's bodyguard, leaning against the far wall.

"I guess Joe said it's okay to bring Big Bad."

Sal nodded. "I was takin' a leak just before you got here. Takin' a leak always makes me think of Joe. So I called him."

Big Bad had his hand inside his jacket.

"You still use the 357?" I asked.

Without changing the expression on his face, Big Bad glanced at Sal through reptilian eyes. Sal said, "It's okay; they're with me."

Both Ungers gave him a look. Then they looked at each other. Garrett seemed more nervous than his older brother.

All eyes suddenly turned to the doorway as Quinn entered, dragging Double X behind him. Double X continued to hold his neck with one hand while pawing the air with the other. Still trying to tap out, I figured. Quinn released his prey, and Double X hit the floor face-first. Quinn locked the door behind him.

Sal jumped to his feet, suddenly excited. "Wait a minute!" he said. "I *seen* this before! At the movies, right? *Weekend at Bernie's*, right?" He pointed at Double X. "You're the guy! You're Bernie!"

From his post across the office, Big Bad watched with amused ambivalence.

By contrast, Chris Unger was outraged. "What's the meaning of this?" he demanded. Unger stood tall, assuming the defiant stance befitting his status of legal heavyweight. His hair was silver and gelled, and he wore it combed straight back. He had on a navy Armani suit, a crisp white broadcloth shirt, and a bright red silk tie.

Those who fear attorneys would have been shaking in their boots at the sight of him, but this was a different crowd. Unable to get the reaction he'd expected, Unger sat back down at his desk, which probably cost more than the house I grew up in. It wasn't just the desk that was intimidating—everything in his office exuded power, from the dark cherry paneling to the trophy wall littered with photos of Unger posing with presidents past and present, not to mention the Hollywood elite. Clearly, this was a man willing to pay the extra fee at fundraising events to secure the vanity shot.

"I need to speak with your brother," I said. "It'll just take a minute."

Chris Unger opened his mouth to protest, but saw Double X trying to tap out and changed his mind.

Chris obviously spent a lot of time admiring Double X's fighting ability on the circuit in the quad cage, because he was visibly shaken to see the former baddest man on the planet reduced to his current state.

Double X must have caught a glimpse of the disappointment in his employer's face, because he tried to form the words "sucker punch." It sounded more like "suction pump."

Chris Unger suddenly found his voice. "Garrett, don't say a word. I'm calling Joe DeMeo." He reached for the phone.

"Augustus?" I said.

Quinn picked up the unoccupied chair and used it as a battering ram to smash the window. He put the chair down and picked Chris Unger up like a rag doll and carried him to the window.

Garrett Unger jumped to his feet.

"Put him down!" Garrett yelled.

Chris waved his brother off, tried to keep the calm in his voice. "Let's all just relax," he said. "Look, gentlemen, we've all seen this a hundred times in the movies. You can threaten me all you want, but in the final analysis, we all know you're bluffing. You have no intention of throwing me out the window, so let's just sit down and—"

Quinn threw Chris Unger out the window.

# 40.

SAL RAISED HIS eyebrows and said, "Holy shit!"

I addressed Sal while keeping my eyes glued to Big Bad. "Are we going to have a problem with you over this?" I asked.

"Fuck no," said Sal. "Tell him to toss Bernie, too!"

Double X's eyes went wide. He stopped gasping and lay perfectly still, trying to make himself as small as possible in the room. I wondered if this type of behavior was acceptable in the quad cage.

Garrett Unger, Greg and Melanie's former attorney, remained where he stood, ashen-faced, dumbstruck. He grabbed the corner of Chris's desk for support and stared at the window, his mouth agape. This was a man whose source of power derived from thoughts and words—which might explain why his lips and mouth were moving a hundred miles an hour as he mumbled sentences none of us could understand.

Garrett Unger slowly eased himself down. Though his body quickly conformed to the contours of the chair, I wasn't convinced his mind was suitably focused.

Quinn turned to face him.

"Wh-wh-what do you want to know?" Garrett asked.

"Think about it," I said.

"B-But ... I c-c-can't."

I looked at Quinn. "Augustus?"

Quinn took a photograph out of his pocket and tossed it

into Unger's lap. The picture had yesterday's date stamped on the lower right-hand corner, along with the time the photo had been taken. It was a simple photograph, depicting a typical family scene: an afternoon lunch at Denny's, a small boy sitting at the table playing Nintendo DS while his older sister sat beside him, lost in her teenage thoughts, their mother talking to the waitress.

In other words, Garrett Unger's wife and children.

"Wait!" said Garrett Unger. He'd just lost his older brother, but the photograph helped him understand he was a brother second, a husband and father first. He began collecting himself. He took a couple of deep breaths and said, "This information doesn't leave the room, okay?"

I don't know what type of people Unger was used to dealing with, but I hoped to hell they occupied a higher rung on the honesty ladder than Sal, Big Bad, Quinn, and me.

"You have my solemn word." I said, solemnly.

Big Bad laughed out loud.

Quinn said, "Yeah, sure. Whatever."

Sal said, "Talk or fly."

Unger nodded. "Okay, okay. I can give you his name."

That comment surprised me. "Whose name?" I said.

"Arthur Patelli."

"Who?"

"The guy who set fire to the house. That's what you're after, right?"

I shook my head. "You can't be this stupid, even for a lawyer. But I don't have the time to straighten you out right now."

I looked at Sal. He held up his hands and said, "Lawyers, Christ Almighty. What you gonna do, huh?"

I said, "Garrett, look at me."

He did.

"You want to save Joe DeMeo or your family?"

"What?"

"DeMeo or your family. Which one?"

He looked down at the picture in his lap. "How can you even ask that question?" he said.

"Well, you're an attorney."

He nodded. "I'll do anything to save my family. Please don't hurt them. Just tell me what you want."

Sal said, "Guys, I don't wanna—whatcha call—eat and run, but you just tossed a law partner out the window, and even if no one in this fancy shithole saw it, someone on the street did."

I looked at him. "Good point. We'll take Garrett with us and trust you to come up with a cover story for DeMeo."

Sal asked, "You brought a car?"

I shook my head. "We'll take Chris's car."

Sal said, "If you had his car keys you could." He laughed. "Who's gonna jump out the window and get the keys?"

"My guess, they're in his desk drawer," I said. "In my experience, a man who wears an Armani suit doesn't want bulging pockets."

Big Bad slid the desk drawer open, fished out the car keys, and dangled them from his ham-sized hand.

"Good call," Sal said. "Don't forget the cameras. They get us coming and going."

"Quinn will take care of the cameras," I said.

Speaking to Quinn, I said, "Augustus, will you do me a favor and clean this mess up while I get Garrett in the car? I'll send the elevator back up for you in a minute."

I grabbed the mumbling Unger, and we followed Sal and Big Bad into the private elevator and down to the partners' parking garage. Big Bad found Chris's Mercedes by pressing the remote and following the chirp. He opened the trunk and helped me toss Garrett inside. I scanned the garage for external security cameras and found none. I guessed the partners didn't want video proof of their meetings with criminals or perhaps dalliances with call girls. I didn't ask what happened to Chris Unger's secretary, but I had a feeling Sal's car had plenty of traction in the back.

Augustus joined us a moment later, and we drove out of the garage and into traffic. I called Beck Building security and said there was a bomb in the building set to go off in two minutes.

"Who are you!" the security guard demanded.

"In the quad cage, I'm known as Double X," I said.

I gave them a few minutes to complete the evacuation of the building. We hit the interstate heading north on 75, and Quinn placed a call to the detonating device.

From the interstate, we had a wonderful view of the top of the building as it exploded and burst into flames.

Big Bad called and said, "Double X gone to that big quad cage in the sky."

# 41.

"WHAT ABOUT MY family?" Garrett Unger asked.

We were at headquarters in Bedford, Virginia, in the interrogation room. Lou stood by the door with his arms crossed, wearing a bored look on his face. Quinn was listening to a jazz mix on his iPod. I tossed Unger a disposable cell phone.

I said, "You're going to stay here as my guest until you get a call from Joe DeMeo. If Joe's smart, he'll give you a password to some of his numbered off-shore accounts. Lou already set one up for me. When you get the passwords from DeMeo, you're going to transfer the funds from DeMeo's account into mine. When Lou gets confirmation that the money's where it should be, I'll remove the threat to Mary and the kids."

We all waited for him to ask the question we knew was coming. He didn't disappoint. "What about me?" he asked.

"That's a toughie," I said. "On the one hand you were plotting to kill me a couple hours ago, and that displeases me. On the other hand, I need you alive in case someone at the bank requires oral or written confirmation for the transaction. As DeMeo's attorney, I'm sure you can produce whatever is needed to affect the transfer."

He was looking at me in a pitiful way.

"I won't lie to you, Garrett," I said. "You were a major player in the killing of Greg, Melanie, and Maddie Dawes.

Because of your participation, Addie's life has been shattered."

"Killing me won't bring them back," Unger said. "All I did was allow it to happen. If I hadn't, DeMeo would have killed my family."

"You were in a tough spot," I said, "and you're still in a tough spot. As you say, killing you won't bring them back. But money's the great healer, and enough money will help all of us cope with the loss."

"I'll do whatever you ask," he said.

I thought about that for a minute. "Garrett, we'll see how it all plays out. If you help me get at least twenty million dollars from Joe DeMeo, I won't kill you."

He looked at Quinn. "What about him?"

"Same thing."

"You'll let me walk?"

"Hell, I'll even have someone drive you home."

"Can I take a cab instead?"

"That's fine, whatever."

"Can I call my family?"

"Not until this is over."

He nodded. "In the meantime," he said, "where will I sleep?"

I said, "Quinn and I are going out of town in a couple hours. Until I get back, you can sleep in my bed."

"That's very generous," Unger said. "Thank you."

I waved my hand in a dismissive manner. "Think nothing of it," I said, wishing I could be there to see his face when Lou escorts him to my subterranean prison cell for the night.

# 42.

COLBY, CALIFORNIA, WAS a small town, and it wasn't unusual to spot Charlie Whiteside coming out of his shrink's office on Ball Street. It was no secret that Charlie's depression had gotten him washed out of the Afghanistan war. Used to be, pilots of unmanned aerial vehicles, UAVs, had it easy. Charlie could sit in an air-conditioned room at Edwards Air Force Base and launch remote-controlled killer drones while munching fast food. He'd put in a day's work studying live surveillance footage, lock onto the occasional target, press the button on a joystick—and be home in time for dinner with the wife and kid.

In fact, it seemed such an easy way to fight a war that in the early weeks of therapy, it had been difficult for his shrink to understand just what it was Charlie was whining about.

"You're a guy," she said, "who's had to deal with frustration and ridicule your entire life."

Charlie had closed his eyes as he ran the highlight reel through his mind. "And much worse."

Charlie wasn't exaggerating. While his parents had been normal, it had taken Charlie many years to grow to his full height of thirty-two inches. His father, having dreamed of spawning a scholarship athlete, found it impossible to derive joy from any of Charlie's accomplishments. For her part, Charlie's mother had accepted his condition from the beginning—but with a stoic detachment and much embarrassment. While neither parent clinically abused him, neither did they embrace or nurture him. They took care of him in a casual way, met his physical needs. But had anyone cared to notice—and none did—it would have been clear that Charlie's role in the family dynamic had been relegated to that of accessory in his parents' lives.

It was in public school that Charlie Whiteside first learned true pain and suffering. But that was a different issue, and his shrink, Dr. Carol Doering, had been satisfied early on that Charlie had made peace with his childhood. He'd overcome the neglect, the taunting, the bullying on his own, without therapy, and had somehow managed to put those terrible formative years behind him without carrying any serious emotional scars into his adulthood.

Which is why this whole depression thing about flying killer planes from a comfortable armchair five thousand miles removed from the action seemed out of whack with Charlie's coping mechanism.

In the early sessions, Dr. Doering had found it difficult to identify with Charlie's condition because she had an emotional connection to the very subject of his complaint. She tried to keep her personal connection out of the therapy, but one day she let her guard down and it just popped out.

"Charlie," she said, "let me tell you something. My brother's an F-16 fighter pilot stationed in Iraq. He dodges enemy fire all day, and at night he sleeps in a tent in blistering heat under constant threat of attack."

"Yes, ma'am," Charlie had said. "I'm not meaning to compare my service to his. He's a true patriot. While I love my country, I'm simply not physically able to serve overseas, so this is the only job I could take where I felt I could make a difference."

Carol Doering felt her face flush. "I didn't mean to imply…"

"It's all right, ma'am, I know what you mean. Does your brother have a wife and kids?"

"He does. Let me just apologize for my temporary lack of professionalism and get us back to your situation."

"It's connected," Charlie said.

"How so?"

"I understand that your brother is putting his life on the line every day to help preserve our freedom, and I mean him only honor and no disrespect."

"But?" Carol said.

"But when your brother approaches a target at six hundred miles per hour, he drops his payload and keeps flying and never sees the result."

Carol cocked her head while pondering the thought. She still didn't have a grasp on his point. After all, no one was shooting at Charlie when he fired his missiles from a desk at Edwards Airforce Base.

"When I fire my missiles," he'd said, "I watch them from release to impact. They're quite detailed, ma'am. I see the actual result of what I did.

"I see them all," he continued, "the bodies of the guilty and the innocent. The terrorists and the elderly. The women and the children.

"Then I drive straight from work to my daughter's piano recital."

That had been their breakthrough day, and Charlie punctuated the event by adding, "We all serve in our own way. I'm just having trouble with my way."

Dr. Doering helped Charlie get reassigned to a civilian job, where his experience could be put to good use. Charlie's attorney threatened the military into helping with the transition. They installed in Charlie's guest room, free of charge, all the computer equipment necessary for him to fly UAVs for the California Coastline Weather Service.

In return, Charlie signed a release. It had been a rare concession on the military's part, but Charlie's attorney explained what would happen if Charlie wound up on a witness stand: military records would be opened to public scrutiny, particularly classified photographic evidence depicting the graphic details of Charlie's armchair service.

Charlie settled into his new career with enthusiasm but quickly found the job excruciatingly boring. While the horror of his military job had taken its toll on his emotional well-being, he now realized that being a significant part of the War on Terror provided a constant adrenalin rush he was not likely to find studying cloud formations.

Which is why when Charlie was offered an interesting proposition by a fellow little person, it wasn't the financial component that caught his interest so much as the idea of adding excitement to his professional life.

Two hours after accepting Victor's proposition, Charlie verified his checking account balance and thought, *Now that's what I'm talking about*! The next morning, he flipped the switches and fired up one of the company's weather drones. His drone began the flight in the usual way, following a typical coastal flight pattern, filming video, and capturing raw data for analysis by the weather crew. Charlie had been with the company long enough to know when the ground guys were just going through the motions, when they took their breaks, what they found interesting and what they didn't.

He knew he could divert the drone ten miles inland, make several passes over the DeMeo estate, and be back chasing clouds before anyone was the wiser. Just to hedge his bet, Charlie had previously videoed thirty minutes of boring coastline that he now transmitted directly to the ground crew while his drone was recording footage of Joe DeMeo's estate. The DeMeo job would take less than ten minutes, which would give Charlie almost twenty minutes to get the drone back to the area of coastline where the fake footage had been recorded. Then he'd replace the fake footage with live shots from the drone.

# 43.

"IT'S A LARGE area to cover," Charlie Whiteside said, "and there appears to be a lot of activity."

We were at his place, reviewing the surveillance videos and stills he'd downloaded from the weather drone.

The photos revealed a nice set-up for Joe, what I'd call a luxury fortress. His twenty-thousand-square-foot residence was situated on top of a prominent hill. If you were picturing a target, the house would be the bull's eye. The next ring of the target would be the ten-foot-tall reinforced concrete wall that protected the main house and two guest cottages and enclosed about two acres of land. The target's next ring was cordoned off by a chain-link fence that guarded roughly ten acres. That fence was surrounded by more than two hundred acres of wooded scrub worth tens of millions of dollars.

The land ranged from gently rolling to steep drop-offs. The outer acreage was thickly wooded with sparse underbrush, a cleared forest with a carpet of soft grass and pine needles.

According to Lou Kelly, it had once been a top-flight corporate retreat due to its proximity to the old highway, its raw physical beauty, and its isolated, tranquil setting.

Joe's residential compound was accessed by a dirt and gravel road maintained by the state. The entrance to the property was a scant eight miles south of Ventucopa, fourteen miles northeast of Santa Barbara, near the center of what most people think is part of Los Padres National Forest.

Charlie was right about the level of activity. Joe DeMeo was running scared, and the proof could be found in the number of gunmen guarding his compound. From what I'd heard, Joe's place had always been well guarded, but this was a ridiculous amount of security. We knew he had about a dozen guns, nine of which had surrounded the cemetery where I'd met him less than a week ago.

The drone showed he had another eight men stationed between the chain-link and concrete fences. These eight had guard dogs on leashes, which told me they were on loan from a private security company. Joe was paying the big bucks and taking no chances.

It would have been nice to have someone on the inside, so I had Sal offer Joe some of his shooters. But Joe wasn't in a trusting mood and felt it wouldn't be prudent to invite a rival crime family inside his inner walls.

Especially one that had recently survived a bombing.

After the Beck Building went up in smoke, DeMeo voiced concerns about Sal's loyalty. Sal gave an Oscar-winning performance of indignation, replete with threats. In the end, Joe DeMeo had no good reason to doubt his story, and one reason to believe it.

Sal had told DeMeo that I must have followed Garrett Unger all the way from New York to Cincinnati, because by the time Sal's driver got him and Big Bad to the Beck Building, the place was in flames and the whole block had been roped off.

Joe DeMeo cursed extensively before saying, "You telling me you weren't even there? You never made it to the meeting?"

"That's what I'm sayin'," Sal said. "You don't believe me, you can check the tapes. I been there before, and Chris had cameras all over his private suite area. You call security and check the tapes. I ain't on them."

"That's a pretty convenient test," Joe DeMeo said, "considering the security cameras were destroyed by the explosion."

"No shit!" said Sal. "What a rotten break."

DeMeo's reason for believing Sal's story: just before the meeting, Sal had called Joe and said he wanted to bring Big Bad to the meeting, since the Ungers had a bodyguard.

"I just want—whatcha call—détente."

"Yeah, whatever," Joe had said.

"You need to clear it with the Ungers first?"

"Fuck the Ungers. Just get to the meeting."

"I'm on my way," Sal had said.

A few minutes passed, and Sal had called Joe to tell him he was sitting in his car a block away from the Beck Building but the area was roped off because the Beck was on fire.

"I just called Chris Unger," Sal had said, "and he ain't answering."

Joe had tried with the same result.

It was a plausible chain of events. The way Joe figured it, Sal wouldn't be making demands about bringing his bodyguard if he didn't intend to show up at the meeting. But that didn't mean he trusted Sal.

A few hours later, they had had another conversation.

DeMeo said, "According to witnesses, Chris Unger jumped—or was thrown—out of his window."

"You think he jumped like them people in the World Trade Center?" Sal asked.

"My stooge in the CPD says their witness puts Unger on the sidewalk more than a minute before the bomb goes off."

Their conversation had gone on like that awhile, according

to Sal, but the bottom line was, Joe DeMeo was starting to panic. So he put together a small army and stationed them in and outside the walls of his estate. It would be a formidable challenge, but I was gearing up for it.

My phone rang.

"I've got the architect," Quinn said. "I'm in his house right now."

"Good. Bring him to the campground."

Quinn paused.

"What's the matter?" I asked.

"What about the wife?"

"I thought she was out for the afternoon."

"Bad timing. She forgot something and came back to retrieve it."

"Retrieve," I said.

"Yup."

"Bring her, too."

Quinn paused.

"Jesus," I said. "What else?"

"He doesn't have the plans."

"Why not?"

"It was part of the deal. Joe made him turn over all the blueprints."

I sighed. "Bring him and the wife, anyway. We'll tease them both with the ADS beam until he remembers what I want to know."

"You got the Hummer yet?" Quinn asked.

"I'll have it by the time you get there."

# 44.

DARWIN BELLOWED AND blustered and raised nine kinds of hell when he heard what I was up to, but I believed he was secretly pleased I was planning to bring down Joe DeMeo. I decided to test the theory.

"I can kill him," I said, "but I can't take him alive without your help."

"Why should I care if he's dead or not?"

"If I take him alive, you can turn him over to the FBI for the hotel bombing, along with all the evidence we'll find in his house."

"There won't be any evidence. Anyway, when the time comes, I'll grab the other guy, the one who works the whores."

"Grasso? He's one of Joe's guards. Lives in one of the cottages. Again, without your help, he's not going to come out of this alive."

"What about the whore?"

"Paige. Her name is Paige," I said.

"Whatever."

"Paige is probably dead by now."

"Maybe not," he said.

"I hope not. Even so, her testimony alone won't be strong enough to put him away for the bombing."

Darwin thought about it. "What do you want from me—and it better not be much."

I knew whatever I told him would make him blow his stack, but really all I needed was a Pulsed Energy Projectile System (PEPS) weapon mounted on a Hummer.

"You're insane!" he shouted.

"You can fly one to Edwards in a cargo plane," I said. That's just down the road from me."

"I know where fucking Edwards is," he said. "Didn't you just fly there with three ADS weapons?"

"Yeah, but I need the PEPS."

"Let me guess: you want it by tomorrow."

"Actually, I need it by six tonight."

"You've lost your fucking mind."

"Oh, c'mon, Darwin. There's nothing you can't do."

"Except keep you on a leash."

"Look, I know it's not going to be easy and no one else in the country could do it—but you're Darwin!"

"Fuck you!" he said. "It can't be done. Period."

"I'll be there at six tonight," I said. "Impress me."

"Go to hell!" Darwin said.

# 45.

HUGO AND HIS army of little people had made their base camp six miles east of Highway 33, near an ancient forest ranger lookout stand. I brought the Hummer to a stop about thirty yards from their campground and waited for Quinn.

"The fuck is that?" Quinn said as he pulled up alongside the Hummer.

"These are circus people," I said. "That's one of their circus wagons." To be completely honest, it was a bright red Winnebago covered from one end to the other with circus paintings.

"I thought you were kidding about them being a circus act."

"Nope."

He looked at me. "We going in or what?"

"Hugo's a military man," I said. "He'll probably want to invite us into the camp."

"Victor and Hugo and the circus people," Quinn said.

"And us," I said.

Some of the little people started milling about in the distance, staring at our strange-looking vehicle. They were wearing colorful shirts and baggy trousers. They were pointing and chattering as others joined them.

"What do you suppose they're saying?" asked Quinn.

"Follow the yellow brick road," I said.

Quinn stared in disbelief.

"Are you in fact telling me we're going up against Joe DeMeo, twenty shooters, and eight dogs with this bunch of clowns?" Quinn asked.

We looked at each other. They were in fact clowns. We burst out laughing. I don't know, maybe it was the stress, maybe we were just glad to be working together again on a major assignment.

"I can see it now," Quinn said. "The little people put a big flower on their shirts. When the goons bend over to sniff the flower, it's really a squirt gun!"

I said, "When they shoot their popguns, a big sign comes out that says BANG!"

"And Joe says, 'Who are these clowns?' and someone says, 'The fuck do I know? Ringling Brothers?'"

I said, "Joe DeMeo, captured by midget circus clowns! Any chance they'll make fun of him in prison?"

Hugo approached. "What the fuck is that thing?" he asked.

The PEPS weapon—pulsed energy projectiles—like ADS, was originally developed for crowd control. Accurate up to a mile away, it fires directed bursts of pulsed energy to vaporize solid objects. If fired near a target, it heats the surrounding air until the target explodes. The resulting shockwave will knock down anyone in the vicinity and render them helpless for a minute or more.

After explaining this to Hugo, he said, "If we have that, why do we need the ADS weapons?"

I explained that while PEPS would knock down walls and disorient people, it wouldn't necessarily disarm them or render them helpless.

"The ADS weapon is different," I said. "It offers an instant, permanent solution to the problem of resistance."

Hugo turned his attention to Quinn. "You are one ugly bastard," he said. "No offense," he added.

Quinn said, "I got this way from eating shrimps. No offense."

Looks were exchanged between the two.

"You want a piece of me?" Hugo snarled.

"Looks like that's all there is."

"Hey," I said, "we're all on the same team here."

Hugo noticed the architect and his wife tied up in the back seat of Quinn's car. "Who are they?" he asked.

"They're going to tell me two things: the layout of Joe's house and how to breach his panic room."

# 46.

I'D COMPLETED MY chat with the architect and his wife and just begun the final run-through with the circus army when Sal Bonadello called.

"Joe's making a move on your wife and kid."

I'd expected that. In a normal world, I would have had Callie take Janet and Kimberly to my headquarters for safekeeping, but this wasn't a normal world; it was Janet's world. I trusted Callie to protect them, but I feared Joe might firebomb the house from a distance.

So last night I'd placed a call to Kimberly and explained the situation. I told her to find a way to get her mom out of the house until I called. I told her wherever she went, she'd be safe because Callie would follow them.

"You got enough guys to handle the threat?" I asked Sal.

Besides getting me into Chris Unger's office, this was the part of the plan where I needed Sal's help. I wanted his men guarding Janet's house in case anything went wrong.

"DeMeo put a contract on you for a million bucks. Told all the families, then called me, said grab your family and hold them hostage."

"You think he sent some of his guys anyway?"

"I do. It would be just like that rat bastard not to trust me."

"You running that charity and all."

"The Mothers of Sicily," he said. "So, did you get your

family somewhere safe?"

"I hope so."

"Is your wife pissed at you?"

"Ex-wife. And yeah, she's pissed. Like always."

"Ain't they all," he said.

I finished briefing the circus performers. Quinn checked their equipment. Hugo and I called Victor and gave him an update.

Next, I called Kathleen.

"How's it hanging, cowboy?" she asked.

"Boring stuff, these Homeland conferences," I lied.

"Anyone famous there?"

"Besides me? Not really."

"You're probably hanging out with one of those pretty high school girls who couldn't get into the movies."

"Like, that's so totally random," I said.

She laughed. "Don't work too hard, lover boy. I'm expecting the full treatment when you come home."

"And you'll get it," I said.

"Speaking of which …"

"Can't say yet. Sometimes these things last a couple days, sometimes more."

"Until then," she said, and we hung up.

And so it was time.

# 47.

THERE WAS NO getting around the noise. Between the Hummer and the Winnebago, we were screwed if we tried to drive within a mile of the chain-link fence.

That's why I needed the PEPS weapon.

Hugo, Quinn, and I were in the Hummer. The architect and his wife were in the trunk of Quinn's rental car, and the little people were in the Winnebago. Quinn was a tight squeeze in any car, and tighter than normal in the Hummer.

"Try not to breathe on me," Hugo said to Quinn.

"Why did you bring a Winnebago?" Quinn asked. "There are only ten of you. I thought you could get at least thirty in one of those little clown cars."

"We could," said Hugo, "but where would we fit the net and trampolines?"

"Good point," Quinn said.

I drove slowly to the highway, the Winnebago close behind me. Then I headed south while the clowns sat tight. I drove past the dirt and gravel road that led to Joe DeMeo's place, and Quinn caught a glint of something: a belt buckle, gun barrel, or cigarette butt. Whatever it was, there were probably two of them guarding the road.

The highway curved a half-mile beyond the DeMeo entrance, and I drove a quarter-mile farther, cut my lights, and turned around. I didn't expect any traffic, since Highway

33 cuts through the national forest and it was well past closing time. Still, I angled the Hummer several yards off the shoulder just to be safe. We eased out of the vehicle. Quinn and I took rifles and camouflage blankets. Hugo stood behind the Hummer to keep an eye out for any oncoming cars or cagey DeMeo soldiers.

Quinn and I moved soundlessly up the road to the area where the curve began. There, we set our rifles down, put on our night-vision goggles, and dropped to our bellies. We slid the next few yards quietly and waited.

We spotted the dots of light at the same time.

Cigarettes.

We reversed course, picked up our rifles, and checked to make sure the silencers were tight. These were state-of-the-art CIA silencers, which meant we could shoot the guards and make less noise than a mouse peeing in a cotton ball.

We separated. Quinn began moving silently through the forest, circling behind the men guarding the road, while I made my way slowly through the high ground, opposite DeMeo's entrance. If everything went according to plan, we'd catch them in a crossfire. But these things never go according to plan, and I didn't want to take a chance on one of us snapping a twig or rousing an otter or making some other sound that might alert the guards.

When I was in position, I covered my head and shoulders completely with the blanket and texted the signal to Quinn and Hugo and the circus clowns. Then we went dark with the phones but set them to twitch. I placed mine in my shirt pocket.

My night-vision goggles made it easy to keep an eye on the guards while they smoked, but I was too far away to trust a shot.

It took two minutes for the Winnebago circus wagon to arrive. As the lights washed over the highway, the guards stubbed out their cigarettes. The Winnebago made a clanking noise and stopped about fifty yards from the entrance. After a moment, two little people climbed out with flashlights and lifted the hood as if to check for trouble. I had hoped at this point that the guards would approach the Winnebago so I could shoot them in the back, but they were well trained. They stayed put.

My plan didn't require them to approach the little people. The whole circus wagon ruse was designed to create enough noise so Quinn and I could get closer. As the clowns took turns trying to fire up the engine and hollering directions to each other, I inched my way closer and knew Quinn was doing the same. Finally, the hood slammed shut and the clowns climbed back in the wagon and started revving up the engine with gusto. I probably covered twenty yards undetected during that sequence. Then the clowns turned their radio up full volume and started singing circus songs as they rode steadily down the highway, past the entrance, through the curve, and out of sight.

While they did that, I covered another fifty yards, maybe more. Now I was close enough to attempt a kill shot. I lined up my rifle and waited for the cigarettes to light.

And waited.

Two minutes passed. I had expected at least one of the guards to walk out onto the road to make sure the clowns hadn't stopped, but neither of them moved or made a sound or relit their cigarettes. These were some incredibly well-trained guards, I thought.

Then my cell phone twitched.

I slowly slid my camouflage blanket back over my head,

eased my cell phone out of my pocket, and brought it up to my face under the blanket. Making absolutely certain no light would be emitted from the keypad, I held my breath and opened the phone. I didn't dare speak, not even a whisper.

"You can come out now," Quinn said. "I killed both of them."

I let out my breath. "Did you check to see if there were any others?"

"You didn't just ask me that," Quinn said.

"Right. What the hell was I thinking?"

We made our way back to the Hummer and congratulated the clowns on their performance.

"And then there were eighteen," Hugo said.

"So far as we know," I said.

I started the Hummer's engine but kept the headlights off. The Winnebago turned around and got behind us and followed us back up the road to the entrance, where we headed down the dirt and gravel road toward Joe DeMeo's place.

# 48.

THERE WAS ONLY one entrance leading to Joe's house, and you had to pass through the chain-link fence to get there. Charlie Whiteside and I had calibrated the distance to the first fence pretty carefully, so I stopped when I got three-quarters of a mile from it. Any closer and I would probably give away my position.

Quinn had both the guards' walkie-talkies, and so far we'd been lucky. No one had asked for an update. I figured we were due, since most security firms go with a fifteen-minute crew check and we'd used all of that and more.

We all slid out of the Hummer and listened for barking dogs. Hearing none, Quinn took his rifle and headed east of the compound. Hugo took mine and headed west.

I climbed on top of the Hummer and gave my gunners time to get as close as they could before the dogs picked them up. I'd hoped they'd get at least halfway there, but the dogs were very alert and the barking started almost immediately. I fired up the PEPS weapon and signaled the circus wagon to make tracks.

Suddenly, the walkie-talkies crackled and came alive with the sound of frantic voices. We'd caught them off-guard, so score one for us, but we were still a long way from winning.

The circus wagon veered off the road to give me clearance for a shot. I took it and heard screaming and yelping. I set my cell phone to speaker and turned up the volume. Then I jumped back in the Hummer, flipped on the headlights, and started the engine. The clowns kept their headlights off and continued making their way to their position, left of the hole in the fence I'd just created.

I cranked the Hummer to about forty and barreled down the road and came to a stop a quarter-mile from the entrance. I climbed back onto the roof and gave my clowns time to get their equipment together.

Quinn told me he was in position. We figured Hugo would take longer. His legs were much shorter, and the gun was pretty heavy for him. Still, he was feisty as a rooster, and I knew he'd do well.

I heard some shots, which meant DeMeo's security team had oriented themselves enough to make me their target. The dogs, being smaller, would take longer to get to their feet. The shots continued. There was a protective shield of bulletproof plastic surrounding the front of the PEPS weapon, so I wasn't overly concerned about being hit. Quinn must have squeezed off a couple of silent shots because his voice came over my cell speaker, saying, "Two more down—security guards."

The clowns were taking more time than I anticipated. I wondered if any had been hit. I aimed my weapon to the right of the circus wagon and fired off another burst. I yelled at the circus people to hurry, though it would have been impossible for them to hear me.

The circus clowns had brought several small trampolines and a giant net used to catch falling trapeze artists. Hugo checked in just as the clowns dragged the net across the road, covering the hole I'd made with the initial blast. They tied the ends to the posts and pulled the center of the net away from the hole to make a large chute. Then they ran back to the

Winnebago and grabbed their trampolines and knives, for these were knife-throwing midgets.

I climbed into the Hummer and drove another hundred yards. Then I climbed back onto the roof and waited for the remaining security guards to make their stand and for the dogs to make their charge.

Nothing happened.

"I got one," said Hugo.

"Two more on my side," said Quinn.

The dogs charged through the fence and got tangled up in the circus net. I fired a burst near them, which heated the air and knocked them all down again. I didn't think there would be much fight left in the dogs at this point, but I couldn't take a chance on being wrong and having them kill some of the clowns. I could have shot them, but why kill the dogs if I didn't have to? The guards were different. They were here by choice, so they were fair game.

The clowns untied the net, closed it off, and dragged the dogs behind the Winnebago, out of the line of fire.

"There's one guard missing," I said into my cell phone. "Anyone got a bead on him?"

They did not.

I climbed into the Hummer and used the walkie-talkie. "Joe, I'm coming to get you and your men. Seven security guards are dead. One remains alive. I'm directing this to the guard: Come out unarmed with your hands up and we'll not harm you. This is not your fight, and you're in way over your head. You've got thirty seconds to let us know where you are. Then we're going to kill you."

The clowns got the main gate open and carried their trampolines in, flanked on both sides of the chain-link fence by Quinn and Hugo.

The last guard came out with his hands up. Hugo put a plastic twist-tie on his wrists and looped several more around his hands and a support pole to secure him to the chain-link fence.

Then Hugo and two of the clowns went back to the Winnebago, fetched the ADS weapons, and carried them into the area we had captured. They stopped while we regrouped. Our next barrier was the concrete wall. The problem for Joe and his men was that we had effectively made them prisoners within the wall. Our problem was the entrance gate gave Joe and his men opportunities to potshot us. My biggest concern before getting the drone photos was if Joe had thought to put ledges on the inside of the walls. Had he done so, his men could have manned the walls and shot us as we approached, but the drone confirmed there were no ledges.

I drove the Hummer very slowly through the main entrance and aimed the pulse ray at the entrance gate. Quinn and Hugo flanked me from thirty feet on either side and trained their rifles on the same target. They squeezed off a few rounds to discourage Joe's men from trying to take advantage of the clowns' momentary vulnerability. If they tried to drive through the gate, I'd blast them with the PEPS weapon. Otherwise, I meant to keep them bottled up. I wasn't worried about them using their cell phones because who were they going to call? Not reinforcements. Joe already had all the shooters he could trust. Not the police. If they showed up they'd be able to search his house and no telling what they might find in there.

But on the chance Joe might call the police anyway, Darwin and Lou had notified local dispatchers and 911 operators that Homeland Security was on the premises and any calls requesting aid to Joe's address should be diverted to Lou Kelly.

I had Hugo turn around and keep an eye out behind us, just in case.

The clowns carried three trampolines and three ADS weapons, keeping the Hummer between them and the entrance gate. On each trampoline were throwing knives and electric drills with extended circular concrete drill bits measuring an inch in diameter.

Here's what we had: three clowns at each of three stations on the right side of the residential entrance gate. Each station had a drill and a trampoline, a cache of knives, and an ADS weapon. Quinn was guarding the front, Hugo the back. I had the PEPS weapon trained on the front entrance gate.

The clowns started drilling holes in the wall.

My cell phone rang.

"What the fuck are you doing?" Joe DeMeo asked.

"The deadline for my money came and went," I said.

"All this because of the little kid who lived?"

"That and the hotel," I said.

"You might want to rethink it," he said. "I've got your wife and kid."

"No, you don't."

"I've got their house surrounded. One word from me and they're dead."

"What's the address?"

He told me.

"That's not my family's address," I said.

"They're at a friend's house. I've got it wired to blow."

# 49.

"YOU PROBABLY DON'T believe me," Joe said, "so hang on and I'll conference you with the guy who's going to kill Janet and Kimberly tonight."

I listened to the high-pitched whine of the drill bits while waiting for the connection to go through. I didn't think Janet and Kimberly were in trouble because Callie was with them and she hadn't called. Sal's men were guarding Janet's house, where Joe's men would have gone first.

On the other hand, it always gives you a sick feeling when someone threatens your child's life.

Joe came back on the line. "Sal, are you there?"

"I'm here," said Sal Bonadello.

I breathed a sigh of relief. Then Sal said, "Creed, it's over. I got your blondee trapped inside with your bitchy ex and your bratty kid and the family that owns the house. I got gasoline all over the outside walls and Molotov cocktails ready to throw."

I didn't say anything.

Sal said, "You think we got a deal, like I'm—whatcha call—monitoring Janet's house, but your blondee followed your kid to a friend's house. Then your wife showed up, and now they're all inside and the blondee is so busy trying to keep everyone calm, she don't even know we're here. So this is payback time, my friend. For livin' in my attic and jumpin' through the fucking ceiling and shooting up my bedroom and scaring the shit outta my wife, you lousy prick."

"I saved your life."

"The life you put in danger in the first place."

I didn't say anything. Joe DeMeo said, "Creed, you've taken a shine to that girl in the burn center. So I've decided to burn your kid, too. And if she tries to run out the door or jump out a window, we're going to shoot her."

"Unless?" I said.

"Unless you put down your weapons and come to the front gate. All of you."

Two of the clowns had gotten their drills through the wall. The third drill made a shrieking sound as it hit a steel reinforcing rod. That clown moved the drill a few inches to the left and started over.

"I'm afraid I can't do that, Joe."

"You'd let your wife and kid die?"

"Ex-wife."

"Still," he said. "Your kid?"

I sighed. "You're going to kill them, anyway, Joe. And me, too, if you get the chance."

"It's your little girl, for Christ sake!"

"Which will give me that much more incentive to boil your body with the special weapon I'm bringing into your home."

"Say goodbye to your family, Creed."

"You tell them for me," I said. "I've got work to do."

The first two clowns put the nozzle of their ADS weapons into the holes they'd drilled. The third clown was nearly finished with his second attempt. We all waited for him.

Hugo walked over to me while keeping his eyes trained on the area behind us. "I heard that bastard on your speaker phone," he said, "and I heard what you said to him."

"And?"

"Are you okay?"

"That's the question I've been asked all my life."

The last hole was completed, and the last ADS weapon was fitted to it. At each station, a clown attached the power packs and flipped the switches. At the same time, a second clown jumped on each trampoline several times until he could see over the wall. When they felt safe enough, they angled their jumps and landed on top of the wall. Then the remaining clown at each station tossed them six knives, two at a time. The clowns on top of the walls placed the knives in their knife belts and scampered along the wall top until they reached the area where the second-floor roof overhung the wall. They jumped on top of the roof and got into position behind each of the three back gables.

Then I climbed down from my perch, pulled a tear-gas gun from the back seat, and tossed it to Quinn. While I covered the entrance with the PEPS weapon, Quinn made his way to the gate. Once there, he started pumping tear gas into each window in the house.

I was surprised by the lack of gunmen in the yard. Once the fighting started, they all must have hidden in the house. The PEPS weapon will do that to people. Even so, why wouldn't they station themselves at the upstairs windows? Maybe they were all hiding in Joe's panic room. I hoped so. That would make it much easier for me.

I heard a scream. "Got one," said one of the rooftop elves. "Trying to climb out the back window onto the roof."

I heard several blasts of gunfire coming from the front of the house. Quinn ducked behind the wall just in time. Then I heard the types of screams one can only make when exposed to the ADS beam—except there were four of them.

"Got one," said another rooftop elf. "Same idea, different window," he added.

We heard an engine start up in the garage.

"Stay at your posts," I yelled into my cell phone.

Quinn sprinted back to his post where he'd set his rifle down. He picked it up and aimed it at the front gate.

When the gate started to open, I fired up the PEPS weapon. Joe's car came flying toward the entrance at an angle, and I gave him a full-power blast that melted his tires and caused his car to flip and slam into the corner of the gate. Several men jumped out and started to run, including Joe DeMeo.

They got about two feet before the ADS beam found them.

"Shut off the beams!" I yelled. I drove the Hummer through the gate, slamming Joe's Mercedes out of the way to clear a path for Quinn and the three clowns who were standing by with the rest of the knives. There were four guys on the ground. We gutted the two who had followed me and Joe at the cemetery the previous Saturday, and twist-tied Joe and Grasso's wrists behind them.

Joe spit at me and missed. "I should've stayed in the panic room," he said.

"It wouldn't have made a difference," I said. "I'd have taken that machine off the truck and aimed it at the wall. You saw what it did to your car. Imagine what it would have done to your panic room."

"If you knew where to aim it," he sneered.

"You got me there, Joe."

"By the way," he said, "your family's dead."

"So you say."

The first four that were hit by the ADS ray were dead, which was to be expected, having been exposed for several minutes. My personal best was less than twenty seconds, so I could only imagine their suffering.

We guessed we'd gotten all of them, and if not, I didn't care. We gathered up all our equipment and headed back to the campground. We'd beaten nearly twenty armed men and eight attack dogs without taking a single hit in return. That's a hell of a campaign, I thought.

Back at the campground, there was just one thing left to do: humiliate Joe.

It has never been my style to humiliate my vanquished enemies, but Hugo insisted it was a time-honored clown tradition, so I didn't stand in their way. He grabbed a seltzer and sprayed it in Joe's pants while the other clowns formed a circle, interlocked arms, and sang, "A little song, a little dance, a little seltzer down your pants!"

They had so much fun they all took a turn spraying Joe and Grasso. Before long, their pants were a soggy mess.

"You're fuckin' nuts!" Joe screamed again and again. "But I got you, Creed. I killed your kid!" he shouted. "I killed your fuckin' wife!"

"Ex-wife," I said.

# 50.

OF COURSE, JOE hadn't killed Kimberly or Janet, and neither had Sal Bonadello. Sal's conference call with Joe and me had been part of the plan. It gave Joe what he thought was a bargaining chip, gave him a false sense of security. When I kept coming after him in spite of the threat to my daughter, he came to the conclusion I was certifiable. He reasoned, if I didn't care enough about my own kid to try to save her, what chance did he have with me? Joe, already in a panic, must have felt like a trapped rat. At least I thought he'd feel that way, and I hoped to flush him out.

Because, truth is, I really didn't know where his panic room was hidden, and he had a hell of a big house. As it turned out, the architect and his wife knew nothing about a panic room. If Joe had one, the architect guessed it had been added by the second architect, the one who revised the original plans and completed the construction effort. That guy had disappeared shortly after completing work on Joe's house.

Lou had pulled the building permits and gave us the name, but apparently DeMeo had told the second architect not to file the revisions. Quinn and I felt terrible about kidnapping and torturing our architect and his wife with the ADS ray, but they were okay now. Hopefully they'd be able to look back on the experience some day and laugh about it. If not, who would believe their story anyway, right?

Our captured included the architect, his wife, the security guy, Joe DeMeo, and Grasso. That's a lot of people to deal with, so I did what I always do when I've got a mess to clean up.

I called Darwin.

Darwin sent a company cleaning crew to Joe's house, and the clowns kept an eye on the architect and his wife and the security guy until the cleaning crew could round them up. Meanwhile, Quinn and I tied DeMeo and Grasso to the sides of the Hummer and made them run a few miles with their pants around their ankles to amuse the clowns. When we got tired of that, I pulled over to the side of the road and put a gun to Joe's head and made him call Garrett Unger at headquarters. Joe claimed he couldn't remember the passwords, so I made him run a few more miles. Unfortunately for Joe, he kept falling and spent most of the time being dragged. Then I repeated the process again and again until he remembered enough to make me square with Addie and Quinn and Callie and Sal Bonadello.

After Joe came through with the passwords, Quinn tied him and Grasso to the PEPS weapon on the roof. Then I hauled them off to Edwards to meet Jeff Tuck, my eccentric L.A. operative. Jeff couldn't understand why it took so long to drive thirty miles to the base. I told him we got a late start.

Joe and Grasso had been dragged half to death, and their faces and bodies showed the effects. Jeff took one look at them and said, "Relatives of yours, Augustus?"

To me, he said, "Do I want to know why their pants are sopping wet?"

"I wouldn't think so," I said.

"You got any dry clothes they can wear so they don't ruin the jet seats?"

Quinn and I gave Jeff our camouflage blankets and watched him wrap them around the two waifs. I remembered the two-thousand-dollar suit and tie Joe wore last week at the cemetery and thought, *You never feel the splinters on the ladder of success until you're sliding back down.*

Jeff flew Joe and Grasso to Washington and turned them over to Darwin's security staff, and Quinn and I took one of the company's Gulfstream jets back to headquarters.

# 51.

"IT WAS THE suit, man. I swear to God, she loved the suit."
This was Eddie Ray, telling his story about the girl he met in
sporting goods. "Words can't describe her."

"You were probably drunk," said Rossman, and the others
laughed. The old friends were hanging at Daffney Ducks, the
neighborhood watering hole. Eddie Ray had grown up and
lived his entire life—forty-six years—within five miles of this
place.

She'd been shopping for a birthday present for her dad. A
fly rod. It couldn't be just any rod, had to be the best. Eddie
Ray was so stunned at her beauty, he'd just stood there
without saying a word. She'd said, "That's a great-looking
suit you're wearing. Is it an Armani?"

"Laugh all you want," he said to his drinking buddies, "but
I've got a lunch date with her tomorrow."

"Tell us where," said Lucas, "and we'll all give her a ride."
He made an obscene gesture with his hands and hips.

More laughter.

"She ain't like that. This is a high-class broad. Seriously."

The blonde beauty had asked about his suit, and he
couldn't just stand there and say nothing. Eddie Ray had
choked up the courage to say, "I'm not sure of the label, but I
got it at the J.C. Penney's." She'd nodded, impressed. Things
were going good, so he tried for a joke. "But it cost a hell of a

lot more than a penny!" he'd said, then added, "Pardon my French." It hadn't mattered about the profanity. "I like that," she'd said. "You're funny."

Now, back at the bar, buying a round of drinks for his skeptical buddies, Eddie said, "I'll take a picture, and you can judge for yourself."

"Make sure you get the front end," said Rossman. "I've always wanted to see lipstick on a pig."

"I'll take a picture, all right," said Eddie Ray, "and when you see it, you're gonna shit!"

They'd talked a few minutes, and he'd picked out the best rod in the store for her. She'd been impressed by his knowledge of the sport. He'd asked her name, and when she said, "Monica," he said, "I knew a girl named Monica once, back in high school. Real pretty, she was." Monica had smiled a sly smile and said, "I bet she was your girlfriend," and he'd winked and said, "You'd win that bet for sure." They'd laughed, and she'd said, "You probably had lots of girlfriends in high school if you had that cool mullet back then," and he'd modestly said, "No more'n my share, I expect." Then he'd told her about being on the football team and how he blew out his knee that last season, and by then they were checking out and he couldn't help but give her the employee discount, meaning, he bought the rod and let her reimburse him, which she did with cash. Cash he was now blowing on drinks for his friends.

"Hold up," he said to his friends. "I can only do the first round. I gotta save my dough for my date tomorrow."

She'd been so grateful for the discount, she felt she should do something to repay him. "Have dinner with me tonight," he'd said, wondering how those words had escaped from his mouth. She'd said, "Hmm. I can't have dinner, but if you feel like driving to the city tomorrow, I can meet you for lunch."

Eddie left the bar early to get himself together for the big date that promised to change his life.

The guys kept drinking and talking, and Lucas tried to take bets on whether or not Eddie Ray's lunch date would show up tomorrow. No one was taking. They decided Eddie Ray had been the victim of a great-looking broad who was playing him for the discount.

They were wrong.

When Eddie Ray got to the restaurant and asked for Monica, he was handed a small envelope by the hostess. Eddie's knees went weak, and he had a sinking feeling in his heart. It was a classy rejection, he thought, but a rejection just the same. Of course, there was always a chance she'd gotten tied up with something at the last minute. If so, she wouldn't have known how to contact him.

So there was a glimmer of hope, Eddie decided. He took the note, walked to an empty chair, sat down, and tried to fight the feeling of rejection that had permeated his life since the day his knee blew out.

The note said she'd ordered a private lunch for them in suite 316.

Eddie raced to the elevators and pressed the button. He didn't care if it seemed too good to be true. He'd seen several movies where the gorgeous party girl wants to get away from her life and winds up humping the pool boy or the maintenance man. Eddie wasn't kidding himself; he knew this wasn't going to be the start of a lasting relationship.

He also knew that when a girl asks you to her hotel room, you don't say no. She was practically promising him sex, probably after a nice lunch and some flirty conversation. As he knocked on the door, he thought, *in less than two hours, I could be banging the most beautiful girl on the planet Earth.*

Callie had other plans, of course.

"Come in," she said. "The door is unlocked."

Eddie entered the parlor area of the suite, noticed the flowers on the table, the champagne bucket, the flute glasses, the fresh-squeezed orange juice, the chocolate-covered strawberries. He could hear soft music coming from the bedroom. Callie stood across the parlor, leaning against the wall, dressed to the nines in a yellow sundress, hands in her pockets, cutting an angle as practiced as any American model.

Eddie let out a low whistle.

"I gotta hand it to you, Monica. You do know how to set the mood."

"I've taken the liberty of ordering lunch. I hope that's okay."

Eddie Ray liked to order his own food, but what the hell, this wasn't about eating. Still, she was probably some kind of model, skinny as she was, and he didn't care much for chick food. He looked again at the champagne and the orange juice and the flowers. All this, he thought, and not one beer. What were the chances she'd order him a hamburger and fries, he thought. Zero, right?

Eddie Ray said, "Whatever you've chosen will be perfect, I'm sure."

"I take you for a guy who likes his steak and potatoes," she said.

Eddie's face lit up, and he said, "Can I pour you a drink?"

"If you'll join me," she said.

They had one, and it was a sissy drink, but it wasn't that bad. He relaxed on the couch, and she made him another. This one tasted stronger, and he was starting to feel the effects of drinking without eating first. He figured he'd leave this part out tonight when he told the guys at the bar about his big date.

She smiled and said, "When you finish your drink, I'll give you a kiss."

"I'll drink the whole damn bottle if you take off your dress," he said with a wink, then wished he hadn't.

"Why, Eddie Ray!" she said, but she said it with a laugh, so he guessed they were still okay.

"I was just kidding," he said. He gulped down the rest of his drink, and she said, "Now, about that kiss." Eddie couldn't believe his luck.

Eddie Ray stood to collect his kiss and got about five feet before making a strange face and grabbing his chest. He took a couple of steps sideways and staggered into the wall.

She asked, "Are you okay?"

He looked at her and said, "I don't know what's happening." He sank to his knees and fell on his side, his face contorted in pain at first, then agony.

Callie pulled a chair next to him and sat. "You don't have much time," she said, "so pay attention."

Eddie had lost all feeling in his feet and hands. "What," he gasped, "have you done?"

"I've poisoned you," she said.

"But why?"

"I did it for Monica. She wasn't your girlfriend, by the way. She was five years younger than you. Fifteen, the night you raped her."

"What are you ... talking about?" he said. He was having difficulty speaking, but right now it seemed his voice was the only part of his body that was working.

"You were hosting a keg party at your house," Callie said. "The party had moved to the front yard. Monica was walking home from a dance class at the high school. You knew her

267

from the neighborhood and called her over. You grabbed her and raped her on your front lawn and threatened to kill her if she told anyone."

"H-how do you know all this?"

"She was a bit snooty," Callie said, "but she was a friend of mine. She had class. Unlike you."

"Help me," he said.

"Fat chance. Here's my best offer. Give me the names of two people who ruined your life the way you ruined Monica's. If you want justice, this is your chance. But speak quickly, because you're about to pay for your sins in a permanent way."

He named his coach and the kid from Woodhaven, the one who took the cheap shot on the football field a full second after the whistle had blown.

Callie wiped down any and all surfaces she might have touched, including the orange juice lid, the bottle, and the champagne bottle. Then she placed the champagne cork and flutes in her duffel, along with the note she'd written that she fished out of his pocket.

Callie stopped for a moment, inspecting the room. Deciding it was sterile, she headed for the door, pausing only long enough to step over Eddie Ray's shuddering body. She was done here, was tired of being Monica.

# 52.

KATHY ELLISON had nearly finished walking her golden retriever, Wendy, around her neighborhood circle when she saw a hulking man standing beside a parked sedan directly in front of her. It was mid-morning, a beautiful sunny day, and theirs was a gated community in Marietta, Georgia, just outside Atlanta. Crime was virtually nonexistent in neighborhoods such as Kathy's, where all houses were priced in the million-plus range.

Even so, the man standing in her path was so huge and his face and head so grossly disfigured, she stopped in her tracks some twenty feet away. Wendy noticed him, as well, or had picked up on Kathy's fear as dogs will sometimes do. The hair on Wendy's back slowly began to stand on end. She let out a long, low growl. Kathy decided the sensible thing to do would be to turn around and go home the way she'd come.

As she spun around, she heard the man call her by name. Kathy froze in her tracks, stunned, frightened. There was no reason for this monstrous man to know her name.

"Please, ma'am, don't be afraid," he said as he approached. "I don't blame you for being upset. I have that affect on everyone at first. I can't help the way I look. Believe me, I've tried."

Quinn kept talking as he drew closer. "The best thing to do is just not look at me." By now, he was standing next to her.

Wendy, poor thing, was shivering with fear, wetting a puddle into the pavement.

"Kathy, my name is George Purvis, and I'm afraid I have some bad news."

Kathy hadn't moved from the spot where she froze after hearing him call her name. She also refused to look at the man standing beside her. That way, she wouldn't be able to identify him, so maybe he wouldn't have to hurt her.

"I'm very sorry, Mr. Purvis," she said. "I don't wish to be rude, but you're frightening my dog and me. I don't think I want to hear your bad news. Can I just go home?"

Quinn dropped to one knee, held his hand out for Wendy to sniff. She clamped her jaws on his wrist, growling, tearing his flesh apart. Then she started tugging his hand side to side as if she were trying to break the neck of a large rat.

"Oh my God!" shrieked Kathy. "Wendy, no! Stop it!"

Wendy released his hand. "I'm so sorry, Mr. Purvis. She never behaves this way."

Quinn just shrugged. "It's okay, ma'am. I don't really feel pain the way most people do." He noticed her staring at his bloody hand. Seeking to remove the distraction, he stuffed it in his pocket.

"Even so," Kathy said, "I'm so sorry." She took a deep breath, turned to face him, tried hard not to recoil in horror. She looked into his face, and this time saw more than she expected to find. Her eyes watered thinking of his pain, the emotional scarring. "What's the bad news you wanted to tell me?"

Quinn looked in both directions before answering. Still on one knee, so as not to tower above her, he said, "It's about your husband, Brad."

"What about him?"

"He gave me fifty thousand dollars to kill you."

Kathy started hyperventilating. She felt light-headed. Her ears began ringing. The only reason she didn't faint was because she didn't want the monster to touch her—and he surely would. She moved her eyes about, seeking help, trying to decide how best to get away from him.

"Please don't run. I'm not going to do it."

"What?"

"I'm not going to kill you."

"Why not?"

"I've been watching you for the past couple of days, and I've been watching your husband. I've come to the conclusion he's the one who deserves to die, not you."

Kathy looked into his face to see if he was just playing with her. She could tell nothing from his expression, but then, his face didn't really seem capable of displaying much beyond horror. She felt, at least for the moment, he was not planning to hurt her. "Why on earth would my husband want to kill me?" she asked.

Quinn said, "Did you ever watch *Seinfeld*?"

"The television show or the comedian?"

"The show."

"Sure. All the time."

"Me, too. Did you ever see the show about Opposite George?"

"Where he starts doing the opposite of everything he's done before?"

"Right. And everything started working for him, remember?"

"Yes," she said. "He goes up to the girl in the coffee shop, tells her he's bald, unemployed, and lives with his parents."

"Uh huh, and she likes him! Then he has the job interview

271

and does everything wrong and winds up working for the Yankees."

Kathy said, "Yeah, I love those shows. I still watch the reruns sometimes. But what does this have to do with not wanting to kill me?"

"It's like Opposite George. All my adult life, I've taken these kinds of jobs, never asking questions, never wondering about the motives, never thinking about the people who had to die. What's it ever gotten me? Nothing but misery. I have to work, and this is all I know. Long story short, your husband called a guy who called a guy."

"And now you've come," Kathy said.

"Right," said Quinn. "Only this time, I started thinking, what if I take the money and don't do the hit? What's the worst that could happen?"

Kathy didn't know how to answer that.

"I watched you, and I may be wrong, but I think you're a nice person."

"Well thank you, Mr. Purvis."

"Actually, my name is Quinn."

"Okay ..."

"It's not your fault that Brad is screwing around on you."

"What?"

"Yeah, he's sleeping with this young girl who works at Neiman Marcus in Buckhead, at the jewelry counter. Her name is Erica Vargas. I'm thinking that's why he wants you out of the picture, so he can fuck her all the time instead of just twice a week."

"Please, Mr. Quinn. Your *language*. It's appalling!"

"Oh, sorry. Anyway, I think Brad's a jerk and you could do better."

"Thank you for the compliment, Mr. Quinn, if that's

indeed what it was. But I'm afraid there's been a terrible mistake. I find it inconceivable that Brad would take a lover."

"Happens all the time."

"Yes, well, I'm sure it does, but not to passionless men like Brad. As for him being capable of murder? Impossible."

Quinn's hand was suddenly a blur as he snatched Wendy and headed for the sedan. Kathy bolted after him.

"Stop!" she said. "What are you doing?"

"I'm taking Wendy for a little ride. You can join us if you'd like."

"Please, Mr. Quinn. You don't want to do this. Look at her. She's terrified."

The giant kept moving toward the car.

"Remember what you said about Opposite George!"

Quinn held the passenger door open. "I've already explained my position on that," he said, "but some things must be seen to be believed. Climb in. If we hurry, we can catch them in the act."

Kathy looked around. "What has happened to our security guard?"

Quinn waved his injured hand dismissively. "He's, uh, tending to a family emergency."

Though Quinn had said it casually, he failed to anticipate the terrifying images that suddenly raced through Kathy's mind. She began shaking so violently, Quinn feared she might slip into shock.

"Kathy, I promise you, everything's fine. Think about it: if I wanted you dead, you'd already be halfway to heaven." He patted the seat. "Now climb in and stop worrying. I'll have you and Wendy back home in no time."

Kathy didn't want to go with the giant. In fact, getting in his car would be dead last on her list of things to experience in her lifetime. But she couldn't bear the thought of losing Wendy. She took a deep breath and reluctantly climbed into the car and hung her hopes on the idea that perhaps one of her neighbors had seen enough to phone the authorities.

Quinn put the car in gear and handed Wendy to her grateful owner. True to his word, Quinn didn't hurt either of them and was in fact very conversational during the drive to Buckhead. It was not yet noon and traffic was light, and before long, Kathy felt the car stop. She turned her attention away from Wendy and looked out the window.

"What happens now?" she asked.

"We wait."

Kathy followed Quinn's gaze to the café across the street, the charming one that offered a view of cozy furniture through the front window—the cozy furniture upon which Brad sat with a young hottie.

Quinn, Kathy, and Wendy settled into their seats for the duration of the lovers' meal, then watched Brad and Erica stroll hand-in-hand to the nearby hotel. They waited in the car in silence for about an hour. Then Quinn spotted the lovers exiting the hotel. Brad gave Erica one last embrace.

"Can you drive us home now?" Kathy said.

He did. Before getting out of the car, Kathy said, "You know that thing you were telling me about, the whole Opposite George thing? I think this just might work out for you."

Quinn wondered what Donovan Creed would have said to keep the conversation going. He came up with, "How so?"

"I'm the one with all the money in this relationship, not Brad, but there is a pot full of insurance and a big inheritance coming Brad's way if something happens to me."

Quinn knew where this was going.

Kathy continued. "You can keep the fifty thousand dollars from my husband," she said, "and I'll add another fifty thousand to it. Do you understand what I'm asking?"

"You want me to kill your husband."

Kathy laughed. "Heavens no! I've got far too much invested in the prick. Plus, I really do love him, and I certainly wouldn't welcome the close scrutiny the media and police would bring."

Quinn was wrong. He had no idea where this was going and told her so.

"Don't you see?" asked Kathy. "I want you to kill Erica."

Quinn nodded absently. "I know a guy who says we all have at least two people in our lives who we wish had never been born. These two people changed the course of our lives for the worse, and we never got over what they did."

Kathy said, "Your friend is probably right about that."

Quinn said, "Apart from Erica, was there anyone else in your life who you wish had never been born?"

"Oh heavens," said Kathy. "What a horrible question to ask!"

"Just hypothetically."

"Well, I hate to speak ill of the dead," she said, "but did you see that media circus about Monica Childers a few weeks ago?"

Quinn nodded. "Did you know her?"

"She was my step-daughter. She made my life a living hell."

After helping Kathy achieve a peaceful demise, Quinn placed her into a shallow grave in the North Georgia woods, went back to the mall, and waited for Erica to leave her station. The store wasn't busy, but there were people milling around. Quinn waited until the area around the jewelry counter was vacant. He placed a small package by the cash register and walked out of the store.

Erica finished up in the bathroom, walked back to her station, and checked the area to make sure the fill-in girl hadn't left any paperwork for her. Satisfied, she turned her attention to the small gift-wrapped package with her name on it. There was a note: "Please accept this with all my love. I'm filing for divorce today. Love, Brad."

Erica let out a squeal of delight. This was her dream come true, what she'd been working for all these months. Working the jewelry counter at Neiman's, she was tired of watching other women casually make purchases that eclipsed her annual salary. Her friends chided her for always dating married men. She couldn't wait to show them the fruits of her labor!

She carefully unwrapped the package, slowly lifted the lid.

And days later, clean-up crews were still finding remnants of her flesh in the strangest places.

## 53.

I WOKE UP first, so I went into the kitchen and set the oven to four hundred. While it preheated, I filled a blender with milk, flour, eggs, butter, salt, and vanilla and almond extract. I let that churn on high a full minute, found Kathleen's muffin pan, and sprayed it with non-fat cooking spray. I poured the batter into the muffin slots, popped them in the oven, and set the timer for twenty-seven minutes. Then I placed some butter on a plate to soften and headed back to Kathleen's bedroom, where I belonged.

"What was all that racket?" she asked.

"I'm making us popovers for breakfast."

"You can't make popovers at home. They always fall before you take them out," she said.

"Not mine."

"Only fancy restaurants can make popovers that stay puffed up."

"Only fancy restaurants and me," I said.

"If you're wrong and I'm right, will you take me somewhere fancy for breakfast sometime?"

"Do you have a place in mind?" I said.

"I'd like to have breakfast at Tiffany's," she said.

"Actually, I think Tiffany's is a jewelry store, not a restaurant."

"You're kidding!"

"I'm afraid not."

"I've never seen the movie. I just always assumed…"

"Don't worry," I said. "My popovers won't fall. We won't have to eat somewhere fancy."

"Darn," she said.

Somebody famous once said that you can kiss your friends and family goodbye and put a lot of miles between you, but you'll always be with them because you're not just a part of the world; the world is a part of you.

Or something like that.

The point is, I never missed anyone the way I missed Kathleen this last trip. When I found my way back to her modest duplex with the faded green siding, half attic, and half basement, and she jumped into my arms and wrapped her legs around me and squealed with joy—well, I knew this must be what all the poets make such a fuss about.

"How long do we have before the popovers fall?" she asked.

"Forever, because they never will. I have it down to a science."

"So what you're saying, you're a chef scientist."

"We all have a specialty," I said.

"My specialty is math," she said.

"Math?"

She gave me a sly smile. "That's right. As in, how many times can one thing … go into another." She arched an eyebrow seductively.

"Before a cooking timer goes off?" I asked.

"Hypothetically," she said.

"I'm not certain, but I'm willing to expend a great deal of effort toward helping you solve that equation."

And so we did.

The bell interrupted our research, and we agreed to continue the experiment after breakfast. Kathleen took a blanket off the bed, wrapped it around her, followed me into the kitchen, and watched me take a pan of perfectly formed popovers from the oven. We filled them with softened butter.

"Oh ... my ... God!" she squealed. "I've always wanted a man who could cook, and now I've got something even better: a man who can bake!"

We each ate two, and afterward, Kathleen looked as though she wanted to say something.

"What?" I said.

"I want to tell you something, but I don't want to run you off."

"You won't run me off. Unless you've got another lab partner."

She took a deep breath and said, "I want to adopt Addie."

I didn't know what to say, so I just said, "Really."

"I love her, Donovan, and she loves me. I've always wanted a child of my own, but Ken beat that physical possibility out of me years ago. Anyway, it's like I'd be choosing her over all the other children in the world, you know? And she needs me."

"What about Aunt Hazel?" I asked.

She lowered her eyes. "That's the problem," she said. "Hazel doesn't want her, but she doesn't want me to have her."

"Why not?"

"She thinks I can't provide for Addie. She thinks Addie should be turned over to an adoption agency where she can be placed with a proper family."

"You mean like a husband and wife?"

She nodded. "And enough money to adequately care for

her needs."

"What did you say?"

Kathleen took my hand in hers. "I told her the chances of a perfect family adopting Addie were slim and that I might not have a husband or money, but I can give her all the things a little girl needs."

"Well said."

"But she still won't sign off on me, even though Addie begged her to."

"You want me to have a talk with Aunt Hazel?"

Kathleen said, "Would you mind terribly?"

"I'll do it today," I said.

We sat there in silence awhile. Then Kathleen said, "Donovan?"

"Uh huh?"

"Will you still see me if I adopt Addie?"

"Why wouldn't I?"

"A lot of men would rather date gorgeous, young, big-boobed women that aren't single mothers."

"Yuck," I said. "Not me!"

On my way to Aunt Hazel's, I reflected on the enormity of the accounts I'd seized from Joe DeMeo. He was far wealthier than I'd anticipated, and in fact, money was still pouring in at a healthy clip. I supposed the contributors hadn't yet heard the news of DeMeo's fall. After paying all costs of the campaign, I had enough left over to give a million dollars each to Lou, Kimberly, and Janet. Janet seemed quite pleased to get a share, I thought, even though she said it was a drop in the bucket compared to what I'd cost her in misery.

I thought about Garrett Unger and how he was scheduled to be arrested this morning. I hadn't said anything about it to Kathleen, and I hadn't mentioned the million dollars that would be wired into her personal account by 2:00 pm today, or the trust I was setting up for Addie that would be funded with the initial ten million I'd clipped from DeMeo. These were all surprises that were sure to make breakfast at Tiffany's seem pale by comparison. Not to mention the biggest surprise of all—when Kathleen finds out I'm not just a baker, but an accomplished cook as well.

Traffic was moving, but slowly. I looked out the window and saw the small piles of black snow, the only visible remnants of a brutal winter. We plodded our way under a bridge, and I noticed several bums huddled together under blankets, trying to sleep. I wondered what had happened in their lives that brought them to this bridge on this day.

I had my driver pull over. I got out of the car and approached the bums. "I've got something for you," I said.

It took a minute, but the three men roused themselves to sitting positions. There was no way to tell how old or young they were, but they were equally filthy. I handed each of them a hundred-dollar bill, and they all said "God bless you, sir."

The first guy held up a small bottle of blackberry brandy. There was maybe a sip left in it. "You want to sit and have a drink?" he asked.

"Another time," I said, but I didn't leave.

"That's mighty generous of you mister," one of the guys said. "Mighty generous, indeed."

Another one said, "Know what I'm gonna do with my hunnerd?"

"What's that?" I said.

"I'm gonna go to a fancy bar and get drunk on the finest whiskey money can buy."

I nodded.

The second guy said, "I'm gonna get me some pussy. Been

a long time since I've had pussy."

I handed all three of them another hundred dollars and said, "Now all three of you can get drunk and get some pussy."

The third one said, "I'm a woman, you dumb shit."

One of the others said, "Mm hmm, you right, Agnes. He is a dumb shit."

I was about to apologize, but my cell phone rang. I waved goodbye to my new friends and climbed back in the car to take the call.

"Mr. Creed...I've got...some...good news...and some... bad news."

"Hi, Victor," I said. "Bad news first."

"The social...experi...ment has...run its...course," he said.

"I'm okay with that," I said. I'd known it was just a matter of time before we got to a bunch of leads that were already dead. "What's the good news?"

"I've got...another...idea...that is...in...credi...ble and ...I want...you to...partici...pate."

"Is there money in it for me?"

"Lots."

"Will this interfere with your plans for world conquest?"

"It might...delay...them some...but it...will be...fasci... nating. In fact...it is...the most...amazing...thing...you will ...ever hear...in your...life!"

"I'm listening," I said.

He told me.

And when I heard it, I had to agree.

A total stranger offers you $100k,
the only condition is that someone
else has to die...

# LETHAL
# EXPERIMENT

# JOHN LOCKE

# PROLOGUE

THE SMALL HOUSE was old and cramped by furniture that seemed even older. A transaction was taking place at the kitchen table, where the three of them sat. A slightly foul odor seeped in from the living room. Trish didn't know it yet, but the next few minutes would change her life. She cleared her throat.

"We were hoping to get eighteen thousand dollars," she said to the loan officer.

The young blond loan officer wore her hair combed back with a part midway above her left eye. "No offense," she said, "but it took more than eighteen thousand dollars of stress to put those dark circles under your eyes. Not to mention the car in your driveway, the condition of your home, the fact you've been turned down by every lender in town…"

Trish swallowed, seemed about to cry.

The loan officer's face was visually stunning, with flawless skin, impossibly high cheekbones, and sandy blond eyebrows that arched naturally over electric, pale gray eyes. Her name was Callie Carpenter, and she was wearing driving gloves.

Trish's husband Rob wasn't looking at the gloves. His eyes had found a home in Callie Carpenter's perfectly proportioned cleavage.

"You know the vibe I'm getting?" said Callie. "Pain.

Frustration. Desperation. There's love in this home, I can feel it. But it's being tested. I look at you guys and I see the vultures circling your marriage."

Trish and Rob exchanged a look that seemed to confirm her words.

Trish said, "This sounds all New Age to me. I'm not sure what this has to do with our loan application."

Callie looked at the chipped coffee cup in front of her from which she'd declined to drink. She sighed. "Let me put it another way: how much money would it take to remove the stress from your lives, allow you to sleep at night and help you remember that the important thing is not other people and what you owe them, but rather the two of you, and what you mean to each other?"

Trish had been quietly wringing her hands in her lap, and now she looked down at them as though they belonged to a stranger. "I'm afraid we have no collateral."

Rob said, "The banks got us on one of those adjustable rate mortgages that turned south on us. Then I lost my job. Next thing you know?"

Callie held up a hand. "Stop," she said. "Would a hundred thousand dollars get you through the bad times?"

"Oh, hell yeah!" said Rob.

Trish eyed Callie suspiciously. "We could never qualify for that type of unsecured credit."

"This wouldn't be a conventional loan," said Callie, getting to her favorite part of the story. "It's what I call a Rumpelstiltskin Loan."

Trish's voice grew sharp. "You're mocking us. Look, Ms…"

"Carpenter."

"… I don't particularly care for your sense of humor. Or your personal assessment of our marriage."

2

"You think I'm playing with you?" Callie opened her briefcase, spun it around to face them.

Rob's eyes grew wide as saucers. "Holy shit!" he said. "Is that a hundred grand?"

"It is."

"This is ridiculous," Trish said. "How could we possibly pay that back?"

"It's not so much a loan as it is a social experiment," Callie said. "The millionaire I represent will donate up to one hundred thousand dollars to any person I deem worthy, with one stipulation."

"What's that?" Rob said.

Trish's lips curled into a sneer. She spoke the word with contempt. "Rumpelstiltskin."

Callie nodded.

Rob said, "Rumpel—whatever you're saying, what's it mean?"

Trish said, "The fairy tale. She wants our firstborn unless we can guess the name of her boss."

"What?" Rob said. "That's crazy. We're not even pregnant."

Callie laughed. "Trish, you're right about there being a catch. But it has nothing to do with naming a gnome or giving up future children."

"Then what, you want us to rob a bank for you? Kill someone?"

Callie shook her head.

"So what's the catch?" Trish said.

"If you accept the contents of this suitcase," Callie said, "someone will die."

Trish said, "All right, that's enough. This is obviously some type of TV show, but it's the cruelest way to punk someone I've ever seen. Here's an idea for the next one: get a normal-

3

looking woman instead of a beautiful model. And don't use all the flowery New Age language. Who's going to buy that bullshit? Okay, so where's the camera—in the suitcase?"

The suitcase.

From the moment Callie lifted the lid, Rob had been transfixed. He'd finally found something more compelling to stare at than Callie's chest. Even now he couldn't take his eyes off the cash. "Do we get some sort of fee if you put this on TV?"

Callie shook her head. "Sorry, no TV, no hidden cameras."

"Then it doesn't make sense."

"Like I said, it's a social experiment. My boss is fed up with the criminal justice system in this country. He's tired of seeing murderers set free due to sloppy police work, slick attorneys, and stupid jurors. So, like a vigilante, he goes after murderers who remain unpunished. He feels he's doing society a favor. But society loses when any person dies, no matter how evil, so my boss wants to pay something forward for the life he takes."

"That's a crock of shit," Trish said. "If he really believed that, he'd pay the victims' families instead of total strangers."

"Too risky. The police could establish a pattern. So my boss does the next best thing, he helps anonymous members of society. Each time my boss kills a murderer he pays society up to one hundred thousand dollars. And today you get to be society."

Trish was about to comment, but Rob got there first. He was definitely getting more intrigued. "Why us?"

"A loan officer forwarded your application to my boss and said you were decent people, about to lose everything."

Trish said, "You represented yourself as a loan officer."

"I did."

"And you're not."

"I'm a different type of loan officer."

"And what type is that?"

"The type that brings cash to the table," Callie said.

"In a suitcase," Trish said.

Trish looked at the cash as if seeing the possibilities for the first time. She said, "If what you're saying is true, and your boss is paying all this money to benefit society, why tell us about the killing at all? Why not just pay us?"

"He thinks it's only fair that you know where the money comes from and why it's being paid."

Rob and Trish digested this information without speaking, but their expressions spoke volumes. Rob, thinking this could be his big chance in life, Trish, dissecting the details, trying to allow herself to believe. This was a family in crisis, Callie knew, and she had just thrown them the mother of all lifelines.

Finally Trish said, "These murderers you speak of. Is your boss going to kill them anyway?"

"Yes. But not until the money is paid."

"And if we refuse to accept it?"

"No problem. I'll ask the next family on my list."

Rob said, "The person your boss is going to kill—is there any possibility it's someone we know?"

"You know any murderers?"

Callie could practically hear the wheels turning as Rob and Trish stared at the open suitcase. Callie loved this part, the way they always struggled with it at first. But she knew where this would go. They'd turn it every way they could, but in the end, they'd take the money.

"This sounds like one of those specials, like 'What Would You Do?'" Trish said, unable to let go of her feeling this was all an elaborate hoax.

Callie glanced at her watch. "Look, I don't have all day.

You've heard the deal, I've answered your questions, it's time to give me your answer."

Her deadline brought all their emotions to a head.

Trish's face blanched. She lowered her head and pressed her hands to either side of her temples as though experiencing a migraine. When she looked up her eyes had tears in them. It was clear she was waging a war with her conscience.

Rob was jittery, in a panic. No question what he wanted to do—his eyes were pleading with Trish.

Callie knew she had them.

"I'll give you ten minutes," she said briskly." I'll put my headphones on so you can talk privately, but you'll have to remain in my sight at all times."

"How do you know we won't contact the police after you leave?" Trish said, wearily.

Callie laughed. "I'd love to hear that conversation."

"What do you mean?"

"You think the police would believe you? Or let you keep a suitcase full of cash under these circumstances?"

Rob said, "Are we the first, or have you done this before?"

"This is my eighth suitcase."

Again they looked at each other. Then Rob reached over, as though he wanted to stroke the bills.

Callie smiled and closed the top. "Nuh uh."

"How many people actually took the money?" he asked. There was a sheen of sweat on his upper lip.

"I can't tell you that."

"Why not?" Trish asked.

"It could influence your decision and impact the social experiment. Look. Here's what you need to know: when someone takes the money, my boss feels he's gotten the blessing of a member of society to end the life of a murderer."

"This is crazy. This is just crazy," Trish whispered, as if daring herself to believe.

"People die every day," Rob said. "And they're going to die whether we get the money or someone else does."

Trish looked at him absently, her mind a million miles away.

"They're giving this money to someone," Rob explained, "so why not us?"

"It's too crazy," Trish repeated. "Isn't it?"

"Maybe," Callie said, putting on the headphones. "But the money—and the offer—are for real."

## 1.

"AND YOU, MR. Creed," she said.

I looked up from my mixing bowl. "Ma'am?"

"What do you do for a living?"

"Apart from making brownies? I'm with Homeland Security."

Her name was Patty Feldson and she was conducting a home study as part of the adoption process. My significant other, Kathleen Gray, was hoping to adopt a six-year-old burn victim named Addie Dawes. Addie was the sole survivor of a home fire that claimed the lives of her parents and twin sister. Ms. Feldson had been watching Addie and Kathleen play dolls on the living-room floor. Satisfied with the quality of their interaction, she turned her attention to me.

"Do you have a business card?" Patty said.

"I do." I took my wallet from my hip pocket and removed a card that had been freshly printed for this very occasion. I handed it over.

Patty read aloud: "Donovan Creed, Special Agent, Homeland Security." She smiled. "Well that doesn't reveal much. But it certainly sounds mysterious and exciting. Do you travel much, Agent Creed?"

I wondered how well we'd get along if I told her I was a government assassin who occasionally performs freelance hits for the mob and for an angry, homicidal midget named Victor.

"I do travel. But I'm afraid my job falls short of being mysterious or exciting. Mostly, I interview people."

"Suspected terrorists?"

I layered the batter into Kathleen's brownie pan with a silicone spatula and swirled Addie's name on top before placing the pan in the oven.

"Apartment owners, business managers, that sort of thing." I closed the oven door and set the timer for forty minutes.

"What's in the brownies?" she said.

I felt like saying marijuana, but Kathleen had warned me not to joke with these people. She was in the home stretch of the adoption process and I intended to do all I could to help her.

"You remember the actress, Katharine Hepburn?" I said.

"Excuse me?"

"This is her recipe. I found it in an old issue of the *Saturday Evening Post.*"

"Oh," she said. "I'd love to have it!"

"Then you shall."

A home study is a series of meetings you have to go through as part of the approval process for adopting a child. Kathleen had provided all her personal documents, passed the criminal background check, made it through all the appointments and provided personal references. But at least one meeting is required to be in your home, and all who live there (Kathleen) or spend nights there (me) had to be in attendance.

Patty Feldson wasn't here to do a "white glove" interview. She'd already made a positive determination about Kathleen's ability to parent. All that remained was to see what sort of person the boyfriend was. She knew, for example, that I had a daughter of my own, who lived with my ex in Darnell, West Virginia. If she'd done any digging she also knew that while

9

PREVIEW

I've always been emotionally and financially supportive, I hadn't spent as much father-daughter time with Kimberly as I should have.

Patty moved closer and locked her eyes on mine. Lowering her voice, she said, "There's a big difference between being a father and a dad."

*Right*, I thought. *She's done her research.*

"I had to learn that lesson the hard way in my own life," I said. "And this might sound funny, but Addie's the one who inspired me to build bridges with Kimberly. We're closer now than ever before."

Patty nodded. We were both silent a moment, waiting to see who would speak first. In case you're keeping score, she did.

"Addie has become a special needs child," Patty said. "She's been traumatized physically and mentally and she's going to need a lot of nurturing."

"I understand."

"I hope so, Mr. Creed, because it's going to put a lot of stress on your relationship with Kathleen. Have you thought about your role in all this—I mean, *really* thought about it?"

Addie was an amazing kid. Funny, affectionate, brave — over the past few months she'd become special to both of us. Special wasn't the right word, she was more than that. Addie had become essential to our lives.

"I love Addie," I said.

She nodded and paused a few seconds. "I felt you must, Mr. Creed. What you've done for her and Kathleen speaks volumes."

Patty knew I'd recently given Kathleen a million dollars and put another ten million into a trust for Addie. What she didn't know is that I'd stolen all that money and more, from

10

a West Coast crime boss named Joe DeMeo.

After witnessing another hour of unparalleled domestic harmony, Patty Feldson gathered Addie, the recipe, and half a pan of brownies.

"You're a shoo-in!" she gushed to Kathleen.

"I'll see you again tomorrow, darling," Kathleen said to Addie. Addie swallowed before speaking, to lubricate her throat. We had grown accustomed to the procedure, the result of her vocal chords being permanently damaged by the fire that nearly took her life.

"At the hospital?" Addie finally said in her raspy, whisper of a voice.

"Uh huh."

Another round of hugs was in order and then they were gone. I looked at the lovely creature that had defied all the odds and fallen for me.

"This might be the last time she'll have to leave you," I said.

Kathleen dabbed at the tears on her cheeks. "Thank you, Donovan." She put her hand in mine and kissed me gently on the mouth. "For everything," she added.

Life was good.

An hour later Victor called me on my cell phone. A quadriplegic little person on a ventilator, Victor's metallic voice was singularly creepy.

"Mis...ter Creed...they took...the...money," he said.

"The couple from Nashville?"

"Yes, Rob and...Trish."

"Big surprise, right?"

"When you get...a chance I...would like you to...kill the ...Peterson...sis...ters."

I paused a minute, trying to place them. "They're in

11

Pennsylvania, right?"

"Yes, in…Camp…town."

I assumed my best minstrel voice and said, "You mean De Camptown Ladies?"

Victor sighed. "Really…Mis…ter Creed."

"Hey, show some appreciation! In France I'm considered a comedic genius."

"You and…Jerry Lewis… So, will you…go to… Camptown and…kill the…Petersons?"

"Doo Dah!" I said.

# DONOVAN CREED

DONOVAN CREED works as an assassin for an elite branch of Homeland Security. When he isn't killing terrorists, he moonlights as a hit man for the mob, and tests torture weapons for the Army. Donovan Creed is a very tough guy.

To discover more – and some tempting special offers – why not join our mailing list? Email creed@headofzeus.com

# DONOVAN CREED

LETHAL PEOPLE
JOHN LOCKE

LETHAL EXPERIMENT
JOHN LOCKE

SAVING RACHEL
JOHN LOCKE

NOW & THEN
JOHN LOCKE

WISH LIST
JOHN LOCKE

A GIRL LIKE YOU
JOHN LOCKE

VEGAS MOON
JOHN LOCKE

THE LOVE YOU CRAVE
JOHN LOCKE

## COLLECT THEM ALL